HIDDEN

JACOBS FAMILY SERIES
BOOK 1

VANNETTA CHAPMAN

Cover design: Ken Raney
Interior design: Caitlin Greer
Printed in the United States of America
First printing, 2014

ISBN-13: 978-1502318473
ISBN-10: 1502318474

Praise for *HIDDEN*

"Vannetta Chapman's characters are so real, her story so compelling, and her faith so genuine, you won't be able to put this one down! I loved it."

~ Jennifer Beckstrand, Author of *Huckleberry Hill*

"Vannetta Chapman never fails to pull readers in and keep them hooked until the final page. *Hidden* will be no exception. Well done!"

~ Mary Ellis, author of *The Lady and the Officer*

"Vannetta Chapman's *Hidden* gives us a glimpse into a world where domestic and international terrorism lurk around every corner, but it's the evil that's personal and intimate that ultimately provides the true test of her well drawn characters. A lovely romance between a complicated woman and a big hearted man, tension that builds steadily to a fever pitch, and a story of faith rediscovered make *Hidden* an engaging read."

~Kelly Irvin, author of *Hew Hope Amish* series

In memory of my grandfather:

Benjamin Van Riper

For the Son of Man came to seek and to save the lost.

—Luke 19:10

"Moral wounds have this peculiarity - they may be hidden, but they never close; always painful, always ready to bleed when touched, they remain fresh and open in the heart."

— Alexandre Dumas, *The Count of Monte Cristo*

Prologue

Livingston, TX
Fall, 1990

D ana Jacobs tried to scream, but no sound came. A small hand slipped into hers and pulled her away from the violence playing before her like an interminable, looping video. She turned and looked into the terror-filled eyes of her sister. Erin tugged again, pleading silently. A ragged, brown teddy bear hung from her other hand, nearly forgotten.

Dana scooped up the three-year-old, mindful that the bear found its way into her arms as well. She backed away from the cries of her mother and fled into the night.

They went into the woods, far enough away to escape the sounds and sights of the house. At ten years old, Dana outweighed her sister by nearly forty pounds, but her fear made her weak.

She prayed as she stumbled along the path.

The tall, old pine finally loomed in front of them. She placed Erin on the ground beside it.

"I have to go back," she whispered, even as she worked to unclasp the grip Erin had on her neck. "You're okay. You have Snooky. I have to go help Mama."

She pushed the bear into her sister's hands.

The smell of him reached her before his words—the unmistakable stench of liquor and sweat.

"And how do you plan to help her?"

She drew herself up to her full four-foot height and turned in the darkness to face her father.

One

Taos, New Mexico
May, 2008

D ana woke from the dream with a sob, drenched in sweat, heart racing, with bedding twisted around her legs. It took only seconds to realize it was a dream—the dream, again. After eighteen years, her father still haunted her. She went through her usual ritual of deep breathing, counting, lowering her heart rate.

She threw off the covers and walked to the kitchen in the darkness. Finding the glass of water she'd left on the counter, she downed its contents in three swallows. The liquid was a relief to her throat. It did nothing to soothe the ache in her heart.

The clock on the wall chimed 5:00 a.m., mocking her.

She picked up her cell phone from the counter, but resisted the need to call Erin to check on her. Instead, she flipped the switch on the coffeepot and went in search of her sweats. She had plenty of time for a run and a shower. She would still arrive at the Department of Homeland Security two hours early, but then that was normal as well.

Two

B en pulled the two-tone, Chevy truck into the shopping strip and fought the urge to verify the address on his confirmation letter. Checking was pointless. He knew he had the right address. Parking in front of the only tenant still in business, he pushed the manual transmission into first gear and pulled the keys from the ignition.

A defunct, coin laundry sprawled to the right. It had been closed long enough for several nests of birds to take up residence under the awning. Some kid's single, lost sock remained pinned between a plastic chair and the dirty, front window.

Facing the street was an old gas station, the kind with a service bay. Ben was only twenty-seven. He didn't remember stations where they also worked on your car, but he'd heard about them. Their ruins still dotted the rural roads of Montana. He smiled to think there was something Taos held in common with his home state, thanked God for this measure of assurance, and walked into his new place of employment—the Office of Homeland Security.

A bell jingled when he pushed through the door, and the grin on Ben's face spread even wider. A bell?

"Can I help you?"

The man's hair wasn't regulation; in fact, it was pulled back into a ponytail. Didn't fool Ben. He recognized a guard when he saw one. Everything from his bearing to the alertness of his gaze confirmed as much. Starched white shirt, black tie, and a smile that stopped just short of friendly completed the picture.

"Benjamin Marshall. Reporting for duty."

Without turning his head, Ben felt all activity in the office stop. A dark-skinned woman at the tactical board turned to stare at him. An older guy monitoring radio traffic threw a glance his way, then went back to his logs. A giant of a man with a full, red beard dropped a sheaf of papers on a desk and walked toward them.

Ponytail man reached across the counter, offering a firm handshake, but no warmer smile. "Clay Statler. Glad you found us."

"Wondered if I was at the right place," Ben admitted. "You keep a casual appearance outside."

"Don't want to draw attention." The voice sprang as if from a boom box.

Ben had never considered himself a little man. He'd struck six feet his freshman year in high school and topped out at six two by the time he graduated. He was on the lanky side though. College had added some weight to his frame. Six years serving in the desert had carved away the extra and refined the rest into solid muscle. He wasn't large by most standards, but he was solid.

When he turned toward the voice at his shoulder and saw the red-bearded man looming beside him, he almost stepped back.

"Jackson Boggs." The big man grabbed his hand and commenced to pumping it. "Folks call me Red. You're ten minutes early—that's good. Shows initiative. Come meet the rest of the Monday morning crew."

Ben followed him behind the counter.

"Nina Jones." The woman's voice lilted in the Apache way. Her gaze was direct, though she was a good ten inches shorter than he was. "Welcome."

Dark eyes stared up into his, eyes wiser than her years. Ben remembered that was common for Native Americans in this region. It was as if the sorrows of their ancestors had been passed down. Her black hair was braided, and still it fell past her waist. Bronze skin accentuated high cheekbones.

"Thanks, Nina. I'm glad to be here."

"Humph. He says that now—in May. Get him to shoveling snow in November and we'll see how glad he is." The old guy on the radios removed his headset and thrust out a hand speckled with age spots. "Captain Finney. Most folks call me Captain."

"Pleased to meet you, Captain. Think you'll find me fairly handy with a snow shovel come November."

Captain grunted and rubbed at his right eyebrow, which was white and nearly met his left eyebrow in the middle of his forehead. "Seems I read you've been in the middle of the Arabian Desert the last six years. Not much cause for a snow shovel there."

"Yes, sir." Ben looked around the office. The place was more high tech from this side of the counter than it appeared from the front door. "Raised in Billings though. Did my share of snow shoveling growing up, and every time I came home on leave."

Captain grunted, which Ben decided to take as approval, and picked his headset back up. It seemed to be a signal of sorts. Everyone else went back to work. Clay stepped to a closed door at the back of the office and tapped on it. The room had windows facing out over the rest of the office. Half-closed blinds covered them. Ben glimpsed a woman with long hair pulled back, hanging well past her shoulders.

"Time to meet the boss," Red said. His giant paw came down, slapped Ben on the back, and propelled him toward the inner office.

Ben heard himself being introduced. He moved forward, again offered his hand, and smiled automatically in the way that was second nature to him.

For the briefest slice of time, everything stopped.

Later, it would remind him of those pivotal junctures in combat—moments of total clarity when all of his senses centered on one thing and only one thing. In this case, that thing was his boss, Miss Dana Jacobs.

It wasn't her beauty that blocked out all else, though Dana Jacobs had no doubt been called beautiful before. It certainly wasn't her clothing. She wore a plain, white, cotton blouse over black pants.

Thick, brown hair was pulled back from her face, revealing finely arched brows, a classic nose, and lips that were full and touched with the faintest of colors—or perhaps the pink was natural. She was tall as women went, only five or six inches shorter than he was, and though she was slight, she gave the impression of strength.

But what held him speechless were her eyes. They were impossibly round, large, and spoke of the many battles she'd fought. As foolish as it sounded, even in his head, their color reminded him of amber waves of grain.

When her hand touched his palm, the world around him came into focus again.

He did not doubt God had brought him back to Taos. And he hadn't questioned why. Now he wondered if the reason for his return stood before him, chestnut hair pulled back, tired gaze quietly assessing him.

Certainly, he had a job to do, skills that were needed, but perhaps there was more. Was he to befriend her, guide her, protect her, or marry her? Regardless, it seemed that for a time his path was destined to run alongside that of Dana Jacobs.

Three

D ana motioned Ben to the chair in front of her desk. "Have a seat."

Clay hadn't moved from the door. He stood there still as a stone sentinel. "Anything else?" he asked.

Dana's crew was faithful and a mite overprotective of their boss.

"No. Thank you, Clay."

With a nod, he was gone.

Dana sat, but her posture remained perfect. She picked up the folder in the middle of her orderly desk, placed her thumb over the tab—MARSHALL, BENJAMIN—and opened it. The two-by-two-inch military photo looked several years younger than the man sitting in front of her.

The man who had bounded through her office door then stopped so abruptly was a complete surprise, which was why she pretended to study his file. She hadn't expected sun-bleached hair, curling at the neck. He'd apparently taken something of a break since arriving stateside. Mr. Marshall's entire physical presence was a bit of a jolt. He was overdressed in a suit that looked like it hadn't been worn more than twice. Topping six feet and solid, he had the energy and demeanor of a Labrador pup.

Though he sat with a military posture, his right leg jiggled continuously, as if waiting were a trial for him. His brown eyes seemed to take in everything, while his face remained focused on her. He reminded Dana of a runner ready to sprint the moment the gun went off.

Scanning the file, a file she'd read thoroughly twice, she voiced the portions she had questions about. The pieces she needed to understand. "US Army, one tour in the Middle East. Usually lasts four years, but you extended it to six."

She looked up and was surprised by his open smile. While she'd been reading the file, he'd been studying her. She slapped the folder shut and sat back. Mr. Marshall looked like a Midwestern boy through and through. So why did he want to spend a year in Taos, New Mexico?

He didn't squirm under his new boss's scrutiny. She gave him points for that.

"Why the extension?" she asked.

"My unit needed me."

When she didn't move on, he added, "We weren't finished."

"But you are now?"

He laughed and the sound surprised her. It was relaxed and genuine.

"I'm finished with the Army, but some good men are still over there. I always knew I wasn't a lifer. I gave what I could."

The answer sounded true, so Dana moved on. "Montana State University. Your grades were good, not great. You certainly didn't need to join up. Could have gotten a job in business."

"Didn't interest me at the time."

"I see you were in the Cadets all four years. Why?"

"My father was." He shrugged. "It wasn't family pressure so much as I grew up on those stories. They didn't disappoint. The Corps was a good filter for my education—"

"Which was in chemistry. Rather an odd combination."

Dana sat back a fraction of an inch as she became engrossed in his story.

"I've always been fascinated with matter, both how it stays together and how it blows apart."

Again the smile and those chocolate-colored eyes. With brown-turning-to-blond hair curling playfully above his collar and a charming personality to boot, he added up to a Casanova. Dana did not need another one of those on her staff. The last one had stirred up the locals, brought down the district manager, and finally been reassigned to El Paso. He was probably wooing señoritas even as they spoke.

"I don't get to choose applicants, Mr. Marshall."

"You can call me Ben."

Dana squared the folder so that it was perpendicular with the edge of her desk. "You applied online, correct?"

"Yes, ma'am. Then interviewed on the West Coast."

"And I don't doubt your expertise in—"

"Explosives."

"In explosives is what you claim it to be."

"I'm handy in plenty of things."

"I'm sure you are." Dana smiled, but in her heart she wished division had sent her an old guy, or another woman. She wasn't prejudiced. She didn't need the headaches of a restless, young man in their small town. "I've read your file. I know about your commendations. Truth is, we're one of the quietest branches of first responders for the Department of Homeland Security."

"I don't mind quiet."

"*Now* you don't. I'm sure you're tired after six years in the Middle East. But by November, you'll be bored and restless. That's when you'll start causing me trouble."

"You're the second person to mention November to me." Ben looked around her office, then back at her, and smiled. "You people don't seem to like winter much. You should try it in Montana. *We* have winter."

Dana sighed and tried to call up more patience. He seemed determined to stick.

"May I speak freely, Miss Jacobs?"

"This isn't the military, Mr. Marshall. Of course you may."

"The moment you need a good explosives man isn't the best time to go looking for one. I don't bore easily. Most of the time in the desert, nothing happened. Combat—it really is long bouts of nothing punctuated by moments of terror. I can't remember who said that."

"It's a very old sentiment."

"Well, it's a true one. The point is, ma'am—"

"Please don't call me ma'am. Miss Jacobs or Dana will be fine."

Ben shifted uncomfortably. "The point is a job that doesn't see much action suits me fine. I know how to stay alert in spite of slow times. And I'm good at what I do."

"An expert with explosives." Dana sighed, still unconvinced he was the perfect fit for her crew, but without the authority to overrule her district boss.

Ben held up both hands and wiggled his fingers. "Still have all ten."

"I won't ask to see your toes."

Dana stood and walked over to a black screen that covered most of the south wall of her office. When she touched it, the screen glowed and came to life. The surge of pride she felt at seeing her designated area was immediately followed by the overwhelming responsibility she had for keeping its residents safe.

"Our area extends north to the Colorado border, east to I-25, west to Farmington, and south to Santa Fe where we overlap with the Albuquerque branch."

Ben had joined her at the map. He whistled appreciatively at the technology of the interactive display. "This is live?"

"There's a twenty-second delay, but yes, for all practical purposes, it's live. As you can see our area is green, which indicates no current threats." She palmed the bottom right corner of the panel and the map zoomed out, showing the entire southwest United States. "The yellow spots indicate reported but unconfirmed threats."

"Abilene? What type of threat would there be in Abilene?"

"It could be anything. Today's happens to be at the wind farms." Dana zoomed back in to her territory. "Our area is fairly wide for a staff of twelve, plus me. We run three shifts of four. Shifts overlap one hour—eight to five, four to one, and twelve to nine. As we're talking, the late-night shift is in the back, writing up their reports."

Dana touched the panel again, and it resumed its flat-screen appearance. She perched on the corner of her desk and expected Ben to sit in his chair. Instead, he remained standing, legs slightly apart, arms clasped behind his back—military stance. For some reason, it irritated her.

"We've had military men here before, Mr. Marshall."

"Call me Ben."

"Ben, I do appreciate your service to our country. But in the past servicemen have not been satisfied working in this office."

Ben cocked his head to the side. "Why would you say that is?"

"We are first responders. Our task is to respond, contain, diffuse, and when possible arrest. If we do our job well, the media is not involved and the residents are not aware of the threat. We carry firearms, but we rarely use them."

Dana paused and looked to the right of the flat screen. Three framed photos hung there. The man in the middle had also been former military. Looking at him, she realized that was what made her uncomfortable about Ben Marshall. Rules of engagement were different here, and it was difficult for military guys to adjust. She'd failed to convey that to Josh in some way, and he'd died because of it. She didn't want the burden of another death on her conscience. They were piling up faster than she could have nightmares about them.

Ben Marshall was a man she'd rather not get close to, rather not know, certainly rather not care about.

But working as a team meant caring about each other. She thought of what she owed the three men on the wall and how to explain their sacrifice to this new, green recruit.

"Our ops vary—biological, chemical, conventional."

"Nuclear?"

"I won't lie to you. There have been three such attacks in the continental United States—all diffused before the media caught wind of what was happening. In two of the three cases, some of our people were exposed to the material and died."

"Here?"

Ben's face was serious now. It was the first time the smile had completely left. It wasn't replaced by fear, but rather a calm acceptance. Dana realized whether she liked him or not, he would be good in his job.

"No. I'm not at liberty to say where, but it wasn't here. My point is we do not have the luxury of going into a situation in full hazmat gear as that would create a widespread panic. It's our job to avoid frightening the general population as much as it is our job to diffuse the threat."

She glanced again at the wall of honor, then looked at Ben, studied him fully. "Do you understand what I'm saying?"

"Yes, ma'am. I read the fine print. I signed the release."

Dana took a deep breath, stood, and walked to her door. Opening it she called to Clay.

"Take Mr. Marshall to the back and introduce him to the night team before they leave. Then pass him over to Captain. We'll start him on the radios."

Ben stepped to the side so she could pass back into the office and he could walk out. She knew he was almost her age—only one year junior—so why did he look so young? No doubt he had seen as much death as she had, possibly or more in his years overseas. Yet he again wore that goofy grin. Perhaps he was a fool. He didn't strike her as such. And there had been the moment of complete seriousness between them.

Time would tell.

As he followed Clay out of her office, she called him back. "Mr. Marshall. We try to blend in with the citizens of Taos. You need to lose the military look, if that's possible."

"Look?"

"The way you stand." She waved her hand at him. "The way you... are. Try to act more normal."

Ben smiled. "Yes, ma'am."

"And stop calling me that." She began typing on her laptop, pulling up e-mails.

"Sure thing, boss."

Dana resisted the urge to roll her eyes. "You can dress more casual."

"That's a relief."

"Shut the door, please."

He did. Only then did she allow herself to watch him walk away and wonder again what she was going to do with the likes of Ben Marshall.

Four

B en shed the jacket and tie immediately, then spent the rest of the day with Captain. The man was a curmudgeon, but he knew his job. Ben had run across his type more than once in the military. They were so accustomed to being disrespected by the world at large, they anticipated and adjusted accordingly before it happened.

Captain stared out at him from under shaggy eyebrows. "You think you understand the notation system in the logbooks?"

"Yes, sir. You explained it well."

"Explaining it is one thing. You following it is another."

"I'll do my best."

Pale blue eyes peered into his. Ben waited. Captain stood and handed the logbook to George from the midshift team. George was a short guy, probably Ben's age, and prematurely balding. He'd hooked into the board with the official headset, and he waited patiently for the logbook.

He'd been waiting for twenty minutes, watching Ben get grilled. Ben understood he would endure ribbing about Captain's training techniques later.

Ben's training headset had also been plugged into the board. He'd unplugged and begun to store it when George showed up. That had been a mistake. Captain had taken the set and begun quizzing him.

"Which side does the local dispatch come through?" Captain asked, holding the headset between them.

"Right side."

"What's the procedure if you hear a level one or level-two call?"

"I override local dispatch, say we are responding to the call, then notify Miss Jacobs."

Ben knew he'd answered inadequately by the way Captain rubbed his left eyebrow and stared up at the ceiling. George tried to cover his laugh with a cough.

"What about logging it in?"

"Right after I call Dana, I mean Miss Jacobs."

"Wrong, Marshall. *Before* you call Jacobs. It has to go in the books immediately. As you're talking to dispatch, you're writing in the logbook."

"Yes, sir. I remember you telling me that now."

Captain waited. Ben had the feeling he was trying to gauge whether or not he should bother asking his new recruit another question.

"Left ear?"

"Upper level feds—regional and national."

"Eyes?"

"On the monitor at all times, reading transcriptions, looking for anomalies."

Captain shook his head, as if Ben had answered wrong, but he didn't correct him. He rewound the cord around the set and stored it.

"And you think you can do all three things at once?"

"Yes, sir. I do."

For his answer, Captain turned and walked away.

George waited until the older man had disappeared into the back break room before he allowed his laughter to slip between them.

"Tough break, pulling Captain first."

"Have to start somewhere," Ben said.

"Make it through Captain's sour attitude, and you'll probably enjoy meeting up with a terrorist." George leaned back in the chair, right earpiece firmly in place, left raised above his head so he could talk with Ben. Lights on the monitor board would indicate any incoming calls if by some chance he didn't hear them—which he would.

Ben could tell George took his job as seriously as everyone else, but he'd learned to do it with a little less intensity.

Ben stretched, popped his back, then hopped on to the counter. He was ready to go home, but then again he hadn't actually checked into his apartment yet. This office, on the other hand, already felt like where he belonged.

"We've lost a few over the years to Captain. Wouldn't want to see him run you off." George followed Ben's gaze. Clay and Dana stood at her door. Both were studying something in a folder.

"What's Clay's story?" Ben asked. He had officially met all the staff now, and Clay seemed the stiffest to him.

Captain's bad humor he'd find a way around. Clay he couldn't get a handle on yet.

"Clay? He's all right." George picked up a stress ball and tossed it from one hand to the other.

"He seems protective of her," Ben noted.

George took a moment to answer. "We all are," he finally admitted. "Clay maybe a little more than the rest. He's been here the longest. He's participated in some of the tougher ops with her."

"Have something to do with the three guys on the wall in her office?"

"Yeah. He was on that one. It was bad." The light on the monitor beeped. George straightened and righted his headphone. "Take care, man."

George tossed him the stress ball, then logged the nightly report.

Clay no longer stood at Dana's office, so Ben detoured by on his way to the break room.

He approached her door quietly, not wanting to disturb her. Watching her read over something in a folder, he couldn't help but notice how tired she looked. What time did she arrive in the morning? No doubt well before her shift.

When he tapped lightly on the open door, she looked up and pasted on a smile.

"I was headed out," Ben said. "Wanted to stop by and see if you need me to do anything else."

Dana looked slightly puzzled. "No. Your shift is over, Ben. You can go."

Some of her brown hair had escaped from the clasp that held it back. He wondered how long it had been since she'd worn it down, felt the sun shine through it. Then he realized he probably shouldn't be having such thoughts about his boss, and *that* thought made his smile grow even broader. It seemed to rattle her more.

"Was there something else?" she asked.

"If you're staying, I could go and get you a sandwich."

Dana tilted her head slightly, as if the thought of eating hadn't occurred to her. "That won't be necessary, but thank you."

"All right then. Have a good evening." Ben turned to go and nearly walked into Clay.

The man must have a monitor aimed at her door. Which was fine too. There were some things you couldn't guard against. Ben was no knight in shining armor, and he had no idea where this urge to sweep his boss off her feet had come from. But he wasn't going to let Clay Statler stop him. Besides, at the rate she was going, she would fall off her feet. He'd merely have to manage to be in the general vicinity so he could catch her when it happened.

Climbing into his truck, he rolled down the window and watched the sun set over the mountains. This was God's country. He'd felt it as a young man eight years ago. The certainty of it still vibrated in his bones.

Something was tugging him toward Dana Jacobs. He felt no urgency to understand why. As his dad was fond of saying, "God will reveal His hand, but not until God is ready."

In the meantime, Ben had an apartment to settle into and a job to learn. Not much more a man could ask for.

VANNETTA CHAPMAN

Five

Dana went on Ben's first call Thursday morning so she could watch him. She told herself it wasn't unusual. She kept a close eye on all new assignees—as much to keep them out of harm's way as to be sure they were performing adequately.

There was more to it than that though. Over her last five years as lead responder in Taos, she'd learned the importance of team chemistry. She needed to hold back and see how Ben worked with the others when things came down to the wire. She wanted to watch him under pressure. A reference was one thing, but references never told the whole story.

So when he appeared at her door early Thursday morning dressed in khaki pants and a button-up denim shirt, she didn't hesitate.

"Intercepted a call from the high school to local enforcement. An unidentified backpack was left near the front, central fountain. It's not one of their approved brands."

It had been a long week—tedious almost—as most of their weeks were. She searched Ben's face and was pleased to see no eagerness, only quiet acceptance.´

"I'll ride along," she said as she stood, retrieved her firearm from her drawer, and slid it into her paddle holster.

Ben nodded and disappeared into the gear room.

Dana stepped into the main room and looked up at the assignment board. "Nina, I want you here at the door. Captain, stay on the radios. Clay and Red, you're with us."

Everyone moved like the gears in a clock. They were in the van within two minutes of Ben stepping into her office.

The high school was located in the center of town. Red parked the van across from the building and stayed with it. Everyone else stepped out simultaneously. No one had spoken on the way over. Everyone knew their roles—it was a textbook call—and Dana hoped with all her heart it was a false alarm.

An electronic billboard proclaimed HOME OF THE TIGERS. As they neared the building, Clay peeled off toward the main doors where the principal waited just inside as he had been instructed. Ben and Dana walked straight toward the backpack.

Dana still hadn't said anything, but she watched Ben closely. His shoulders were loose and his pace purposeful. He wasn't running toward it. No one watching would have thought to panic. In fact, any students who happened to be looking out a window might think he was a father coming to pick up a missing backpack.

He didn't slow down until he reached the pack, then squatted beside it and studied it.

Dana knelt across from him. She waited a full thirty seconds, then asked, "What do you think?"

Ben shrugged. "Few bombers dot their i's with hearts."

She moved around to his side. In light-blue, permanent marker someone had written Jaimie, and both i's were dotted with hearts. The letters were tiny though, and the pack was faded denim. She wasn't sure she would have seen it.

Ben turned on his hand scanner, ran it over the pack from top to bottom, then left to right. "It's not hot."

He stood, grabbed the pack, and draped it over his shoulder.

They walked back to the van at the same deliberate pace and reached it at the exact moment as Clay. They were quiet on the return trip, and Dana gave Ben points for his reticence as well. Many newbies celebrated too early before the mission was actually over.

Back at the office, Ben took the pack to the decon room, placed it on the table under the hood, and x-rayed it.

He was back at Dana's door in an hour with a list of contents.

"How sure are we about this?" Dana didn't look up, merely continued studying the printout. Ben stood at military rest in front of her—feet spread, arms clasped behind him. She wondered again when he'd figure out she wasn't his sergeant.

"One hundred percent."

She looked up, skeptical.

"Ma'am."

Not the answer Dana wanted.

"Boss." Ben shifted uncomfortably, but a smile tugged at his lips.

She was convinced he knew he irritated her. He'd done his job well though. She had no critiques other than with his answer.

"I doubt you can be 100 percent certain, Ben. However, if you're over 95 percent sure there are no explosives in the pack, then you may open it and explore the contents." Dana handed the inventory back to him.

"Yes, ma'am." He touched the corner of the sheet, but didn't immediately pull it away. "Captain's going out for burgers. Would you like something?"

"No. But thank you, Ben, for asking." She let go of the sheet, pulled the next folder to her, and opened it, plainly signaling for him to leave.

"It won't hurt if they see you eat," he said softly.

Dana stared at the sheet in front of her, seeing but not comprehending the words on the page. She forced herself to count to ten, made it only to four, then looked up.

"I appreciate your concern over my dietary needs, but I'll pass. Thank you."

She made sure to look him directly in the eyes and speak clearly. Possibly the man didn't pick up on subtle, social clues.

Ben cocked his head and studied her, glanced out the window, then ran his hand over the top of his head, further disturbing the mess of hair there.

"If you change your mind, let me know. I can go back and get you something. Or I can share." He turned and walked out the door.

She had dared to breathe a sigh of relief that he was gone when he stuck his head back around the corner.

"Or I'll give you mine, because I ate breakfast. I don't really need it."

Before she could answer, he was gone.

She looked down at the folder again, tried to remember what it was about, and finally gave up. Turning to her computer screen, she called up her e-mail and pushed Ben Marshall from her mind.

Thirty minutes later, she was talking with Clay when Marshall called her on the phone. "What is it, Ben?"

"I think you're going to want to see this."

"Something from the pack?"

"Yeah. We have a problem."

Six

B en glanced up as Dana and Red walked into the room. "What did you find?" Dana stood beside the table where Ben had set the contents of the backpack. She didn't disturb anything, though he could tell she was mentally noting and cataloging each item. When she'd reached the end of the table, she turned her inquisitive gaze to Ben.

He thought again of how those eyes seemed so guarded. They took in everything, but gave away very little. He wondered if she was worried or merely cautious.

Red had plopped onto a stool, which groaned under his weight. "I do love a mystery," he muttered, stroking his beard.

"Great, because we have something of a puzzle." Ben walked to the northern most end of the table.

"I did a handheld scan on site. Once we returned, I did a computed tomography. Then I brought the list of contents to you, boss."

Dana shot him a look of reproach at the name, but a slight nod of her head indicated he should continue.

"Why don't we use a dog to sniff for explosives?" Red interrupted. "They had one over in Las Cruces."

Ben nodded. "We had one in my first unit overseas as well. I personally like using canines, and we can talk about going that route. The dogs we worked with had incredible accuracy, however, there are disadvantages. A dog can only work a one-hour duty cycle without a break, and he can't communicate what type of explosive he's detected."

"It's certainly something we can discuss," Dana said. "Both of you can write up your recommendations, and I'll consider them."

Ben looked back at the table. "What you see in front of us is identical to what was on the original list. There were no surprises in content. Items are numbered in the order they came out of the pack. All of it is pretty standard for what you'd expect to find in a teenage girl's things."

Ben moved down the table pointing but not touching as he spoke. Though he wore gloves to keep his fingerprints off the material, he preferred to handle items as little as possible. He knew from experience what was at risk each time a piece of evidence was physically touched. Valuable clues could be lost to a past or potential crime. For reasons he was about to explain, he now thought they were in the middle of exactly such a situation.

Though it wasn't necessary, he identified each item as he walked by it. "Tiger sweatshirt, iPod—with no obvious content on it—makeup bag, which appears to be filled with makeup, paperback copy of *The Grapes of Wrath*, and a spiral notebook."

He had reached the end of the table, so he stopped and looked up at Red and Dana.

Red sat with his hands resting on his knees. Dana still stood as when she'd come in. Ben had noticed her posture was always perfect. She frowned slightly and shook her head.

"It all looks normal to me."

"I thought so, too, but I tested for explosive residue anyway—per the procedure manual." Ben picked up a handheld light, slightly larger than a security wand the FAA uses at airports. "We have several ways to do this, but I decided to use laser technology that has been effective in card readers."

"Cards?" Dana looked at him skeptically.

"Fare cards, like when you take the subway. These readers are being tried in the US, but they've been installed across England. In order to gain access to mass transit, the passenger slips his card into a machine. The card is read to confirm he has paid, but it's also scanned to detect any residual amount of explosives."

"I didn't realize we had this technology," Dana said.

"The patent was only approved in 2006," Ben explained. "The laser heats the object to a critical temperature, which is how it identifies the residue."

"Hold this blue light for me, Red?"

"Sure thing." The big man jumped off the stool, took the light, and held it over the Tiger sweatshirt.

When Ben walked to the wall switch and turned off the overhead lights, the letters on the sweatshirt glowed as if they were being held under a black light. On his way back to the table, Ben retrieved three pairs of goggles and handed a pair to Red and Dana. The third pair he kept for himself.

"If there was any residue burned by the laser, we'd see it with the light and these goggles," he explained.

Dana put them on. "What color will it be?"

Ben smiled. "Black smudges mostly, but you shouldn't have any trouble seeing them. They'll look like burn spots."

Taking the light from Red, he began moving down the table. When he reached the end, both Dana and Red looked up at him—relief clearly etched on both their faces.

"No spots," Red said.

"Ben found something else though." It wasn't a question. Dana's gaze met his.

Even through their goggles, he looked into her beautiful, amber eyes and knew she understood him. She trusted he had a good reason for taking the long route to show them what he'd found.

"Yes, I found something else. I had a hunch something wasn't right about this. The laser actually does two things. It reveals explosive residue, but it also reveals fingerprints. Regardless what type of explosive someone uses, it is all composed of sticky, microscopic particles. No matter how you wash your hands, it sticks to the whorls in your fingerprints. Your hands will look clean, but the residue is there nonetheless. It remains there for twenty-four to forty-eight hours."

"How many people know this?" Dana asked.

"Very few. I didn't know it until last year when I began reading the patent information on this laser."

Dana motioned for him to continue.

Ben walked back up to the head of the table. "Something bothered me, but I couldn't figure out what. I had to walk up and down the table a second and then a third time. Then it came to me. Red's right. There was no explosive residue."

He looked up uncertainly, as if he needed to explain what he did next. Red tugged at his beard. "Military can hone a man's instincts."

"Maybe that's what it was. I don't know. I decided to apply an application of vapor of iodine."

"To reveal fingerprints," Dana said.

"Yes. I know I had no cause to at that point, but something kept nagging at me." Ben turned on the blue light again. "Of course, fingerprints won't show on cloth."

Both Red and Dana moved in closer.

"All of the other items are covered with prints as you would expect. Probably whoever owns this stuff loans her things to her friends. Most everyday items have so many fingerprints on them, you can't lift off any one clear print. For instance, a phone or a doorknob is too covered with prints to be a good source of evidence."

"Or an iPod," Red said.

"This is disgusting." Dana leaned in until her nose was practically under the blue light. "All those swirls are fingerprints? It looks so… dirty."

"Yeah. Most things are dirty. They're covered with signs we've handled them. Lots of people have left their DNA on these things. All except for this."

Ben stopped at the spiral, held the light over it, and waited for their reaction. At first, no one said anything. Then Red and Dana started talking at once.

"Maybe it's brand new," Dana suggested.

"Or she wiped it off," Red said.

"Or we need to turn it over," Dana added.

Ben looked at them both, tried to read their expressions, what was going on in their minds. It was difficult with the goggles they were wearing. He chose his next words carefully.

"Even if the spiral were new, someone bought it. The person at the store had to stock it on a shelf. The cashier would have handled it. Mom or Dad would have brought it home. Someone put it in the backpack."

Dana tucked her hair behind her ear. It was the first time Ben had seen her touch her hair in any way, and he knew she was rattled. He forced his attention back to the table.

"And if someone tried to wipe them off?" Red asked.

"Then it would be smudged. As you can see, it's not. This item is clean."

"So how is that possible, Ben?"

"I'm not sure," he admitted. "My guess would be someone took this straight off an assembly line before it was touched by human hands. They used gloves as I am. Then they put it in the bottom of this pack."

No one spoke as they considered the scenario he painted. In the quiet and darkness, the buzz from the blue light seemed to stutter then amplify, as if it held the answers to their questions.

Dana broke the silence by asking what they all wanted to know. "But why?"

"I haven't looked inside yet. I wanted to wait until you were here."

Dana looked up at Ben, then at Red. "All right. Well, it's just paper. We know it won't explode. There's no sign it contains ricin or any other toxic agent. Are we in agreement?"

Both Ben and Red nodded.

"Open it."

Ben handed the blue light to Red, then reached forward with his gloved hand and opened the spiral.

The three of them stared down at the page.

No one said a word, as they each worked through what they could possibly be dealing with.

Pasted across the first page, in two-inch letters cut from a magazine, was a single word.

BAM!

Seven

"We are not going to assume this is a joke," Dana said. "Red, I want you on the iPod. Use every program we have. I want to know if there are any more hidden messages."

"Wouldn't the laser have fried the memory?"

"Yeah, it would have," Ben said. "I saved a back-up, though it looked blank to me. I'll send it to you."

"I'm on it then. I can also get the serial number and contact iTunes. Find the retail store where it was sold." He walked off, stroking his beard and mumbling.

"Good work, Ben. Get the specifics of this spiral to Nina. See if she can find a plant anywhere in northern New Mexico."

"Sure thing, boss."

Dana picked up the phone next to Ben's computer and punched in Clay's extension. "Have you finished with the high school surveillance tapes?"

Dana pulled her hair back out of her way and wondered again if she should cut it off short. "Forward what you have to my office and meet me there in two minutes."

Hanging up the phone she walked back to Ben. "I want you to come with me."

"Sure."

He looked surprised, but didn't ask why. There were advantages to having a soldier under her command.

"Ben, I want to ask your opinion about something."

Dana sat on the stool and let her gaze drift along the items on the table. Each new development concerned her more. The perpetrator was playing with them, had chosen the school as their point of contact. The thought infuriated her, but as usual she swallowed her anger.

"Do you think this was a prank?" she asked.

"No."

"Why?"

"It's a little too well planned for my tastes."

"How do you mean?"

Ben walked around the table, arms behind his back, as if he were surveying his unit. "The items on top were harmless enough. If we hadn't been called, someone would have walked away with a sweatshirt and an iPod."

"Red will come up empty?"

"I think so."

"Go on." Dana tilted her head, wondering where his thinking would diverge from hers.

"The message was for all practical purposes harmless. Again, if someone else had found it—a laugh, a rip of the page, no harm done."

"But we were supposed to find it."

"Yes, we were."

"And you know that because…"

"No fingerprints. When we do a microscopic analysis on the cutout letters, it won't reveal any particular newspaper or magazine. It's extremely difficult to do that kind of work without leaving fingerprints."

Ben stopped pacing, stood in front of the blue denim backpack, and frowned. Dana realized it was the first time she'd seen the expression on him.

"A man's war cloaked in a child's things. It's an evil guise." His words were soft, spoken more to himself than to her.

She blinked—had to look away.

It was as if he had reached in and read her mind.

"Let's go view those security tapes," she said.

Eight

C lay had the wall-sized flat screen in Dana's office on and the surveillance video prepped.

She walked around her desk and took a seat, resisting the urge to pace. Ben stood, military stance, behind one of the chairs. Clay waited at the screen, remote control in hand. If he was surprised Ben was present, he didn't show it.

"Preliminary report?" she asked.

"You're not going to like what I found." Clay nodded at Ben who turned off the lights.

It occurred to Dana again that her staff was accepting Ben as one of the team, though he had been with them less than a week. Even Clay, who protected her more fiercely than a well- trained pit bull, acknowledged Ben was a good fit for them.

"The security cam on the front of the courtyard has our best view. I've checked two others, but they don't show any additional information. The time lapse you're seeing begins the evening before at 6:00 p.m."

"Well before dark." Dana leaned forward in her chair to study the teens gathered in front of the school. Looking so happy and carefree, they might as well have been from another planet. They in no way resembled what she remembered of high school.

"What are they doing there in the evening?" she asked.

"I checked with Principal Miller. A drama practice had released at five forty-five. If you watch the top left quadrant..." Clay used a laser pointer to indicate the persons he wanted them to notice, "...you'll see the two chaperones."

Clay touched the remote, and teens began moving in a comic, fast-forward fashion. "Everyone had gone by six fifteen. As you can see, no backpack."

A digital clock in the bottom, right-hand corner of the screen showed the progression of the evening as Clay continued to fast-forward.

"The surveillance runs continuously?" Ben asked.

"It doesn't. It can be activated in one of two ways. Motion sensors, which did not happen all evening. Or preset, periodic checks, which Miller had asked the security guard to set at hourly intervals—standard procedure during the school year. Those five-minute hourly checks are what you're seeing now."

Each scene showed an empty area in front of the school. When the digital clock read 6:23 a.m., teachers began showing up. By seven fifteen there was a steady stream of students, and Dana motioned for him to slow the tape down to real time.

"You've been through the entire tape?" she asked.

"Four times."

"Have you pinpointed when it appeared?"

Clay shifted from one foot to the other. "No."

Dana tilted her head and waited.

"It wasn't there at seven twenty-five, but it was at seven thirty."

Dana gestured for him to proceed. Both she and Ben leaned forward.

At seven twenty-five a flurry of students arrived.

"First bell?" Ben asked.

Clay paused the tape. "Yes. They have a warning bell at seven twenty-five and then a tardy bell at seven thirty. That's why you see this mad rush of activity. Everyone drops off at once."

On the tape it was indeed solid teenagers, with a few teachers on the fringes. The spot Clay had been pointing at was in the center of the open area in front of the school, actually in line with the flag pole. Even slowed down, it was impossible to tell when the pack had been dropped. As Clay said, it simply wasn't there, then it was.

They watched it twice. A wave of students pushed through, no one slowed down, the area cleared out as the tardy bell rang, and left in the wake was one denim backpack.

Dana sat back and tapped her fingers against her desk. "So a student left it."

Clay shrugged, rewound the tape again to seven twenty-five, and then paused it.

"Fast-forward to seven twenty-seven, Clay. Can you zoom in on this guy?" Ben stood up and walked to the screen. He pointed to a male in a blue-jean jacket, wearing a worn baseball cap. He looked no different than the other boys.

"Why him?" Clay asked.

"I don't know." Ben frowned at the screen. "He could be carrying something in his right hand. It's impossible to tell."

"But so could a dozen of these other people."

They all stared at the screen. Dana looked at the man who had caught Ben's attention. He looked indistinguishable from the others to her. They could see nothing but his back.

Clay ran the tape. As they watched, he disappeared with the crowd, heading toward the front door of the school.

Dana and Clay focused again on the area where the backpack would appear in another ten seconds.

Ben walked to the far left of the screen. "Stop the tape, Clay."

Dana turned to see what had caught his attention. "What is it?"

"This guy. The one in the blue-jean jacket. He's our man."

Now Clay joined him at the corner of the screen.

"He doesn't go into the school." Ben walked back to the right of the screen, demonstrating with his hands as he explained. "He walked in with the crowd—knew when we wouldn't be able to identify him. We know he's a planner, so he would have watched the school, known when the bell would ring, when the crowd was the thickest."

Ben looked to Dana for confirmation. She gave him a single nod. It was all the encouragement he needed.

"He's pre-planned where the backpack will go—in the center of the square, in front of the camera. He continues on with the students, but never intends to go into the school. Here." Ben stopped and tapped the screen. "He veers off and returns to his vehicle."

The room was silent as they all considered the possibility of Ben's scenario.

"Or maybe he's a kid who forgot something in his car," Clay suggested.

"Maybe," Ben agreed. "But when you forget something, you stop, you think for a minute, then you remember you've forgotten something, and you turn around. Back it up and run it at regular speed, Clay. I think we'll see our man's escape is a little more purposeful."

This time Clay didn't look to Dana for confirmation. He hit the remote and rewound the tape to the point of the first bell. Instead of watching the backpack site, they all watched the man in the blue-jean jacket. And what they saw was exactly as Ben had described it. When the man reached the front doors, he never paused. He veered like a jet on a predetermined course.

Dana walked to the wall and flipped on the lights. It was almost time for shift change, and they had a lot of work to do. She picked up her phone and dialed Nina's extension.

"I want all personnel here in ninety minutes. We're going to code yellow."

She hung up the phone and faced the two men in her office. "Clay, I want you to get with Red and do an analysis of this man. Tell me everything you can."

"Sure thing, Dana."

"Ben, work on the message he left. Ninety minutes isn't much, but do your best."

"You've got it, boss."

She half expected him to salute, but he didn't. He'd done a good job—she'd credit him with that. Give him a few weeks, and maybe he'd learn to address her by her name.

Nine

B en went out and purchased copies of all the local magazines, brought them back, and spread them around his lab. He'd barely begun studying the message under his magnifying lamp before he had to stop for the meeting.

Watching Dana clarify the situation to all of her staff impressed him tremendously. She led with quiet confidence. He had detected a general respect for her among the staff individually. When they were gathered as a group, it was more than obvious. Dana was a born leader.

She explained the situation succinctly, didn't insult them by reminding them what their jobs were, and she certainly didn't commit the cardinal sin of wasting their time. The purpose of the meeting was to deliver the most immediate information in the most expedient way.

Afterward, he returned to his lab. He thought he might stay there an hour, then go back to his apartment for dinner. He still hadn't unpacked his boxes. Three hours later his stomach began to grumble. Frustrated beyond belief, he left everything he had with Toby, the night-shift guy, who promised he'd stick with it until morning.

"Call me if you find anything," Ben said.

"If that's what you want."

Toby looked at him dubiously. The man was in his fifties and had a habit of rubbing his bald head when he questioned what someone said. He was rubbing it now, as if it were a bowling ball that needed a new shine.

"It's what I want, Toby." Ben slapped the man on the back and walked out of the room.

The muscles in his neck were knotted and tense. He could use a five-mile jog, but he'd be lucky to find the energy to drive home. Heading toward the break room to grab his jacket, he nearly bumped into Dana.

"Ben, why are you still here?"

"Actually, I'm headed home."

"Which doesn't explain why you're still here." She looked at him pointedly, and he realized again that she was very good at what she did. Dodging her questions didn't work.

"I didn't even notice what time it was," he confessed. "Then my stomach started growling, and I realized I was starved."

Dana walked with him out the rear entrance toward their parking area. "This will probably be a long operation. Don't burn out in the first twenty-four hours."

"Aye aye, boss."

Under the parking area lights, he saw her turn sharply toward him, and he couldn't help but smile. He did enjoy teasing her. Jiggling his keys in his hand, he stopped walking.

"I'll walk you to your car. Where is it?"

Dana shook her head as she looked around. "That's not necessary." She turned slowly in a circle.

As he watched her, the stubborn look on her face turned to one of confusion, then absolute aggravation.

"Something wrong?"

She let out a growl.

"Definitely something wrong. I completely forgot that I took my Honda into the shop. I was supposed to pick it up before five. Good grief." She looked around again, as if her car might appear.

"I'll give you a ride home," Ben said.

Dana shook her head, brown hair slipping over her shoulder. "No. Thank you though."

Ben looked around them, then back at her and waited. He smiled when the realization finally dawned on her that he was her best choice—unless she wanted to take someone off active duty, or call a cab.

"There aren't a lot of cab companies in Taos," she admitted.

"I don't mind. My truck is over here." He motioned her toward the old Chevy.

She gave him a small smile and nodded. "I live in Cimarron Hills."

"I know where it is."

"I remember now. You lived here before when you were younger."

"One summer between my freshman and sophomore year in college." He moved toward the truck, which he'd parked at the end of the lot.

"You're sure this truck will make it to the end of town?"

He managed to look offended. "Of course. Why wouldn't it?"

Dana stopped beside the black-and-white, Chevy truck, but she didn't get in when Ben opened the door. "It looks well maintained, but it also appears to be quite...*old*."

Dana said the last word carefully, as if she was afraid it would offend.

Ben still held the door with one hand. With the other he reached around her and tapped on the top of the cab. "Not only is she old—she's classic."

"Which is a good thing?"

"Extremely."

She sighed, but she did get into the truck. Ben moved around to the driver's side, determined not to waste any time. From the look on her face, she might rethink her decision and take a hike at any moment.

He cranked the truck and slipped it into gear. The moon rising over the mountains graced the sky with a shimmer of light. Ben realized he was happy for the opportunity to have a few moments alone with Dana. He wanted to find ways to help her, but he also trusted that God would provide opportunities in His own time.

He didn't feel a real need to spoil the night with his own voice. Dana looked tired. He suspected she didn't relax very often. Glancing at her in the light of the moon, he thought she was starting to loosen up a little around him. He didn't want to bungle the moment by rambling on about things she'd rather not hear.

From the way she stared out the window, he gathered she was preoccupied with the case. Or maybe she was trying to maintain the professional distance she valued so highly.

Ben slowed the truck as a fox ran across the road in front of them. Dana turned to look at him, a smile lighting her face.

"He was beautiful," she whispered.

"So are you," he said.

Her smile slipped, then fell away. She stared down at her hands, then back out the window as he continued down the road. "You say the oddest things."

"Why is it odd to say you're beautiful?"

She didn't answer, merely shook her head.

"Tell me about your truck. I know we pay you enough for new wheels."

Ben laughed. It felt natural to him, laughing when he was with her. She made him think of home and a long parade of tomorrows and all that might be.

"You don't play fair, Dana Jacobs. You know very well a man can't resist bragging about his wheels."

Dana tugged at her seatbelt, loosening it enough to allow her to angle into the corner of the truck. "Brag away."

"This is a 1967 Chevrolet, with a three-speed manual transmission." Ben rubbed the steering wheel. "It was my granddad's."

"He left it to you?"

"Granddad's still around. He'll turn eighty-seven this year. About the only thing he drives any more is a golf cart."

"When did he give it to you?"

Ben stared out at the stars sprinkled over the mountains. He had a hard time coming to terms with the fact that thirteen years had passed. He was used to getting up each day and doing what needed to be done. Days had piled up that way though, turned into seasons he couldn't recapture.

"Ben?"

"Yeah." He looked over at her and thought again how beautiful she was.

"You were going to tell me when your grandfather gave you the truck."

"Right. I kind of got lost in the memory of it, I guess." He reached over and squeezed her hand that rested on the seat between them. He felt her stiffen—knew he'd crossed into her personal space.

The memory of those teenage years still felt like a fresh wound at times though, reminding him of the isolation he'd struggled so hard against. He pulled his hand away to shift the gears in the truck and noticed when he did that she tucked both her hands under her legs.

"Granddad gave me this truck thirteen years ago. Makes me feel a little old to think of how long ago that was."

"You were fifteen."

"Yeah." Ben laughed again and ran his hand over the top of his head, as if he could ruffle his thoughts into some logical order. "We knew it would take at least a year to get it into running condition. It was nearly thirty years old then and had been parked out behind the barn for quite a while."

"So why—"

"Do you remember your high school years? Going to the school today and watching the kids on the tape…it brought it all back for me. If memories were a taste, for me those years would be bitterness—loneliness shrouded in confusion. Does that make any sense?"

Dana nodded.

"I don't know how my parents survived me. I was a brooder."

"Doesn't sound like the Ben I know."

Ben stared at something in the darkness. "I was a stranger then. Maybe everyone is at fifteen. I would sulk about anything and everything. It wasn't my nature, which made it worse. It was like wearing a pair of shoes that didn't fit, but I'd get up and put them on every day anyway."

"I'm sure you weren't so terrible."

"Oh, I was. My dad couldn't do anything right. Couldn't talk to me. Mom tried, but I wouldn't listen. But Granddad…" Ben let his fingers caress the wheel again. "Well, he seemed to know I was trying to scratch my way out of my old skin. Scared and mad about it."

They approached Cimarron Hills, and he glanced at Dana. "So for my fifteenth birthday, he gave me the keys to this truck. I must have spent more time in the barn with him, working on this truck, than I spent in the house that year. I know I slept more nights there than I did in my own bed."

"And it worked out."

"Yeah. It did. It took more than a year to redo it. I was soon hooked on the project. By the time I left for college, we'd turned it into a work of art."

Ben pulled into the residential neighborhood. Dana directed him down a street to the left, last house on the right. The home was modest, well kept, and tidy. He parked in the driveway. To his surprise she made no move to get out.

"Were things better with your dad by then?"

"Better, but still not good. It wasn't until I moved away that I was able to appreciate what kind of man he was. Distance can help with that sometimes. When I came home the first summer of college, it was as if those poisoned years had never happened. He didn't once hold them against me."

Ben studied Dana in the moonlight, thought he saw a glimmer of tears in her eyes. Reaching again for her hand, he asked, "What's wrong?"

"I think it's wonderful you had a loving family. You're very lucky."

Ben nodded, gently massaging the palm of her hand. "Yes. I'm very thankful for my family. My little brother was a much better teenager than I was. He had a little trouble in college, but he made it through. We stick together."

Dana stared out the window, as if she were searching the darkness for something lost. "What happened when you deployed?"

"To the truck?" Ben laughed. "My brother Jed offered to drive it for me those six years, but Dad bought him a newer model. Jed never did have a handle for mechanical things. Instead, Dad took care of it—kept it until I returned."

"Your truck is sort of a family heirloom."

Ben studied her, prayed for wisdom, then plunged ahead. "Not really, Dana. It's only a truck. I like driving it, because every time I slide behind the wheel it's as if I can see my granddad sitting here. I can practically smell his Old Spice aftershave. But it's still just a truck—nuts, bolts, pistons."

"I don't understand. I thought you loved it." Her voice had grown incredibly small.

He'd met her one week ago, and she was his boss, so he couldn't really explain what he did next. Perhaps it was the intensity of what they'd been through the last twelve hours. He'd experienced that in combat, too—strangers could become brothers in a day. Sometimes a day was all you had.

So he followed his heart, reached out, and tucked her hair behind her ear. "I know men are supposed to love their trucks, but I'd rather not invest that kind of emotion in a thing. You can lose things pretty easily."

"You can lose people too."

"Yes. I know that's true. But they're not really lost to us. Only gone for a time."

Ben waited. Why couldn't he have the words, the right words, to make loss and grief and faith easier for her?

"I understand what you're saying. I wish I could believe it." Dana pulled her hand away and opened the truck door.

"You can, Dana."

"But I don't know how."

She turned to look at him. In the dimness of the dome light, he could see the fear and longing. What had happened in her past to injure her? Something told him it was more than the ops gone bad, more than the guys on the wall. The pain in her eyes spoke of something personal. It nearly broke his heart in two.

Then she exited the truck, shut the door, and walked away.

Ten

D ana was at her desk an hour early Friday morning. She had a ten-year-old Ford sedan she kept parked in her garage, and that was what she drove into work. It wasn't as dependable as the Honda, but it would do until she could ask Clay to take her at lunch to swap out the cars.

She was early, and for once she'd slept well, which was unexpected. She'd thought she might toss and turn all night, especially after the feelings Ben had stirred up. She'd worked hard to be personable with her staff and yet maintain a professional distance.

Somehow she'd failed to convey that to Ben Marshall. Straightening her blouse, she wondered if she should speak to him directly about it or try being aloof. With some men aloofness worked, but they were going to have to work closely together. Sighing, she realized she'd need to speak to him and the sooner the better.

Scanning the larger room outside her window, she saw the day shift coming in, greeting the night people. It seemed everyone was here early. No doubt they were all keyed up about the new investigation. She envied the easy banter they shared with each other, but she firmly believed it was better if she kept herself at something of a distance. While it might be lonely for her, in the end things ran smoother. Personnel respected her authority more and could relax better when she wasn't around.

And to be honest, she didn't need the heartache that came with developing relationships. It only took one glance at the three pictures on her wall to remind her of the truth of that hard-earned lesson.

She stood, straightened her ivory blouse, and walked around her desk. Staff briefing first, then Ben Marshall. Who said Fridays were the best day of the week?

Clay brought her fresh coffee when she walked into the main room. Without her saying a word, the talking died down and folks found a seat. It wasn't as crowded as the day before when she'd called everyone in, but there were still twenty-five staff members in a room that usually contained twelve—thirteen since they'd added Ben to the day shift.

He sent her a casual wave when their gazes connected. She nodded, then took a sip from the coffee. Ignoring the way her heart raced, she reminded herself of the conversation they'd have in a few minutes. Once she was clear about where they stood, he'd tone it down. Then her personal life would once again resume its smooth, if somewhat dull, timbre.

Which was fine. She had enough excitement in her professional life.

"Cheryl, you want to summarize the night shift's progress?" Dana perched on a desk, but was careful to keep her posture straight. She wanted her staff to know they had her full attention.

Cheryl was a beautiful, petite, black woman. She'd been with the Taos office for two years, and she'd proven herself on a dozen missions. She had a sharp mind and a no-nonsense attitude that Dana appreciated. All of it was wrapped up in a soft, southern voice.

"There's little chance we'll find out who the sweatshirt belonged to. No identification inside of it, and the school ordered over three hundred last year."

This sent a small murmur through the staff. Dana took another sip of coffee and nodded for Cheryl to continue.

"Sayeed spoke with Sheriff Dunn's office about the iPod."

Cheryl nodded to Sayeed, who picked up the thread of the briefing without a pause.

The thirty-year-old Middle Eastern man was actually a ballistics expert. Because of his knowledge and experience, he'd made close contacts with the local law enforcement office. Several times they'd requested his help with an investigation. Each time Dana had happily complied.

"The iPod was reported stolen by a freshman girl named Angela Johnson on April 4. She noticed it missing after lunch and filed the paperwork with the school officer. I contacted personnel at iTunes. Since that time the unit has not been accessed."

"Any data at all?" Dana asked.

"Everything was fried to a crisp by Ben's laser," Sayeed confirmed.

Ben ducked his head and everyone laughed. The moment helped to ease the tension that had been crackling in the air like static electricity.

"I was able to use the files he so wisely downloaded before he lasered the drive." Sayeed shook his head. "Nothing had been accessed since 11:24 a.m. on April 4."

"We can assume our perpetrator isn't interested in the music or the sweatshirt then. He only needed props," Dana said.

She quietly studied each person in the room to see if anyone had additional information to offer. Nina's brown hand rose halfway in the air. Dana nodded, and the quiet woman stood. Nina was her detail person. If there was a detail they had missed, she could count on Nina to find it.

"Something about the book bothered me. I attended high school here, and I read *The Grapes of Wrath*. I remember being disturbed by it then." Nina paused, glancing around the room. "My daughter is a senior at the high school now, so I asked her about it. She hadn't read it, which I thought was odd. I called her teacher last night. She's a friend of mine. She said they pulled it off the reading list five years ago. The school board felt the content was too controversial."

Nina sat back down.

Dana sipped again from her coffee.

No one spoke as each person digested Nina's news.

Finally, Dana stood. "Possibly the book is another message from our perp. Nina, I'd like you to write me a summary of the book. I'm afraid I didn't read it either. Steinbeck wasn't pushed too hard in Texas."

This earned her a few smiles, though she could tell the mood of her group had once again turned.

"As I mentioned to a few of you, this is likely to be a long investigation. There are no indications that we are on a critical timeline, which is why I have moved us to a code yellow, not a code red. I expect you to do your job, do it well, and be out of here at the end of your shift." She shot a look at Ben, who had the grace to look sheepish.

"We will not be working extra hours this weekend. If you're scheduled, I expect to see you here. If you're not, I don't want your car in the lot. Cheryl is running lead tomorrow, and I'll be in on Sunday. As for today, I want to focus our efforts in two areas. The first is the manufacturer of the spiral. Look at employees in the past year. The second is the regional database of known felons. I know it's a long shot, but compare height and weight of the person Ben tagged on the tape. Any questions?"

When there weren't, the group broke up. Dana walked by Ben as casually as possible and said, "I'd like to see you in my office."

She didn't slow down to note his reaction. She wanted to get this over with and move on with the investigation. The last thing she needed was personal feelings interfering with her job.

55

Eleven

B en followed Dana into her office, thinking she looked even more beautiful than she had the day before. The woman could put a pair of black slacks and a simple, off-white blouse on the front of a fashion magazine. Whatever she wore managed to come off as classy.

When she turned her penetrating gaze on him, Ben realized Dana's beauty had nothing to do with her clothes. It was her amber eyes, which changed from a golden yellow to a coppery color, depending on her mood. There was a mystery and a depth there that would draw any man in.

"Close the door, Ben."

"Sure thing, boss."

"Have a seat."

Although her expression hadn't changed, something in her tone caused Ben to pause. He shut the door, but stood there, his hand on the knob. "What's wrong, Dana?"

She straightened the folders on her already perfectly neat desk. "There's something I'd like to discuss with you."

Looking up, she pierced him with her stare. Ben had

thought of her well into the night. Instead of unpacking as he'd intended, he'd flopped onto his cot and wrestled with the image of Dana Jacobs.

"Absolutely." Ben sat in front of her, rested his hands on the arms of the chair, and waited. He remembered the look of pain in her eyes the night before, and he knew now was not the time to rush her.

Finally, she cleared her throat, tucked her hair behind both ears, and looked directly at him. "I've been very impressed with your work. I think you're a fine addition to our team, and I'm pleased you've decided to work with us."

Ben had been chewed out enough times to know when he was being softened up, not that they bothered with easing you into a reprimand in the military. There had been a few women though, and then there was his mother. He almost laughed at the memory. One look at his boss and he knew— Dana Jacobs was about to let him have it.

She cleared her throat again. "However, I'm afraid you and I have taken a step in the wrong direction. I am your supervisor, not your coworker. While I value our professional relationship, I need to make it clear what the boundaries are. If I misled you in any way, then I want to straighten it out now. I never allow my personal life and my career to intermix."

She'd been staring at something over his shoulder, but when she reached the last part of her obviously rehearsed speech, she looked him directly in the eyes. She didn't even blink, and Ben had to give her credit. She believed every word she said. At least she thought she did.

When he didn't speak, she again fidgeted with her hair. "Do you have any questions?"

He felt the smile grow on his face, knew he should squelch it, felt certain he was about to head into dangerous territory. As so often before, he couldn't stop himself. Probably wouldn't have stopped himself even if he could have.

He relaxed into the chair and studied her. "One."

"Great. Ask away."

Ben leaned forward, his arms now resting on his knees, close enough to smell the light perfume she wore. "Did something frighten you last night, Dana?"

She froze, much like the fox in the beam of their headlights the evening before. She covered her surprise with a frown. "I'm not sure I know what you mean."

"Of course, you do. We're being honest with each other, and I hear you loud and clear. I'll respect your request. My only question is what about last night frightened you?" He searched her face a moment longer.

When she didn't answer, didn't even move, he stood and walked to the door. Before opening it, he bowed his head slightly and prayed again—silently and quickly—for wisdom. He could almost feel her struggling against the cocoon she'd built around her life. But he couldn't force her out of it.

"Personal lives are *part* of professional lives, Dana." He looked up at the three pictures he knew she treasured. "We can no more separate the two than we can leave our hearts at home in the morning."

He turned then, looked at this woman he could so easily care for, and smiled. "I'm not really sure I'd want to if I could. But I am sorry I frightened you."

With that he turned and walked out of her office.

Twelve

B en's watch only had to beep twice before he was up
and out of bed Saturday morning—if 3:00 a.m. could
be called morning. Glancing around his apartment in the
predawn darkness, he realized his military habits weren't
going to die easily. Not that it mattered. There was no one to
irritate with his rituals.

He padded across the room, in the darkness, and flipped
on the coffee maker. Then he opened the blinds, which
allowed in a small amount of light from the apartment's
perimeter security.

The apartment was an efficiency—tiny by most people's
standards, though much larger than anything he'd had
overseas. The design was old, but solid. It worked for him.

Turning on the water to the shower, he dropped to the
floor and began his regimen of push-ups and sit-ups. By the
time he finished, the water was hot, and he was wide awake.

Twenty minutes later he was in the Chevy truck, headed
toward Nina. Yesterday had been a lesson in frustration. No

one had made progress on the case, and Dana had been careful to steer clear of him.

This was his first Saturday in Taos. He'd asked Nina to arrange the meeting. She agreed without probing for any details as he knew she would. It was the Apache custom to stay out of other people's business. He explained it was important for him to see the father of a close friend, and the meeting needed to take place at the beginning of the day as the sun rose over the reservation's eastern boundary.

It was all he needed to say. She'd told him to meet her at the western edge of El Vado Lake State Park an hour before sunrise.

Ben drove west out of Taos with the window down, his thoughts on his friend and the promise he'd made so many months ago. He was grateful that today he could keep his word. He didn't understand why Joe had to die, didn't presume to know why he had been allowed to live. As he passed through Carson National Forest, he trusted God would give him the words he would need to ease the pain Joe's father must still feel.

Ben didn't consider himself good at comforting others. He only knew he was fulfilling a promise to a friend, and he had no choice in that matter.

Nina's Ford Explorer was parked on the side of the road. She stepped out when Ben pulled in beside her.

"Good morning, Nina."

As every other time he'd seen her, Nina's long, black hair was combed into a single braid down her back. The slacks and cotton blouse were similar to what she wore to work, but covered with a down jacket.

"I spoke with Joe's father. Follow me in your truck. Then you'll need to walk a short distance."

"Thank you."

She nodded once, her expression revealing neither curiosity, approval, nor disapproval.

Even in the darkness, the drive into the reservation meshed with Joe's descriptions and Ben's own memories—a rugged land dotted with piñon-pine mesas, mountains, and ponderosa-pine forests.

Nina pulled over when they'd reached the front of a rundown, gas station. This time she didn't get out of her car. Ben hitched his backpack over his shoulder as he walked up to her rolled-down window.

"Follow the path behind the station. After a mile and a half it circles around to the north side of the mountain. Mr. Tafoya knows you're coming."

Joe smiled. "Thank you, Nina. I appreciate you getting up early on your day off."

"My daughter has her final track meet today. I would have been up early anyway." Nina slipped the Explorer into drive and pulled away into the darkness that was fading into morning.

Ben thought of searching for the flashlight in his pack, but decided he wouldn't need it. His vision had adjusted enough to make out the worn path. The light would merely diminish his night ability to see.

As he walked along the path, his hiking boots pounding against the earth that had been the home of Joe and his family, he thought of that summer so long ago. He had been a boy then, intent on seeing new places. Answering the ad for help at the Days End Ranch had felt like an adventure. He'd met Joe on his first day. They'd become fast friends instantly.

It had been a summer of chasing girls, none of which they'd caught, and fishing for trout, which they'd had better luck with.

Ben glanced up at the sky. Stars were disappearing in the morning light. They reminded him of how much richer his life was for having known Joe Tafoya. Reconnecting in the army had been more than coincidence. It had been destiny.

Rounding the corner in the trail, Ben saw an older man, sitting with his back to him. The man's hair was long, braided, and gray. He wore a padded, flannel shirt to ward off the coolness of the morning. Sitting cross-legged, he faced where the sun would soon rise.

Ben slowed his steps, not wanting to intrude. When Joe's father still didn't turn, Ben lowered his backpack to the ground and sat beside him. He didn't speak, didn't want to interrupt this important moment in the Apache tradition. Joe had described it to him many times as they'd watched the sun rise over the Arabian Desert. So Ben sat beside the father of his friend and waited for the warmth of the sun to crest the mountain and brush his face.

When it did, he felt as if he'd been touched by his friend.

He was startled when Mr. Tafoya spoke. "You must be Ben."

"Yes." Ben shook hands with the man, looked into his eyes, and was surprised to see peace there. He recognized loss as well, but it had been softened by acceptance. "I brought something for you."

He reached into his T-shirt and felt the two sets of dog tags. He didn't have to look to know which one was Joe's. The explosion had scarred the metal. Pulling it over his head, he handed it to Mr. Tafoya.

"Joe and I made each other a promise that if anything ever happened we'd deliver these personally."

Tafoya looked down at the dog tags. His hand was old and wrinkled, more than it should have been for a man his age. It didn't take a genius to figure out he'd spent most of his life working on or around this mountain. The lines of truth were etched there.

He closed his hands around the scarred metal, then slipped his son's military ID over his head. "Joe talked about you a lot the year you were here. You two were always out trying to find trouble, mainly in the form of girls, according to Joe."

"We did our best. Not many girls wanted skinny boys who had their minds more on old trucks and where the best trout were."

Tafoya laughed. "It didn't stop you both from trying."

Ben looked out over the landscape in front of them. It was the land Joe would have worked if he had come home. "Sometimes I wonder if I filled his mind with my stories, my dreams. Maybe if I hadn't come here that summer, he wouldn't have joined up. Maybe he'd still be here."

Tafoya was silent for a time. When he spoke, his voice was strong and brooked no argument. As he spoke, Ben realized he must have struggled with similar questions. "When the Army men first drove up in their official cars, we knew what the news was. They don't come here unless it's to tell us our sons or daughters won't be back. I suppose it's the same for your people as well as ours."

A hawk soared in front of them, dove, and found its prey.

"Later they sent his body and a flag. The flag sits in a place of honor in my home. Joe wanted to serve his country. The Jicarilla Apache people have a long tradition of being hunters, gatherers, and artists. Jicarilla means *little basket maker*. We came to this land from the Canadian North, and for centuries we have flourished here." Tafoya breathed deeply of the clear morning air, then turned his gaze on Ben. "Even when Joe was a young boy he had a strong sense of honor. He would stand up for the little ones in the schoolyard. His Granddad once said Joe would have been a warrior in the old days. It was in his blood to defend. You only reminded him of what he was. I think though, by meeting you, he was able to recognize his calling. In the end, he was able to live his life with honor."

Ben nodded, worked to swallow the lump in his throat.

The old man finally stood and began walking back down the path. Despite his age, he was still quite agile. Ben had to hurry to keep up with him.

"I come here at least once a week to honor the ways of my people, but like Joe I have embraced the teachings of Christ. This is what gives me peace, knowing I will be united with my son and even my wife who went before him. This is why I can work each day and do so with the strength of the hawk and the peace of the deer."

Ben cinched up his backpack.

"I would be dishonest though if I said I don't miss Joe." Tafoya paused on the trail, put his hand on Ben's arm, and looked him in the eye. "Nina says you're living in Taos now."

"Yes, sir."

"I'd welcome a visit if you happen to be out this way."

"My weekends look as if they're going to be free."

The old man's smile widened as he began walking again. "I suppose you have fishing gear in your pack."

"Fishing gear, water, even some lunch. I was hoping you'd join me—go out along the Chama River. Joe and I used to find excellent rainbow trout there."

Tafoya laughed. The heaviness in Ben's heart eased to hear the sound. Somehow Joe's father had found a way through his grief. No doubt his faith had helped him through—his faith and the members of his tribe. Ben had weathered his losses much the same.

"I walk a trail like this easily, but I can't go running off down the river like a young man. You may go as my guest though whenever you wish as long as you share your catch."

He slapped Ben on the back, and they shook on the agreement.

Thirteen

T hree hours later, Ben sat beside the old creek, enjoying his lunch and wondering if the four trout he'd caught were enough. They weren't large, but they would fry up well. He could leave now and give them all to Tafoya, or stay and fish for more, which would allow him to take one or two home.

Finding the old fishing spot along the river had been no trouble at all. He and Joe had visited it often that summer so long ago.

Washing the last bite of his sandwich down with a slug of water from his bottle, he decided one more fish couldn't hurt. The day was still mild, and he couldn't resist the lure of the trout slapping the top of the water.

Pulling the pole off the ground, he checked to make sure the dry fly he'd been using for bait was still securely attached. He was reaching out to cast it into the stream when his cell phone rang.

Checking the display, he saw it was the office.

"Marshall," he said.

"We have a code red," Captain barked. "What's your ETA?"

Ben began disassembling his rod as he spoke. "Three hours."

"Hold please."

By the time Dana came on the line, he'd retrieved the trout and was jogging back down the trail toward his truck.

"Ben? I have to start the briefing in thirty minutes. Call me then, and I'll put you on the speakerphone. We'll leave the minute you arrive."

"Type of threat?"

"Semi-truck, loaded with explosives. Currently parked at Philmont Boy Scout Ranch. We have an anonymous tip they will move within the next six hours."

"Final destination?" Ben increased his pace.

"Unknown."

"Number of hostiles?"

"Two."

"Intent?"

"Unknown, but the caller gave us their route."

"Roger." Ben disconnected, dropped the fish, and doubled his speed to a near run.

Fourteen

D ana understood she had no rational reason to be irritated with Ben, which didn't stop her from wanting to slap the back of his curly head when he hustled into the office two and a half hours later.

The fact that he was wearing a fishing vest and had a touch of sunburn didn't improve her mood.

"Has anything changed?" He studied her as he traded the fishing vest for a Kevlar one.

"The semi has left the Philmont Boy Scout Ranch and is heading south on I-25. We have two spybots tailing it. They will continue to send live transmissions until the vehicle stops, at which point they've been programmed to back off."

Ben nodded and accepted the M24 rifle Sayeed handed him.

"The spybots were able to scan the load they are carrying while the rig was parked." Sayeed pushed two extra magazines of ammunition into his own vest, then passed two more to Ben. "Our best projections are half a ton of dynamite. The bots also confirmed two hostiles, both riding in the front of the rig."

Dana had turned to give last-minute instructions to Captain, but she caught up with Ben and Sayeed as they walked out the back door.

"What did we forget?" Ben asked.

"Me. I'm riding with the two of you." Dana walked ahead and jerked open the front passenger door of the Humvee. She turned in time to catch Ben throwing a quizzical look over the top of the vehicle at Sayeed, who only raised an eyebrow. Fortunately, they both knew better than to argue with her.

Sayeed pulled their vehicle into line with the caravan of five cars.

Dana worked the computer controls on the GPS video panel.

Ben leaned forward from the backseat. "The rig is the red dot?"

"Correct. They're still on Interstate 25 headed south." Dana sat back, slowed her breathing, and focused on what she had to be thankful for. They had not detonated at the scout camp.

"We'll stop them, boss." Ben's voice was quiet and certain.

She turned in her seat and hesitated before replying. His eyes locked with hers, and what she saw reminded her of the first day he'd walked into her office. His words were more than boastful chatter. Ben quite simply possessed an absolute certainty in what needed to be done and his ability to do it. The thought comforted her more than any other had during the last six hours.

She nodded and turned back to the GPS display.

"We should intersect them south of Wagon Mound. Clay's vehicles will cut to the north." Dana traced a route toward Watrous on the display. "We'll go around to the south with the other vehicle and cut them off before the tunnel."

"Have we intercepted any additional communications?" Ben asked.

"Not since this morning." Dana leaned back and stared out at the passing mesas. "We now believe their target to be Alamogordo, but it could be Las Cruces or El Paso. Either way, they won't get past I-40."

Sayeed nodded in agreement. "If we miss them, air cover is standing by to come in and take them out."

"We won't miss them." Ben took a deep, steadying breath.

"I guess you thought you were done with such things," Dana said. "It's not supposed to happen here."

At first she thought he wouldn't answer, almost wished she hadn't let the words slip between them.

"Probably no place is safe from such atrocities now." Somehow Ben stated it as if it were the day's weather forecast, nothing more or less.

To Dana the words felt heavy, full of sadness and someone's loss. Full of responsibility.

"ETA six minutes," Sayeed said.

They all wore communication units. Dana's was currently patched in with the regional office. They in turn relayed what information the spybot was able to gather. The surveillance planes were no bigger than a small bird and could fly within a meter of a target without being detected. A remote pilot *flew* the bird and operated its onboard programs.

"We'll position ourselves under the bridge." Dana pointed to a spot on the display. "State troopers have stopped traffic ten miles further south."

Sayeed unclipped the onboard radio and called to the vehicle behind them, relating Dana's instructions.

Ben again leaned forward to get a better look at the bridge up ahead. It actually passed through a portion of the mountain pass. Dana thought it would provide a good bit of cover for them.

Sayeed pulled to the northern most portion, then parked under the edge of the bridge overhang. They would be able to see anything coming toward them, but no one could see them.

Dana listened to the update from regional, then relayed it through the comm link to her group. "The rig has passed the checkpoint at Wagon Mound. Clay's group is closing in from the north."

She jumped out of the vehicle and walked to the edge of the shadows.

Fifteen

B en fought the urge to pull Dana back into the protection of the darkness. His common sense told him they couldn't be seen yet, but his heart told him to be extra careful with her.

"I'm going on top of the bridge to set up," Sayeed said.

Ben studied the flat road, stretching like a map in front of them. They had a good strategy. It should work, but he preferred to have a backup plan. To the left of the bridge, out in the sunlight and four hundred yards north, were three giant boulders. He touched Dana's shoulder and pointed.

"I want to set up there."

She looked at him in surprise. "Why?"

"Backup. In case something goes wrong."

She tucked her hair behind her ears and frowned. He thought she might argue, but she didn't. "Keep your comm unit on."

He flashed her a smile and was gone.

Jogging down the hot road, carrying the fifteen-pound rifle, Ben realized he might as well be back in Iraq. Like Dana had said, he had thought he was done with carrying a sniper weapon and setting up a cover. On the other hand, wasn't this why he'd taken the job with Homeland Security? To keep American towns from being torn apart like the ones in Iraq had been?

Ben knew that all he'd endured in Iraq had prepared him to serve here. The kids at the local school, Sayeed and Dana, Mr. Tafoya, even his own family in Montana—they all deserved a measure of safety. Dropping down beside the boulders, he felt his psyche gear up for battle. He would do what he had to do to protect those he loved.

Fifteen minutes later, Ben heard Clay over the comm unit. "We have a visual on the rig. He's passed our location and is headed in your direction at seventy-five miles per hour."

"Roger that," Dana said. "Cheryl, bring up the second car from the south in exactly two minutes on my mark. Clay, proceed from the north. I want to pin them at a point where Sayeed and Ben will have a clear shot—between four- and six-hundred meters."

Ben took three steadying breaths and fitted the rifle against his shoulder. With his back pressed against the boulder, he knew he'd be invisible to anyone on the road, but he was worried about Sayeed. The sun might bounce off his barrel given his position above the bridge's northern overhang.

"Three, two, one, mark." Dana's voice was perfectly calm. It occurred to Ben she might have done this before.

A dot appeared in his scope. Everything was proceeding as they'd anticipated... until Clay's voice came back over his comm unit.

"He's accelerating."

Cheryl had pulled her Humvee across the middle of the road and placed emergency flashers on top. Clay had come up behind the rig, and he, too, had flashing lights.

This was the point of no return. Would they fight or stand down?

"He's going to ram you, Cheryl." Clay's voice was disgusted.

"Let him try." Cheryl sounded angry. Ben could picture the petite woman taking on an eighteen-wheeler.

Ben didn't take his eye away from the scope, even when the rig began to slow down in front of Cheryl's Humvee.

"Better decision," she muttered. Stepping out of her vehicle along with three other personnel, she raised her firearm. They were all careful to remain behind the armor-plated vehicle.

Speaking through the loudspeaker of the Humvee, Cheryl said, "Power down your rig and step out with your hands up."

It seemed for a moment they would comply, then Ben saw the faintest glint of sunlight on metal. He heard the ring of gunshots at the same time the big engines of the rig powered up. In a breath, it was racing toward Cheryl like a demon on wheels.

He heard Dana scream for Cheryl's team to get out of there at the same moment the rig hit the Humvee. The next thing he heard was all too familiar—the sound of a rocket-propelled grenade powering up.

Ben felt his heart lodge in his throat. Sweat trickling down his face, he somehow resisted the urge to turn and check on Dana and Sayeed.

He heard Clay scream, "They're going to blow the bridge, Dana. Get out of there."

The next moment ticked by, as if in slow motion. Ben could have no more stopped it than he could have stopped his body from pulling in another breath.

The shoulder-launched, anti-tank RPG streaked from the passenger window of the rig and found its mark obliterating the top of the bridge.

Ben couldn't get a clear bead on the driver or the man in the passenger seat still holding the RPG. Part of Cheryl's Humvee remained stuck on the front of the rig. Something was on fire to his right near the bridge. He prayed with all his heart it wasn't Dana or Sayeed.

Carefully, he sighted in on the rig's fuel line, corrected for speed and wind, and took the shot. Even as the bullet traveled to its target, Ben threw himself behind the boulders for cover.

The eighteen-wheeler exploded directly in front of him. If he hadn't ducked behind the boulders, he would have been cut up worse than he was by the flying debris. But in this, too, his military training took over.

He counted to ten, then dropped the rifle, and ran to find Dana.

Sixteen

D ana woke up to Ben leaning over her. His face was such a mixture of terror and compassion that for a moment it took her breath away. Then she remembered the bridge and the explosion. She struggled against him, determined to sit up.

"Hang on, Dana. You're hurt." Ben brushed some debris off her face.

"Sayeed—" She jerked back from his hand, startled by the realization of how gentle his touch was.

"He's hurt, but he's okay. Clay is with him now."

Ben ran his hand through his hair, clearly frustrated. It took her a minute to realize there was blood running down his face.

"You're bleeding." She tried again to sit up.

"I'm fine. You need to take it easy though." He helped her to a sitting position, but stopped her when she tried to stand. "I think your left ankle is sprained. You were thrown by the blast."

Dana scowled at him. "How do you know it's sprained?"

"Look at it, Dana. It's already beginning to swell. I don't think anything is broken. I'm not a medic though. Hang on until one can get over here."

A deep line had formed between his eyebrows. He looked almost comical. His eyes met hers, and she was reminded of a basset hound she'd had for one summer. It had met her each day after school with that same pitiful look. She couldn't help laughing. He looked exactly like Bowzer.

Ben had been squatting beside her, but as she clapped a hand over her mouth, he sat in the dirt beside her and shook his head. "What?"

"Nothing," she mumbled.

"It must be something. I don't know what you could possibly think is funny."

He was aggravated now, and that made her laugh harder.

"Great. I must not have noticed your concussion."

"So only someone with a concussion would laugh at you, Marshall?"

"Maybe." Ben waved at the destruction in front of them. "Especially after we've blown up a road and a bridge."

"Not to mention the rig."

"The rig is toast."

They sat silently, leaning against the rocks where the blast had thrown her. From their vantage point, they could view the road below. Looking out over the charred remains, all laughter fell away.

"Nice shot, by the way."

Ben gave her a sideways look, trying to hold on to his scowl but not quite managing it. "Thanks, boss."

"Want to update me?"

"Cheryl and her team were able to get out of the way before the rig hit her vehicle. Two of her people were cut by flying debris."

Dana frowned. "How seriously?"

"Superficial wounds. Red is with them now."

"Go on."

"Sayeed's injury is more serious. A bit of debris embedded in his shoulder. Careflight will be here in another five minutes."

Dana had begun to struggle into a standing position as soon as he said the word serious.

"You might consider going on the Careflight as well. Get your ankle looked at."

Trying to put any weight on her left foot proved futile, but she waved his suggestion away. "Help me over to him."

Ben sighed. He didn't argue though. "Sure thing, boss."

He took her arm and wrapped it over his shoulders.

She tried to ignore the feel of his muscles under her arm. The same way she was determined not to notice his smile or the sparkle in his eyes as he snugged her in close to his side.

"Don't get any ideas, Marshall."

"Wouldn't think of it."

"You're enjoying this entirely too much."

"It would be faster if I carried you."

"That is *not* going to happen."

"Whatever you say, boss."

The helicopter landed in the distance as they hobbled down the hill and across the road. She could see Sayeed being loaded on a stretcher.

"You're uncharacteristically quiet," Dana said.

"I was thinking we're going to have a hard time keeping this story out of the news."

Dana waved the idea away with her free hand. "Great idea hitting the fuel line. We'll blame it on a mechanical problem."

Ben paused as they reached the side of the road. "Think we'll ever know where they were headed?"

"Will you and I know? Probably not. Someone with a higher pay grade than us might."

Ben laughed and helped her to where Sayeed was being loaded onto the Careflight chopper.

"Nice shot, Ben." Sayeed grasped his hand. "I owe you."

"There are no debts between soldiers, man. You know that." Ben stepped out of the way so Dana could speak to Sayeed.

Dana told him she would be there when he came out of surgery. She also promised to call his father herself.

As they loaded him onto the chopper, Red hollered, "Call me if you have any good-looking nurses."

Then the doors shut, the chopper rose, and it was gone. An eerie silence filled the afternoon. They looked around at the carnage two men set on destruction had wrought.

Dana tried to step toward the Humvee and stumbled. Clay and Ben reached her side at the same moment.

"Thanks," she said quietly. She stared at the ground, not looking at either of them. Finally clearing her throat, she gazed out over her team. They were a ragtag group, but they had done well. She was proud of them.

Suddenly, she was also very tired.

It would be a long time before she could rest though. Her job didn't stop now that the danger had passed. She owed a lot to the men and women who had risked so much here. First, she had a report to write up, then a phone call to make, and finally, a trip to the hospital. She would be there when Sayeed awoke.

She'd given her word, and she intended to keep it. No matter how exhausted she was.

"Let's go home," she said. Then she let Clay and Ben help her to the Humvee.

Seventeen

The report writing was a relief. Dana was able to lose herself in the facts of the mission. Reducing the previous twelve hours to data made them somehow more palatable. In the process, she could ignore the scars around her heart, wounds that were once more inflamed.

Speaking with Sayeed's father had been difficult. During the conversation she caught herself switching the phone to her left hand so she could rub her chest with her right. Looking down she half expected to see infected wounds—angry, red, and hot to her touch. She knew emotional scars seldom presented themselves so obviously, but her pain felt real—physical.

Sayeed's father spoke flawless English, though with an Iraqi accent. The man's voice was gentle and concerned. He'd insisted on reserving the next plane to New Mexico. Dana had assured him Sayeed was being well cared for, but it didn't lessen his resolve. He would be near his son when he awoke from surgery.

Dana had placed the phone gently into its cradle, and for a moment the loneliness she faced daily had become too much. She covered her face with her hands and allowed the darkness to win and the tears to come.

Of course, Ben had picked that moment to pop his curly head into her office.

She hid her emotions by snapping at him.

He'd wisely withdrawn, but the worried expression on his face had nearly been her undoing.

Now three hours later, she closed the report file, hit the send button, and powered down her computer. With any luck, she'd make it to the hospital before Sayeed was out of the recovery room. The doctors had called and kept her apprised of his progress.

Reaching for her crutches, she pushed down her frustration. The medics had assured her the sprain was slight. Hopefully, she would only need to use them for a few days. She hated the way they slowed her down.

Hobbling across the outer office, she nodded at George.

"Let me help you with the door, Dana." He rubbed the top of his bald head, looking concerned as he pushed the door open.

"Thank you."

"No problem." He offered a weak smile as she awkwardly made her way through.

The darkness outside surprised her. Somehow she expected the day to stretch and accommodate her.

"Do you need me to drive you somewhere?"

"No. Thank you. Since it's my left foot, I'll be fine. I'm going to the hospital now to check on Sayeed."

George didn't say anything else, but neither did he go back inside. He continued to rub the top of his head.

Dana smiled at the familiar gesture. "Problem, George?"

"You look tired, and I'm sure the docs are taking care of Sayeed."

"I'm sure they are. Good night, George."

"Good night."

The drive to the hospital was short, but too quiet. She reached for the radio, found a jazz station, and turned up the volume. Perhaps she could drown out the things that haunted her. Why had this day left her nerves so raw? She felt as if she'd left her skin back on Interstate 25 with the burned-out rig.

A silver-haired volunteer directed her to the correct floor and waiting room. Maneuvering through the elevator doors, she immediately identified Sayeed's father.

"Mr. al-Bakri, I'm Dana Jacobs."

Sayeed's father stood and accepted her handshake. Dana knew Mr. al-Bakri had been raised in Iraq, but had spent the last thirty years in the West.

"Thank you for coming," Mr. al-Bakri said. "I did not realize you had been injured."

"I'm fine. The doctors have been updating me on Sayeed's condition. They said he's doing well and should return to his room soon."

"Yes. We're expecting him anytime."

Dana's eyebrows shot up at the pronoun "we", but before she could ask she heard an all too familiar voice.

"Can I get you a soda or cup of coffee, boss?"

She turned and looked straight into the eyes of the last person she needed to see tonight.

"Why are you here, Ben?" Dana felt her back stiffen. She had to fight the urge to reach up and squeeze her temples, which were now pounding.

Instead of answering, he touched her arm. "Can I help you to a seat?"

"No." Dana clutched the crutches more tightly, as if he might try and take one from her.

She'd had to use crutches twice before. Both times she'd hated them. They made her feel like a hunchback. She tried to compensate by standing straighter, which was impossible bent over crutches. The result was a sore back and an intense headache. She could tell this time would be no different.

Right now she felt a powerful urge to whack something with one of them, and Ben Marshall was standing dangerously close.

His forehead was bandaged where he'd received three stitches, and his arms were scratched up worse than she realized. Dana noted he must have gone home long enough to change into a pair of jeans and a white T-shirt. His skin still glowed with his new sunburn. Why couldn't he stay home? He should be recuperating, not sitting in a hospital waiting room.

Ben sat in the chair beside Sayeed's father and handed the man a Styrofoam cup of hot tea.

"Why are you here, Ben?" Dana repeated the question softly.

"I suppose I feel responsible. If I had shot a moment earlier, they wouldn't have blasted his position with an RPG."

The pounding in Dana's head increased. Her smile felt carved on her face. "Could I speak with you? Privately?"

"Sure. Absolutely." Ben set his soda on the table beside his chair and stood with entirely too much energy.

Dana hobbled down the hall. She didn't speak until they rounded the corner. Unfortunately, the direction she picked led past the newborn nursery. She closed her eyes momentarily, wondered if this day would ever end, then drew in a deep breath.

"Are you all right?" Ben put a hand on her shoulder, which was his second mistake.

"Do not ask me that," she growled.

Instead of answering, he merely nodded and shoved his hands in his pockets.

"What were you thinking back there?" She watched Ben, waited for an answer, and wondered why he chafed those places she'd rather keep buried.

He took a moment before he answered, studying the pink and blue bundles beyond the window. When he finally turned to look at her, she thought she detected laughter tugging at his lips. Surely he knew better than to laugh at her at this hour.

"Do you mean when I asked you if you'd like a drink?"

"This isn't the time to be funny, Ben."

He ran his hand through his hair and all laughter left his expression. "Okay. What did I do this time, boss?"

The look he gave her was challenging. She realized in that moment he would not be one to back down easily.

"What you *did*, Ben, is talk about a covert operation to someone who is not classified to know the details."

He stepped toward her, closing the short distance between them. "What I did was admit my actions weren't perfect this afternoon, and maybe they cost the man waiting back there something. At least I can admit my mistakes. What about you, Dana? Is that what's eating you?"

He searched her eyes. She told herself to look away, not to be drawn into the depth of his gaze. She couldn't though. There was something about looking into Ben's eyes that was eerily like holding up a mirror to her soul.

He reached out and cupped her face in his hand. His fingers caressed her skin, reminding her of freshly laundered sheets against her body. She wanted to sink into it, into him, and never rise.

Instead, she took a step back and nearly fell over the crutches.

Ben dropped his hand and ducked his head for a heartbeat. When he looked at her again, his smile was back in place, his voice husky with emotion.

"I don't think anyone expects perfection. Would we like it? Yeah. Every day I wake up praying I can go through twenty-four hours without messing up, or making you angry, but it doesn't seem possible."

He turned away from her, stepped back toward the windows, and crossed his arms. She thought he wouldn't say anything else and wondered if she should just go.

"Look at them, Dana. They don't have anything to regret yet. They're still in a state of grace."

Almost against her will she moved beside him and looked at the faces of those tiny infants. Something she would never have, never hold.

"Maybe I did break another rule, and I'm sorry. But if by doing so I gave Mr. al-Bakri a measure of peace, if my admitting I'm sorry for not being perfect helps him to look at his son in a few minutes and accept what he sees, I'll take whatever reprimand you want to dole out."

Then he walked away and left her there staring at dreams she'd long ago abandoned.

Eighteen

I t was a few minutes past eleven by the time Ben and Dana said their good nights to Sayeed and Mr. al-Bakri. Sayeed came out more lucid than they expected. The doctors had been able to repair the damage to his shoulder, but he would not be shooting a rifle for several months.

Ben had watched Dana grow paler with each passing moment. He'd already decided to follow her home, whether she was aware of it or not. If he could get away with driving her there, he'd prefer that. Suggesting it would probably earn him a rap on the back of the head, so he didn't.

"You don't have to walk me to my car, Ben." Dana shot him a tired look as they waited for the elevator.

"What if we're parked beside each other?" Ben held the doors open as she passed through.

"I would have noticed your archaic truck. We're parked nowhere near each other."

"Whatever you say, boss."

They stepped out of the elevator into the night and a near empty parking lot. Dana's Honda sat at the far end of the lot, five spaces down from Ben's old, Chevy truck. At this late hour, there were few other cars in the visitor parking.

"I see you managed to retrieve your car."

Dana nodded, but offered no explanation.

He noticed she seemed to be having trouble with the crutches. He'd used them several times during high school.

"Ever been on crutches before?"

"Yes." She spoke so softly, he had to step closer to hear her.

"It helps if you relax into them. Did you ever play the game with your father where he picked you up under your armpits and swung you around? You need to relax like that. If you try to keep your posture straight, you're going to be very sore."

Dana nodded once, but didn't answer.

As they continued across the dimly lit lot, she stumbled and nearly fell. Ben reached out a hand to steady her. He heard her draw a shaky breath, thought he could see the fatigue weighing on her shoulders. But neither of them spoke.

Finally, they reached her car. She fumbled through her purse, searching for her keys.

His first clue she was crying was the sniffling.

"Dana?"

She found the keys, beeped the unlock, but didn't glance up.

"Look at me, Dana."

Her hair had fallen completely out of its clasp. He couldn't see her face, and she wouldn't turn toward him. She also didn't get into her car though. She stood there, frozen, wounded sounds coming from her throat.

It tore at him more than anything else she could have done. He could handle her reprimands, the cold, hooded look she had perfected so well. But this injured thing standing before him, afraid to move, was more than he could resist.

He took the purse from her hands and placed it on the car seat. Set the crutches against the car and pulled her into his arms. Instead of quieting her, his actions intensified her emotions. She cried all the harder, shaking in his arms. Her tears dampened his shirt, then wet it completely.

He didn't hurry her, made no attempt to stop the flow. Brushing her hair with one hand, holding her with the other, he kissed the top of her head and waited.

After two minutes the sobs lessened. After three she drew in a few deep, ragged breaths.

"I am so sorry," she murmured.

"I'm not." He leaned back against the Honda, fitted her to him, and was surprised when she didn't pull away.

"This isn't like me," she whispered.

"It's the adrenaline, Dana." He thought of how soldiers were trained to handle the destruction and carnage they both saw and wrought in the Army. How their training was sometimes helpful and at other times inadequate. Each man had his own way of coping with the things he did. For Ben, it always rested upon his faith and his family.

The question was, what did Dana lean on?

"I could see them," she whispered. "All of them, on my wall. It was as if their bodies were already in the ground, their pictures framed—Cheryl, Captain, Clay, Sayeed."

She drew another ragged breath. "Even you."

"One less thorn in your side." When she didn't laugh, he rubbed her back and wished he could pull the words back. "You can't be responsible for what evil men do, and you'll make yourself crazy worrying about what might have happened."

She sniffled again and rubbed her nose against his shirt. He smiled at the gesture and resisted the urge to tease her. When she peered up at him in the near darkness, he felt something inside his chest drop down to his toes. She looked so absolutely guileless.

"Why were you here tonight then?" she asked.

He wiped the tears from her cheeks and considered his next words carefully. "Sayeed and I share a bond now. I needed to be here when he came around—for him and for myself. He would have done the same for me."

Dana had stopped crying, but she continued to look up at him.

Ben didn't have a lot of experience with women, would never claim to understand them. At that moment he only knew what was in his heart.

He tilted his head and kissed her softly on the lips.

As he'd imagined, she tasted like the honey his mother had served when he was a child.

She pulled away slowly, both of her palms pressed flat against his chest. "I should go."

"I'll drive behind you, make sure you get home safely."

For once, Dana didn't argue.

Nineteen

B en had no idea how to go about courting his boss. He was fairly sure it wasn't called courting. He tried to explain that to his granddad on the phone the night before. Granddad had accused him of splitting hairs and said it all amounted to the same thing. He also insisted Ben take Dana flowers.

Somehow as he studied her during the Monday morning briefing, he couldn't imagine walking in with a bouquet of flowers. He'd get demoted faster than his Chevy could carry him out of Taos on Highway 68.

Which reminded him Dana was his boss, and he shouldn't even be considering a relationship with her.

But that kiss. And the way she'd felt in his arms as she'd cried. Those flowers might be a good idea after all.

"You sure your MRI came back clear?" Red asked as the meeting broke up.

"Huh?" Ben looked around to see if the old codger was talking to someone else.

"I'm talking to you, Marshall. Anyone else in this room have a bandaged head?"

Red threw an arm around him, nearly knocking him over in the process, and walked him to the coffee machine.

"Uh, no. I'm the only one with a head wound, but I didn't have an MRI."

"My point exactly. Perhaps you should have. You're looking a little dazed today." Red poured them both a mug of coffee without asking and slapped one into Ben's hand. "Drink this. It's terrible for your stomach, but the acid reflux is bound to wake you up. You heard Dana, staff is split between the school guy and the semi-drivers. Lots of work to do."

Ben set the mug down without hazarding a drink. "Hang on, Red. Maybe that's the point—to split our group in half. What if these two incidents are related?"

Red ran his long fingers through his beard and took a sip of coffee, staring at Ben over the top of his mug. As he turned the mug in his hand, he shook his head.

"Now I know you weren't listening. Dana said at the beginning there were no connections between the two, then she went on to report on each. After that she divided us up. Did you sleep through the entire briefing?"

"Hang on a minute." Ben grabbed a napkin from the table and pulled a pen from the crossword puzzle cup. "How long has it been since you've seen two incidents of this magnitude?"

Red sat in a chair and leaned it back on two legs, causing it to creak and groan. "Well, we haven't had an explosion like Saturday's round these parts ever, but that was your doing. And we're grateful to you. Don't take me wrong."

The big man frowned into his coffee, then took another drink. "As far as explosives of that magnitude going through our area, you'd have to go back four years."

Ben listed it on the napkin. "And two simultaneous incidents? Big ones?"

Red shook his head, took another sip of coffee, and grimaced. "Nah. Not since I've been here. Heard Clay talk about something in White Sands a few years back, but those weren't related. They proved it when they caught the guys."

"Okay. We're assuming these are not related. Let's for a minute suppose they are. How were we first notified about the trucks?"

"Regional boys called it in."

"And how did they hear?"

"Huh." Red fidgeted in his chair. "I'll have to check with Captain, but I think it was an anonymous tip."

Ben set the pen down and stared at Red. "How would someone anonymously know what was in those trucks?"

Red shrugged. "Maybe a third party had a change of heart. It happens."

"Yeah. Possibly. But three days ago we had twenty-five people on the school guy's case. Saturday we get an anonymous tip and everyone's pulled off."

"Which was the correct call," Red pointed out. "Immediate danger takes precedent. Dana made the right decision, and you know it."

"Exactly my point. She did what she had to do—we know it—and I bet our schoolyard friend knows it too."

"He could have done a lot of things to divert our attention. A lot of smaller things than blow up a bridge and kill two people, not to mention injuring several federal employees." Red stood, walked to the coffeepot, and poured another cup of coffee. "More?"

"No. Thanks." Ben tapped the pen against the napkin. "You're right. This is out of proportion to the schoolyard, unless the schoolyard is a predecessor to something big."

Red frowned and shook his head, but Ben plunged on.

"Something smaller wouldn't have pulled us away. It wouldn't have kept us away."

Red walked back to the table and sat down. "I'm not convinced, but say you're right. How would he have known what we're up to?"

The pause lasted less than three seconds, long enough for their eyes to meet and their thoughts to follow the same path. Ben felt the instant their minds seized on the same answer. They stood and pushed their chairs back, left behind the coffee cups.

Ben had reached the door before he realized he wanted the napkin with the notes. He hurried back to the table, snatched it up, and caught up with Red by the time he'd reached Dana's door.

"Morning, Red, Ben." Dana looked at them with a small, polite smile. "You two need something?"

"We'd like to talk to you," Red said.

"At the coffee shop," Ben added.

"Down the street." Red jiggled his keys in his pockets. "I can drive."

Dana continued to look at them. When she didn't accept the offer, Red added, "Or we could walk."

"Thank you, both. I appreciate it. I'm not very thirsty though, and if I were I'd probably drink some of our coffee."

Ben shot Red a look. He'd known this wouldn't be easy. Walking across the room, he stepped around her desk.

Dana popped to her feet the moment he entered her personal space. The woman was at least predictable. Well, she was predictable in some areas—the kiss had caught him off guard.

"What are you doing, Ben?"

He settled his hand at her elbow and guided her around the desk, slowing so she could reach for her crutches. "Red and I would like to take you out for coffee."

"But I already explained—"

"Is there a problem in here?" Clay stood at the door beside Red, looking fully capable of pulling his service weapon and shooting Ben if he forced Dana into a coffee shop.

Dana seemed to sense it as well. "No problem, Clay. I'm going to step out for a minute with Ben and Red. I'll have my cell phone if anyone needs me."

Clay nodded once but continued staring at them as they exited the building.

Once they were out in the morning sunshine, Dana attempted to turn on them. Ben could feel her bristling with indignation.

"Not yet, Dana. Wait until we're down the road a bit." He walked on one side of her and Red walked on the other. They moved slowly down the sidewalk in the morning sunshine, just another group of coworkers out for a stroll— except Dana hobbled.

"You better have a great story to go with this, Ben."

"Well, he convinced me," Red said.

Fifteen minutes later, she sat twirling her hair and ignoring the coffee and muffin Red had bought her.

"Tell me it's impossible," Ben dared her.

"I'm saying it doesn't seem likely. How could someone know what we were doing?"

"They could have an inside man," Red said gruffly. Obviously angry at the thought, he devoured half a cranberry muffin in one bite.

"No." Dana stirred her coffee again, though it was now quite lukewarm. "I know my people. I know their files by heart, including each of yours."

She looked up and met their gaze. "No. It's not an insider."

"All right. So it's not an insider. They could have bugged the office."

"How? When?" Dana began quartering her muffin. "When you lasered the backpack it would have fried any surveillance equipment. It didn't come in that way."

"Are you going to eat your muffin or dissect it?" Ben asked.

Dana pushed the muffin away. "Stay focused, Marshall."

Red picked up Ben's napkin from the workroom and flipped it over. Drawing a line, he created a crude timeline. "Let's suppose we have a real sicko on our hands. For the sake of argument."

Ben leaned forward, even as he noticed Dana fiddling with the clasp that held back her hair.

"Say he was watching you pick up the backpack." Red made a beginning notch on the timeline. "He saw you bring it back to the office. Probably knows our procedures. Certainly saw the increased number of cars at the lot when we had the full staff meeting on Friday."

"Could have been what triggered Saturday's incident," Ben said, his voice low and angry.

"Wait." Dana picked up her knife and poked at the napkin. "You don't get angry and order a semi with half a ton of explosives. Even if you're crazy. Walmart doesn't stock those. Regional boys received the tip Saturday morning at 11:00 a.m. That gave him twenty-six hours. How did he put his people in place, and why would they even do it? This is crazy. I'm not sure I'm buying it at all."

She dropped the knife, but when she looked at him again, Ben saw the worry on her face. It was the same anxiety gnawing at the pit of his stomach.

"He already had the semi and the men. He just didn't know when he was going to use them." Ben looked at Red for confirmation, then back at Dana. "We saw this often overseas. Adversaries would have several sets of contingency plans like chess pieces on a board. When the need arose, they'd be ready to move them into place.

Dana's hand slapped the table, causing cups and silverware to clatter. "This is not a chess game. This is a town with people who have lives and children."

Ben had seen enough of his mother's temper, not to mention his superior officers', to know when to keep his mouth shut. He waited while Dana chose the next move, fully realizing it was hers to make.

When she stood, her pretty eyes had taken on a wolfish tint. Ben looked sideways at Red. The big man's response was the barest of smiles hidden within the wooly, red beard. They might be up against a formidable enemy, but he would question his game if he could see the commander they were watching.

Dana grabbed her crutches from the empty seat, pushing them under her arms with a scowl, and limped out of the coffee shop.

"We've done it now," Red muttered as he threw ten dollars on the table.

Ben didn't even try to temper the grin on his face. "She is so hot when she's angry."

"Easy boy, that woman is your boss."

For some reason as they stepped back into the bright, morning sunshine and hurried to catch up with Dana, the reminder only energized Ben more.

Twenty

D ana's mind spun at roughly the same speed the earth orbits around the sun. At least that was what it felt like as she stormed back into their building, Red and Ben close on her heels.

They had protocols for a breech in security. She would implement them all. The very idea of being spied on made her feel violated. No one would succeed with infiltrating her teams.

She didn't speak to anyone before entering her office. She did slam the door shut with her foot and go directly to work. Within the hour, she'd sent encrypted messages to the regional office, notifying them of her intended steps, then to her staff detailing each of their responsibilities for the next twenty-four hours.

If data was being compromised, they would find out where the leak was.

She spent the next two hours completing routine paperwork, answering e-mail, and attempting to appear as normal as possible. At exactly twelve noon, she grabbed her purse and headed back out of her office.

She noted Ben was gone as requested.

Clay met her at the door to the break room. "Anything you need, Dana?"

"No. I'm going out for some lunch."

He nodded and moved back to his work station.

Dana was at the rodeo grounds in fifteen minutes. She pulled in next to Ben's black-and-white truck at the far end of the lot. He leaned against the railing, smiling at her.

He wore what he'd worn every day since she'd told him to lose the suit—khaki pants and a denim shirt. She could picture five sets lined up in his closet, hangers half an inch apart on the rod. It wasn't that she thought he had a lack of imagination. It was just so obvious his military training had stuck, would be with him until he had grandchildren on his knees.

His sleeves were rolled up to his elbows and the top button was undone. He looked as if he'd be at home in a boardroom for Microsoft or in the middle of an arena. In fact, she could picture him with a cowboy hat. The image brought a smile to her face.

"You know you look like a rodeo guy."

"Thank you, ma'am."

"What makes you think I meant that as a compliment?"

"I prefer to be positive."

Halfway to him, she stopped and rested on her crutches, reveling in the warmth of the sun on her back. The morning had brought a whirlwind of emotions, but with it a certain satisfaction. At least they were doing something.

Ben reached for his firearm as a Jeep turned into the far end of the lot.

Dana touched his arm. "It's Clay."

Ben nodded and pushed the pistol back into the paddle holster.

Clay pulled in beside their cars. He was wearing his customary black pants, white dress shirt, and tie. Dana couldn't help comparing the two men in front of her and thinking how very different they were.

Before she could follow the train of thought far, Clay was beside them. "Dana, Ben."

His voice was stiff with concern. He hadn't relaxed much around Ben, but neither did he seem hostile toward him since Ben had saved their lives on Saturday.

"We could still be observed here," Dana said. "But I doubt it, especially if you took the route I sent you."

Both men nodded.

"Good. I don't mean to slip into cloak-and-dagger mode. Neither am I going to take risks with any more lives. I'd rather disprove Ben and Red's theory so we can all rest easy."

Clay cleared his throat.

"Did you find something, Clay?"

"Possibly. Two people were left at the office on Saturday morning."

"Captain and Nina." Dana leaned against the metal railing that encircled the rodeo arena.

"Correct. I ran the tapes as you instructed. Two people came into the office after we left. The first was a guy asking for directions—looked to be mid-twenties. Nina gave the directions and they left."

"Plates on the car?" Dana asked.

"Outside cameras didn't pick them up."

"Why?" Ben asked.

"Because there weren't any front plates. When they pulled away, the angle was wrong. We didn't get a clear shot."

A light breeze had picked up, stirring the dust. Dana tucked some stray hair back into place. "And the second person?"

"That's where it gets a little odd. The second person came in when Nina was in the bathroom."

Ben began pacing. "Was this guy lost too?"

"Wasn't a guy. *She* claimed to be looking for a job. Captain tells her we're not hiring, gives her the standard line, etc. She starts asking what kind of business it is, and he reaches under the counter to hand her the city brochure we had printed up. Only there weren't any up front, so he had to walk over to Nina's area to get one."

"This woman was left alone at the counter?" Dana felt the small bit of coffee and muffin she'd eaten threaten to rise up.

"Yeah. I wanted to run a sweep for bugs, but if our perp hears us—"

"No. You were right to wait." Dana looked out over the rodeo grounds and wondered what kind of evil they were dealing with. She could almost sense it brushing against her like the small particles of dust in the air stirred up by the breeze.

"The lost motorist was a feeler," Ben said. "He was sent in to confirm how many people were in the room."

"And the woman?" Clay looked skeptical. "We have a perfect shot of her. We can run her against all the federal databases."

"She won't be on those databases," Dana guessed. "Probably someone he paid a hundred bucks to come in and drop a bug. All right. Clay, don't write this up. I'll send it to regional in my report. Good work."

Clay nodded, stood there waiting for more instructions.

"Don't mention it to anyone else either. Is there any way to confirm whether any surveillance units are in the office without him knowing what we're doing?"

"I can run a silent sweep from my terminal, but if he's hacked past our firewall—which he shouldn't have been able to do—he'll see what I've found."

"What about if you purchase a clean laptop?" Ben stopped in his pacing. "I have software at my place I can load on it. You can bring it into the office in your bag, maybe during the night shift, and never tie into the main system."

"Could work." Clay looked at Dana for approval.

"Do it. Take the rest of the day off, buy the laptop after lunch, and I'll schedule you into tonight's shift. If he's watching our database, he'll see you requested the afternoon off for personal reasons."

Clay nodded and turned toward his car.

"Hang on a minute." Ben pulled out his wallet, found an old receipt, and wrote his address on the back. "Meet me there in two hours. We'll get the software loaded."

Clay took the paper without looking at it, stuffed it in his shirt pocket, and drove away.

Twenty-one

B en watched Dana watch Clay drive away. She hobbled into the afternoon sun. It played on the chestnut color of her hair, reminding him of the fall fields of hay in Montana. The thought made him a little homesick, which surprised him. It wasn't often he wished to be somewhere he wasn't.

He expected her to give him a brisk nod and leave as well, but then Dana didn't always do what he thought she would. At times she was very predictable—operating by the book and to the letter. Other times, she surprised him. It was one of the many things he found fascinating about her.

As if sensing his thoughts, she turned and pierced him with a look.

Ben held up his hands. "Whatever you think I did, it'll be quicker for both of us if I just cop a plea bargain early."

Dana tilted her head and leaned forward onto the crutches. The gesture made Ben want to pull her into his arms, protect her from the meanness lurking in their midst.

"Marshall, I haven't decided what you've done yet, so how can we reach a plea bargain?"

"Huh. You've got me there, boss." He pulled at a weed, growing through the corral bars, and stuck it in his mouth.

Dana moved next to him and peered up into his face. "That's disgusting. You don't know where that grass has been."

His laugh rang across the rodeo grounds. "I think it's *been* right here. Grass never hurt anyone. Want me to get you some? You must be hungry."

"I'll pass. Thank you though." She turned, leaned back against the railing, and set the crutches aside. Then she shocked him completely when she removed the clasp that held her hair and ran her fingers through it, massaging her scalp.

"You can help me though."

"Anything," he muttered.

"Tell me how you knew." Her words were muffled as she leaned forward, head upside down, apparently trying to work away the beginnings of a headache.

"Knew?" Sweat rolled between his shoulder blades. He was too aware his discomfort wasn't caused by the mild Taos afternoon.

She parted the soft curtain of her hair and peered up at him. "How did you know, Ben? That the two incidents were connected? That our office had been compromised? That this, this man—and it's safe to assume it is the man on the video—predicted our every move so well? How did you get into his head?"

Ben forced himself to hold her gaze, tried to concentrate on her words and not the nearness of her. "A few years ago, I stopped believing in coincidences."

She blinked, then stood up straight. "I'm not following you."

"All the time we walk through life and ignore things, write them off as coincidences, refuse to see destiny, or fate, or the hand of God." Noting Dana's frown, he paused. "Call it whatever you want, we'd rather not accept things are pre-planned. It bothers us, makes us feel uncomfortable. So instead we say something like *isn't that a strange coincidence.*"

Dana shook her head and then smoothed her hair down with her hand. He watched her consider and reject what he was saying.

He pushed on. "For instance, is it a coincidence that you've requested a bomb expert for how many years?"

"Four, but—"

"Four years, and the week you get one, the week you get me, this perpetrator pops up with apparently some expertise in explosives?"

Dana's frown split into a smile. "So you're my destiny?"

"I know. You probably expected something different. But would you write it off to coincidence?" Ben studied her for a moment, then shrugged. "I'm not overrating myself as much as I'm saying I see the bigger picture more than I used to."

"And when you saw the semi?"

"I didn't think of it then, but later it started nagging at me."

Ben walked out of the shadow of the arena overhang and into the sunshine. The warmth focused his thoughts. It didn't make them more pleasant, any more than they had been a dozen times before. After a moment, he walked back to Dana, his boots crunching in the dirt.

"In Iraq, you wanted to believe every suicide mission was another nut, acting on his own. It was too much to think it could be a coordinated attack, working away at your defenses, but, of course, that's what it was. As soon as you accepted that truth, as soon as you stepped back and looked at the bigger picture, you could sleep at night again. At least I could."

"This isn't Iraq, Ben." Dana's words were soft as a gentle rain on his skin.

"I know, but an attack is the same thing, whether it's domestic or foreign. We had two hits within the span of a few days, and you want to believe they can't be related."

Dana's hands came up on her hips, once again prepared to argue. He stopped her with a hand on her arm.

"I don't mean you. I mean it's human nature to push the unpleasant truths away. I think that's why hostiles get a foothold early on. By the time we catch up, by the time we realize we're under attack, they've already done quite a bit of damage."

Dana sank back against the railing. "I should have seen it." She stared out across the fairgrounds as she pulled her hair back into the clasp.

"No. You did your job exactly as you were supposed to, which is what he expected."

Dana picked up the crutches and moved briskly to her car. Before she ducked into it, she smiled at him. "Glad he didn't expect you, Marshall. Whether your being here is destiny, or a coincidence, you're doing nice work. I owe you one."

HIDDEN

"Really?"

Dana shook her head. Muttered, "Why did I say that?"

He moved to his truck and grinned at her over the top.

"I gather you have something in mind," she said as she opened the door to the Honda.

"Actually, I do."

"I'm afraid to ask."

"Dinner and a movie?"

"I'm your boss, Marshall. We talked about this."

"I didn't mean we'd eat at work in front of the guys."

Dana's laughter surprised them both. "Taos is a small town in case you haven't noticed."

"We'll go to Red River."

Dana shook her head, got in her car, and started the engine. She did power down the window as she backed out though, which meant the conversation wasn't over.

"Or Raton," he added. "No one would know us in Raton."

She pulled the Honda even with his truck. "I once read a relationship you have to hide isn't worth being in."

Ben squatted beside her window. "Taos then."

"See you back at the office, Marshall."

She drove across the lot, and a small cloud of dust rose up around her car.

Ben found himself whistling as he hurried to grab some lunch before meeting Clay. It occurred to him he probably shouldn't be quite so happy about being turned down, but then he realized she hadn't said *no*.

She hadn't said *yes* either.

Maybe was an answer he could work with.

Twenty-two

D ana pushed open the door to her house and debated whether or not to turn the light on. The need for darkness won.

She dropped her purse on the entry table, leaned the crutches against the wall, and limped to the kitchen. With practice, she could be off the crutches by midweek. Drawing a glass of water from the tap, she considered eating. The thought of food turned her stomach. She only had to remember the surveillance devices Clay and Ben had found, and the sandwich she'd eaten nine hours ago caused dangerous rumblings to rise again. Impossible, she knew. The roast beef on rye was no doubt well digested, but her feelings of nausea remained.

Sinking into her overstuffed chair, she traced the stitching in the red leather with her hand. It had been quite the splurge several years ago when she'd envisioned these rooms being a home. Now it was a place she retreated to when they shooed her away from the office.

Realizing her thoughts were turning morose, she flipped on the table lamp and checked the time. In Texas it would be eight. Possibly, Erin would be home. Reaching for her cell, she pushed two, her sister's speed-dial preset.

Just as she feared her call would transfer to voice mail, Erin answered on the fifth ring.

"Hey, Sis." Erin's voice fell like a comfortable shawl around her shoulders.

"Hey, yourself."

"How are things in the West?"

"Miserable," Dana admitted, flipping off her shoes and propping her feet on the ottoman with a groan. "How's the South?"

"About the same. I went to rescue a dog. Got there and found out the dog was actually a two-hundred-pound pig."

Dana wouldn't normally have laughed so long or until the tears were running down her face, but she had passed tired several hours ago and entered the black world of weary.

"Catch a flight and come help me with this orphan."

"Not a chance."

"Chicken."

"Absolutely. I'm not the one who decided to run an ark."

"I love my work, pig and all."

Dana snuggled into her chair and felt a small measure of satisfaction for the first time since rising sixteen hours ago. "How is Noah's Ark doing?"

"Fine. I'm still the only animal rescue facility in Livingston, so I stay busy."

"That's why you get the pig calls."

Dana heard the sound of a slop bucket being emptied.

"Daisy was a 4-H project no doubt. Or at least she started out as one. Then the family up and moved. Daisy didn't get a seat in the family sedan."

"Did she have a name tag around her neck?" Dana asked.

"I can't call her, Hey Pig," Erin said.

"Sweetie, you've been naming animals since you were old enough to talk." Dana's mind flashed back to a ragged teddy bear. The pain was sharp and dangerous.

"Yeah, but the stuffed ones didn't eat so much." Erin as usual could follow her train of thought better than anyone else. "You should have seen her, Dana. At first I thought there was no animal there. Then I noticed this reddish lump on the ground."

Dana heard the sorrow and regret in Erin's voice. She wished for the thousandth time since moving west that she could be there for her—to share a cup of tea, make sure she was taking care of herself, even carry a slop bucket for her.

"She's a Duroc breed?"

"Yeah. Wouldn't even stand up for me. I had to put her on a gurney and drag her to the truck. If I could get hold of people who neglect their pets... All they had to do was drop her off on the way out of town."

"Maybe they're the ones who called."

"No. I'm sure it was the neighbors. I saw them watching at the window as I drove by."

Dana heard a soft grunt and the sound of crickets in the background.

"Is she eating now?"

"A little. Mostly, I'm happy to see her drinking. One-half to two-thirds of a pig's body weight is water. She didn't have any in the pen where they left her."

"Folks are cruel, Erin." Dana thought of her conversation with Ben on Saturday night. Before she knew it, his words were tumbling from her mouth. "You can't be responsible for what evil or irresponsible people do. Don't make yourself crazy worrying about it."

Erin's silence filled the line across the miles. Finally, her laughter erupted like a kettle boiling over. Dana smiled to herself and switched the phone to her other hand.

"Now what did I say that was so funny?"

"I just want to know who he is. You're a wise gal, but that did not sound like my older sis. Fess up. What's his name?"

Dana grinned in spite of herself, glad Erin wasn't there to see the blush staining her face as bright as the leather chair. "You mean I can't change my attitude about things?"

"Oh, you can, but it's rather sudden for someone who's a confirmed Type-A personality. Now who is he?"

Dana worried the seam on the chair and tried to think of where to start.

"Wow," Erin murmured. "This must be really good if you're having that much trouble spitting it out."

"It's not what you're thinking."

"Ahh."

"Don't *ahh* me, Erin Breanne. Ben is our new explosives expert, and…" Dana sighed, stuck again trying to find the right words.

"Start with a physical description."

"But that's not the part haunting me," she whispered.

"So he's ugly?" Erin's voice was still teasing, but she was no longer laughing.

"No. Of course not. Erin, he works for me. I'm his boss. I can't even be thinking like this."

"I'm your sister. I won't report you. Now tell me what he looks like."

"Good point." Dana sunk lower in the chair, though it meant she was practically lying down. "Okay. He's a good half a foot taller than I am."

"You were five-foot-eight last time I checked. Haven't been shrinking have you?"

"Nope. Not yet."

"All right. That puts mystery man at six-foot-two."

"Ex-military, but you couldn't tell it by his hair. He wears it to the collar, curly and sun-streaked."

Erin laughed again. "Sounds like a surfer dude."

"Right? Except he's from Montana. Last I checked there were no beaches there. But his body is great." Dana giggled with Erin. For a moment she felt sixteen again and wonderful as her worries slid away. "Let's just say he must have kept the military regimen going."

"Gee, Sis. I think I'd forget he's your subordinate. What about his eyes? You know we always said they were the window to the soul, the most important part."

"That's what unsettles me the most."

"You better not say he's creepy."

"Not at all. Worse. They're the most peaceful, serene, beautiful..." Dana switched the phone to her other hand again, wiping her sweaty palm against her pants. "We sound like two teenagers."

"Yeah. Only I have an ark with a pig—"

"And I have a major case to solve."

"How bad is it?" Erin's voice was all seriousness now.

"I've had worse," Dana said with more confidence than she felt. She shook her head, then felt stupid doing so since Erin couldn't possibly see her. "At least I think I have. To tell you the truth, we're not exactly sure what we're dealing with yet."

"Is that why it's bothering you so much?"

"I almost lost some of my team yesterday. This perp, it's like he's playing with my mind. Sometimes I think he wants more than to win."

"And your guy—"

"Ben."

"Ben is helping you with this?"

"Yeah."

"Then thank him for me."

Dana smiled into the phone and realized the knots in her shoulders had eased completely. "I will. You take care of Daisy, okay?"

"Absolutely. I'll call you with an update in a few days."

"I love you, Erin."

"Same here, Sis."

Dana turned off the lamp and sat in the darkness, relishing the fact she had so many people on her side.

It wasn't a coincidence either.

She wasn't sure it was a miracle, as Ben thought. But it was a fact she could take comfort in.

Twenty-three

B en waited and watched Dana for the next week. She showed up without the crutches on Wednesday and stopped limping completely by the following Monday. He figured ten days was plenty of time to recover from a light sprain.

Sayeed had returned to work earlier that day. He'd only be seeing desk duty for six weeks, but his presence in the office gave Ben the opening he'd been waiting for.

Dana's decision to leave the surveillance bugs in place was a brilliant one in his opinion. It put them back on top. Not only did the perp think he was proceeding undetected, but they could now feed him misinformation.

Of course, knowing your every move was being monitored also made for a tense work environment.

Which is one of the reasons Ben found himself keeping such a close eye on his boss. If you paid attention, you could see the stress take a greater toll on her every hour.

Plus he rather enjoyed making up reasons to stop by her office. She was prettier than watching a trout splash in a sunlit stream.

"What now, Ben?" Dana looked up tiredly when he came to her door at three thirty.

"I was wondering if we could talk about that other thing."

Dana looked up at him, but didn't raise her head, reminding him of a librarian he had angered more than once in high school.

She shook her head and turned her attention back to the papers on her desk. "Thing. What thing? You're going to have to be more specific."

"Uh. The thing." He glanced back over his shoulder, then stepped into her office. "You know. The 'you owe me' thing."

This time Dana leaned back in her chair and gave him her full attention. "I owe you?"

"Yeah. For doing such a good job?" Ben smiled, placed his arms behind his back, and waited for her to remember. When she continued to stare at him blankly, he cleared his throat and tried again. "Last week, at lunch. You said I had done nice work, and you owed me."

Dana put her hands over her face. She was either counting to ten or praying for patience. "I'm busy, Ben."

"Everyone has to eat."

When she lowered her hands, he had pulled out the note he'd written on a full sheet of paper. In large letters it read, "Rock climbing and dinner. Need to leave by 4:00. Meet at my place?"

Her eyes grew wider as she read.

He knew he'd surprised her when she didn't answer immediately.

"I, well, I…"

"Great. It's a deal then." He pivoted on his heel and headed for the door.

"I can't leave an hour early." Her tone made it clear she thought he'd lost his mind.

He stopped in the doorway and smiled back at her. "Why not? You got here an hour early. So did I. Shouldn't be a problem—technically." When she didn't answer, he gave her a little salute. "See you there."

And while her mouth was still hanging open, he turned and fled from her office.

He left immediately so she wouldn't be able to find him and offer an excuse. Pulling in front of his apartment, he jumped out and ran up the stairs. He'd changed his clothes and put together a small cooler full of bottled water and snacks by the time she knocked on the door.

"Hi." Her eyes were as big as a doe's. He knew he had to move fast or she would still find a way to back out.

"I already have packs in the car," he said, walking outside where she waited.

"Ben, I don't have—"

"Clothes? Supplies? Courage?" He laughed when a spark of defiance came into her tired eyes. "We'll stop by your place and get some clothes. I have all the other supplies. If you have the courage, we should be good."

"Marshall, do you know how tired I am?"

He reached out, tucked the hair back from her face. "Yeah. I do."

"I should be working. Doing something to catch this creep—"

"Long investigation. Not a critical timeline. Do your job, do it well, and be out of the office at the end of your shift." He could tell that hearing her words quoted back to her was having the desired effect. "That's exactly why I'm calling in my favor this way. Come on. No experience required. What do you say? It's a great way to work off tension."

Dana hesitated, then shook her head as she walked back down the stairs. "If I break something, you're fired."

"You've got it, boss."

He followed her in his truck, retracing the roads back out to Cimarron Hills. While she was inside changing, he transferred the climbing packs he'd loaded into the passenger seat that morning to the bed of the truck.

In less time than he'd have thought possible, she returned in hiking pants and a long sleeve, powder blue, cotton shirt. Her hair was pulled back with a Nike sweat band.

He smiled, but didn't say anything.

"What?"

"Nothing."

"It's something or you wouldn't be sporting a Cheshire grin on your face." She climbed into the two-tone truck as he held the door.

He walked around, started the truck, and maneuvered out of the driveway. Neither of them spoke until he'd merged onto Highway 64.

"I was smiling because you look nice in casual clothes, and you dressed perfectly." Ben glanced at her, but she was busy studying the passing scenery. "Have you climbed before?"

Dana snorted. "No. I haven't. Generally, I have more common sense than when I'm with you."

His laughter filled the truck. Settling his arm across the back of the seat, he touched the back of her neck, then began gently massaging the bunched muscles.

"Then you've hiked."

She tensed beneath his hand, but he waited as he would for a fish to settle on a line.

"I used to hike," she admitted. "When I first came to Taos."

She studied the trees and mountains and eventually she forgot to hold her shoulders up. Ben felt her fall into the memories she wasn't ready to share. He continued to massage the knot in her neck muscles.

"I thought I'd been assigned to heaven. Where else is there so much sunshine and cool temperatures?"

"Not to mention fishing, canyons, cliffs..." Ben pulled his hand away as he signaled to pass a farmer moving his tractor. When he did, Dana relaxed into the corner of the truck and studied him.

"How long were you here before?" she asked.

"A summer. One summer doesn't seem like a long time, but it made an impression on me." He moved his visor to block the descending sun as the road turned north. "In many ways those three months changed the course of my life. But that's another story."

Ben still felt the ache from the loss of his best friend. He could accept God's will in all things, but rarely a day passed by when he didn't remember—and miss—Joe. Shaking the loneliness away, he glanced over at Dana.

"What matters this afternoon is I learned to climb from a very good friend I met then—Joe Tafoya."

"Apache?"

"Yeah. Joe had climbed since he was a boy. I think he took me with him because he enjoyed watching me scrape myself up. I was a slow learner, but I was stubborn."

"You're kidding. You?" Dana yawned and pushed up on her sunglasses. "I guess you outgrew it."

Ben reached for the radio dial, set the volume low, and pushed in the Eric Clapton cassette he kept handy for road trips. "Sarcastic women can usually benefit from a nap."

"Uh-huh." She scrunched further down in the seat, until her head could rest comfortably against the back. Her arms crossed over her stomach, and the frown lines that worried the space between her brows relaxed.

Ben wasn't sure he'd ever seen a sight that made him feel any happier, any more content.

Forty minutes later, he was tempted to keep driving when he reached Cimarron Canyon State Park.

He slowed the truck as he tried to decide whether to make a loop and drive her back. Maybe she was more tired than he realized. When he shifted down the gears, she blinked twice, then sat up and stretched.

"Wow. I was totally out, Marshall. It was either the music or the company."

"I'll send your regards to Clapton."

Ben pulled up to the state park visitor entrance. There was no charge to enter the park. A man of about seventy with a close-cropped white beard wore a tag which said State Park

Host. He asked if they'd like a map, but Ben declined. He did tell the gentleman where they'd be climbing, and the old guy promised to log them into the book.

"Why did you do that?" Dana asked.

"Safety precaution. You should always let someone know where you're climbing just in case."

"In case what?" Dana's voice rose a notch.

"Relax, boss." Ben pointed to three deer, standing near the riverbed.

The does succeeded in distracting her for about ten seconds. "Why didn't you get a map?"

"I have the map." Ben tapped his head. "It's all up here."

Dana glanced at him. "Frightening. I thought I heard something rattling while I was sleeping. Figured it was this truck."

Ben knew then she was rested enough to climb.

The valley began to narrow and the scenery grew even more dramatic as they entered Cimarron Canyon.

"It's beautiful, Ben."

"I love this place. The hiking is great too." He slowed the truck so they could take in the aspen trees growing along the riverbank. As the sheer cliffs of the Palisades came into view, he heard Dana gasp. Looking over at her, he saw the worry lines were back and fully in place.

"Don't worry. We're not climbing there."

She let go of the breath she'd been holding and gave him a nervous smile.

Ten minutes later he parked in the small dirt pullout on the right, stepped out of the truck, and was surrounded by memories as sweet as Dana's smile.

Twenty-four

They sat on the tailgate and had a snack of granola bars and water, then walked the ten-minute hike to Maverick Cliff and began unpacking Ben's equipment. Ben went over the basics of clipping on and rope safety, then helped her into the gear.

Dana stood staring at the fifty-foot-high cliff.

"What did you say it's called?"

"The Block Head." Ben checked Dana's harness one more time. "There are plenty of jugs and in-cut edges."

Dana touched her helmet and peered up at the top again. They had passed a few other climbers. At least someone might hear her body when it fell to the ground, broken and busted.

"This is a bad idea," she whispered.

"Trust me," Ben said. "We'll go slow. You remember how to clip on?"

"Yeah. I've got that part."

"Good. You're going to clip on where I clip on. You'll also be tied to me. You can't fall, Dana. It's like parachuting in tandem."

"Only we're going up." She smiled at the comparison.

"Exactly."

"Unless we fall."

"We won't fall. Are you ready?"

"As I'll ever be."

The south-facing sandstone was warm to her touch. As she climbed behind Ben, she focused totally on where her hand went, the placement of each foot, clipping on carefully. Pressing her body against the cliff, she forgot to worry about what was happening in the office thirty some miles to the south.

And each time she came to a difficult hold, she would reach and find Ben's hand there—strong, firm, tanned. The muscles in his forearm and bicep would flex and tighten as he reached for her, reminding her of a finely honed machine. She never doubted he could help her to the in-cut edge. By the time they gained the top, the bond between them was as strong as the dynamic ropes that kept them from falling to the ground fifty feet below.

"That is an amazing view," Dana whispered breathlessly. Her fingers, toes, arms, and legs ached. And she couldn't wait to do it again.

The sun was nearing the horizon. A painter's cascade of color spread out before them.

"I'm glad you like it, Miss Jacobs." Ben fished in his pack for energy bars and handed one to her.

"I seriously hope this is not your idea of dinner."

"What? You want more? I bring you to the best table, with the best view—"

"But not the best food." Dana grimaced as she tried to swallow the bite she'd taken.

"They do take some getting used to."

"Yeah. They're a little like oats."

"So you've eaten oats, have you?" Ben slugged his bite down with water, then poured the small amount left in his bottle over his head, causing Dana to laugh outright.

"What is it about men that makes them cool off like a dog under a water hose?"

"We're beasts at heart, I suppose. And I'll have you know I do have better dinner plans. First though, you have to go down."

"Not yet."

"No, we can wait a few more minutes." Ben leaned back on his elbows and looked out at the panoramic view.

Dana realized one of the things she appreciated the most about him was his ability to be silent with her. They could share a quietness that wasn't uncomfortable. The sun was dropping like a giant beach ball, and the nightingales were calling to one another. A light breeze cooled the sweat on her face.

Within her soul, something like peace began to blossom.

Then she remembered she still had to climb down.

Twenty-five

D ana peered over the edge and frowned. "Maybe I'll sleep here."

"Until?" Ben reached for his pack and pulled a second bottle of water from it.

"Until the helicopter comes?"

Ben smiled his slow, lazy smile, and Dana knew she was in trouble. Of course, she'd suspected as much the minute she'd climbed into his pickup.

"Trust me," he whispered as he stood and held out his hand to her. He once again checked her harness, then tapped the top of her helmet. "You're good, Jacobs. We'll be on the ground in no time."

Dana pulled on her gloves, readjusted her knee pads, and tried to think of something else she could do to put off the inevitable.

"Ready?" Ben asked.

"No."

"Lean into the harness, sweetie. I'll do all the work up here. Put your feet against the wall, maintain your balance, and I'll ease you down as gently as your mother set you in a cradle."

Dana closed her eyes and pushed down the pain that any mention of her mother brought. When she looked at Ben again, he had turned away and was adjusting his pack and their ropes.

Walking to the edge, he motioned her over. "Let's do it. The sooner we start, the sooner you get to eat."

"I'm not so hungry now," she admitted.

Ben put his arms around her in a bear hug, then pivoted so her back was to the void.

"How will you get down?" Dana asked.

"Don't worry about me. I'm a veteran." Ben backed up five paces.

"I'm not talking about your military status, Marshall."

"Step off, Jacobs. Hold on to the rope and lean into it."

One minute she was looking at Ben's lopsided smile, the next she was suspended in air, staring into a sky as clear as the surface of the river they had passed. Although the sun had set, light lingered. Squinting, she could make out the first of the evening's stars, struggling to find its place among the heavens.

Then she realized she was dropping.

The feeling was exhilarating and terrifying.

If she made it to the ground she was going to kill him for talking her into this. No, first she'd fire him, then kill him. If she survived.

Her feet touched rock, and she heard his words reminding her to relax. A calm assurance chased away her fears. She knew Ben wouldn't drop her. Slowly, almost imperceptibly, she watched The Block Head disappear as she slid down it—like a baby being laid to sleep.

The strangest thing happened in those few moments. She suddenly did remember her mother's smiling face—not with her, but with Erin. She'd been seven when her mother had brought her baby sister home. Looking up at the sky and rock, she could clearly see her mother placing the baby swaddled in pink into her arms.

She'd been every bit as terrified then as she was the moment she'd stepped off the rock face above. All those years ago, her mother had whispered to her as Ben had. "Trust me, Dana."

Erin had been soft and warm. She'd looked up at her, made little cooing sounds, then gone back to sleep.

Her feet scraping the ground brought Dana back to the present. She unclipped the rope as Ben had shown her. She tugged on it twice, and Ben pulled it up. Stepping back, she watched as he made his way down the rock face.

He made it look so simple. Somehow Ben made much of life look easier than it was.

He'd given her something precious tonight though. More than an evening to relax, he'd given her a memory she'd buried somewhere along the way.

Maybe she'd wait to kill him.

"Easier than going up?" Ben asked.

"Much." Dana smiled as he gave her a congratulatory hug.

"You did it," he said.

"Yeah." She picked up the rope and helped him store it back into the pack. She thought of telling him about her mother and Erin, but the images were still too fresh, too raw. Instead, she seized on a safer memory. "Coming down reminded me of an exercise we did during Homeland Security training. It was supposed to help with our trust issues."

"Yeah. They have something similar in the military."

Dana stopped and looked at Ben, suddenly realizing this hadn't been training though. Her life had rested in his hands as she repelled down the cliff. And it was okay, because she did trust him. Not only was she sure he knew what he was doing, but she knew he wouldn't allow any harm to come to her.

"What?" Ben reached up and wiped at his face. "Am I wearing chalk dust?"

"Nothing, Marshall. Let's go."

"Sure you don't want to do it again?" he teased as they walked back to the car.

"In the dark?"

"People do. Lights on the helmets and all that."

Dana shivered. "No, thank you. I wasn't sure I had the courage to do it in broad daylight."

"You have plenty of courage,. More courage than any woman I've ever met."

Dana peered at him in the gathering dusk. "Thank you."

"For what?"

"The compliment. And this. Everything. For knowing what I need when I don't know what I need." An owl hooted as they made their way down the path. They paused to look for it, spotted it on a low branch to the south. Staring straight at them, the Great Horned didn't move or speak again until they continued down the trail. "It does help to get away from the pressures of work. It helps to push myself physically… in a different way. I jog, but lately I can't turn my mind off even when I'm running."

She felt his hand encircle hers more tightly.

"Couldn't think about much while I was afraid of falling to my death," she admitted. "It was nice to forget everything for a few hours."

"Did you manage to work up an appetite in the process?"

"Oh yeah, Marshall. You definitely owe me food."

Twenty-six

B en thought he might starve before they finished pizza negotiations.

He understood women dug veggies. He was a healthy guy himself, or so he thought.

"You've really never had a mushroom on a pizza?" Dana pulled a slice off the platter before Ben could even set it on the table.

Grabbing his own piece, he bit into the warm, cheesy bliss and shook his head no.

"It's good," Dana declared, reaching for her iced tea. "You should try it sometime. I tried mountain climbing for you."

"Rock climbing," Ben corrected. "And you wouldn't agree to sausage. Everyone loves sausage."

Dana rolled her eyes as she continued devouring her piece. He did admire a woman who enjoyed the finer foods of life, though burning a thousand calories probably had something to do with her appetite. For a few moments they focused on the food.

"Great mom-and-pop shop," Dana said as she considered a third piece. "I take it you've been here before."

"Yeah. Joe and I would come here every time we went out to Cimarron Canyon."

Ben felt the pizza stick in his throat, so he reached for his Coke. The sweetness of the drink couldn't wash away the sudden, bitter taste in his mouth.

"Tell me about Joe," Dana said. "If you want to. I mean, if I'm not intruding."

Ben looked across the old, oak table at Dana, knew what Joe would think of her, and couldn't stop the smile that worked its way across his face. It hurt though, like new skin stretched over a fresh wound.

He reached for another piece of pizza. "Joe was great. I guess he was the first real friend I ever had."

Dana looked surprised. "I imagined you with lots of friends in high school."

"I guess I did have—in a way. But those are childhood friends, people you've known since you can remember being you." Ben dropped the half-eaten piece on the plate and wiped his mouth with the paper napkin. "Joe was different. He was the first real stranger to befriend me."

He looked across the pizza place, saw it as it was back then. "I spotted this HELP WANTED ad for Taos, New Mexico. It sounded so far away, so adventurous."

Ben let his gaze wander around the room. The place hadn't changed much in the last eight years. "I was nineteen and had finished my freshman year in college. I didn't want to go home for the summer. Things there were better, but still not quite right."

He stopped, tried to think of how to go on.

"And you had the truck," Dana said.

"Yeah. There was the truck. Plus I knew it all then."

"All what?"

"All everything. Surely knew enough to come down to Taos and work for a few months." Ben laughed and took another drink from his glass. "By the time you deducted what it cost to get here and go back home, plus all we spent hiking, fishing, and chasing girls—I didn't go home with a dime more than I left with."

Dana poked at a piece of pizza with her fork. "But you didn't regret it?"

"Nah. It wasn't about the money. It was never about the money. And meeting Joe, well, it goes back to the coincidence thing we talked about."

"You think it was your destiny to come here and make friends with him?"

Ben pushed the plate of pizza out of the way, and leaned forward. He ran his fingers through his hair and finally looked up at Dana.

"I don't have all the answers. You know? I wouldn't trade that summer for anything. Wouldn't trade time spent with Joe Tafoya. He was one of the best men I've ever known."

Dana had finished eating and was watching him closely, so he pulled out a twenty-dollar bill and set it down on the table. "Let's get out of here."

When they were again in the truck, facing the road and watching the occasional car go by, Ben continued.

"We weren't quite men though, and I think we knew it. We wanted to be. And we had such big plans. Both of us were interested in the same things." He turned and looked at Dana in the dimness of the parking lot lights.

"Like rock climbing and chasing girls?"

"Yeah. Rock climbing we were fairly good at. Chasing girls we somehow hadn't got the knack of." He reached out and pulled her hand into his lap, ran his thumb up and down her palm. "Sometimes I worry I filled his head with the wrong ideas. Even then I knew I was going into the military. Joe, he wasn't so sure. But when I started talking about it..."

Ben wondered if she really wanted to hear this, or if he just needed to unburden himself.

"What happened to him?" she asked gently.

"That's the odd part. We ended up deployed at the same base in Fallujah. What are the chances?" He studied her. "Coincidence? I knew he'd signed up, but I had no idea he was deployed in the area until I walked out of my barracks one morning and heard someone holler my name. Turned around and there he was. I never was so happy to see a familiar face."

"How long had you been there?"

"Twelve months. I was due for a furlough, but I'd been extended to eighteen. Then Joe showed up. Suddenly, it was fine. We were like kids again, but bigger." He looked back down at her palm, ran his finger up and down the lines he could barely see. "Doing what we were supposed to do, and we were good at it. Until..."

Dana said nothing, only clasped his hand.

"I was with him." Ben felt tears sting his eyes and didn't move to wipe them away. "He was going into this barn to

134

look for kids. I had the perimeter. We'd already checked it from a distance through our scopes and with spybots."

He watched her reaction closely as he shared that most intimate of losses he'd shared with so few others. "Joe turned around and gave me this grin. Said he'd be back in five. He walked across the doorway of the barn and it... it exploded into the sky."

Dana reached out and rubbed the tears from his face. "I'm sorry, Ben."

It was the first time she'd touched him on her own initiative, and one part of Ben recognized the victory. Another part of him was still over seven-thousand miles away.

Dana moved closer to him and snuggled into the circle of his arm. "You two needed each other."

Ben swallowed, looked out the front windshield of the truck. "Joe didn't regret going. He told me so the week before. He missed home, but he knew he was making a difference over there."

"Did you come back here because of him?" Dana asked.

Ben didn't answer right away. He shuffled through the prayers and questions he'd had for the last year.

"I can't honestly say why I'm here. I know I don't believe it was a chance happening for me to meet Joe, then reconnect with him four years later. I can't pretend to know why he died over there and I didn't. Maybe I'm here to figure it all out. Or possibly I'm here because this is a good place to be—a place God wants me to be right now."

He felt her stiffen under him, then pull away.

"It's late. We should go."

Ben nodded, started the truck, and pulled out into the night. He'd known Dana wouldn't want to hear his answer, felt any mention of faith would scare her like a rabbit to its hole. But he also knew that hiding his true feelings would be basing their relationship on a lie.

And he did intend to have a relationship with Dana Jacobs, whether she was his boss or not.

Somewhere he could sense Joe Tafoya sitting back and giving him a thumbs-up. No, they'd never been any good at chasing girls, but Joe had predicted the right woman would cross Ben's path one day. And when she did, he'd realize explosives were easy to deal with—comparatively.

Women, on the other hand, had to be handled with care.

Twenty-seven

D ana stood up from her desk Tuesday morning and winced. She was sore in places that didn't have a right to hurt. She was also more rested than she'd been in weeks. Truth was, she'd slept like a baby last night.

She walked around her desk to go in search of a bagel or cup of yogurt. She was so hungry she'd even settle for conning one of those energy bars out of Ben.

Her mind on food, she nearly collided with Captain.

His white eyebrows were drawn in a straight line of concern, and his voice didn't waver as he thrust the printout into her hands. "Intercepted this from local dispatch. You're going to want to send a team out, including Marshall."

Dana read the words and knew it couldn't be a coincidence. Worse, she realized he knew their every move to date and was again one step ahead of them. Maybe she'd been foolish to leave the surveillance devices in place.

"Pull the devices now. General meeting in ten minutes." She pivoted and returned to her desk.

All thoughts of food vanished. First, she sent encrypted messages to her team members. Then she advised her regional office she was entering phase two of their predetermined plan. Eight minutes later, she logged off and walked out into the main room.

Her group was assembled. Ben, Clay, and Nina had already donned Kevlar vests and were loading additional ammunition into them. Red stood at the front of the room, holding a report briefing. Sayeed monitored the GPS board, his left arm still in a sling to protect and immobilize his shoulder. Captain sat at the edge of the group, radio set covering one ear.

Dana marched to the front. "Red, tell us what we were able to learn about the surveillance devices."

"We've had a little over thirty-six hours to trace them. He's using a scatter device, which isn't a surprise. The signal is received, scatters it to three other locations, which then receives and scatters it again. We have a possibility of nine hot spots so far, all in the northern part of the state. Swing shift is working on identifying and monitoring them from home."

"Good. Nina?"

"I'm still following up on the book. *Grapes of Wrath* is basically about a family dispossessed of their land. I've been going through the rolls of people in the Taos area who were forced into bankruptcy over the last twenty years, matching them to the height and weight of the man on the video surveillance—though he was probably a boy then so I've had to account for the time factor. So far no matches."

"Captain, relay to our late night people that I want to increase that parameter to forty years."

"Copy that."

"Clay, what have you found on the types of surveillance he was using?"

"He likes the newest and the best. Unfortunately, they can be bought on the Internet by anyone. Due to the level of sophistication necessary to use them though, I'd say we're talking about someone with a highly technical background."

"Red, keep updating the profile and make sure everyone gets it." Dana pulled herself up taller and gripped the printout in her hand. "Now this, and he knows we're coming."

Dana looked around at her group and drew in a deep breath. She didn't have to look down at the facts on her sheet. Fear had etched them on her heart the first time she'd read them.

"Eighteen minutes ago local dispatch received a call from a concerned mother. UPS delivered thirty bags of fertilizer. She tried to refuse the delivery, but it had been prepaid. Specific instructions were to deliver it to the garage apartment where her teenage son sometimes hangs with his grunge band. Captain intercepted the call."

"Local officers have no record on the kid—officially. Unofficially, there's some domestic disturbance history. Dad left town after a restraining order was filed fifteen months ago. Mom's behind on some payments, but working hard to stay current. Kid's a loner, according to the school resource officer."

Dana shook her head, amazed as always how her people were able to pull together so much information so quickly.

"Ben, anything you want to add before we head out there?"

Ben looked around, his normally easy smile missing from his face. "Ammonium nitrate is an oxidizing agent. When combined with diesel fuel or kerosene it's quite explosive. We know it was used in Oklahoma City."

When no one said anything, Ben added, "Unless someone crashes a truck into the garage or starts a very large fire, we should be okay."

Dana nodded, thinking he was finished, but he wasn't.

"I wouldn't put it past him, Dana. He knew we were listening. Knew we'd intercept this call, and he's probably waiting."

"We can't be sure of that."

"No, we can't. But it is a possibility. This could be a trap."

Dana searched the faces of each of her team members.

"All right. Let's move out. You have comm units from Captain. Keep them live. I'll ride with Clay. Nina and Ben, you're together. Red, I want you to stay with Captain in case he plans to attack here while we're out."

Red touched the Glock in his shoulder harness. "We'll be ready for him."

"Captain, relay a request to local law enforcement. I want a three-block perimeter around the house, but I'd rather it be unobtrusive if at all possible."

"Got it."

"Let's move out then."

Dana met Ben's gaze as she walked toward the back door. She resisted the need to reach out and touch his arm. Somehow managed not to tell him to be careful. Ben Marshall had been dealing with explosive situations all his adult life. She had no doubt he could handle this one.

Driving toward the two hundred block of Brockshire, it occurred to her she no longer believed it was a coincidence he was here when she needed him. She wasn't ready to call it a miracle, but she knew enough to be grateful for a gift when one fell in her lap.

Twenty-eight

B en studied the shabby, one-story, frame house. It didn't look so different from the slums in Fallujah—different building material, same despair.

Near dead flowers suffered in a broken pot near the front door. A child's bicycle lay abandoned in a yard that hadn't seen grass in several years. Scraggly cactuses grew near the street, but no trees adorned the yard.

"Movement in the garage." Ben spoke softly into his comm unit.

Nina glanced at the right-hand corner of the garage, which he indicated with a nod of his head. They were positioned across the street and two houses down where fortunately, there were shrubs to crouch behind.

"Roger that." Dana's voice was calm. "I'm going to the front, try and talk to the mother."

"Bad idea, Dana." The words were out of Ben's mouth before he could stop them.

"Didn't ask for your opinion, Marshall. Clay will cover me. We'll give you and Nina a two-minute head start to circle around to the garage. On my mark. Everyone confirm."

Three clicks filled the silence of the comm unit, though Ben certainly wasn't happy about her plan. He would have laid fifty-fifty odds their perp was either in the house or watching it. He could feel it as surely as he could feel an itch between his shoulder blades he couldn't possibly reach to scratch.

"Mark."

Ben was first and foremost a soldier. At Dana's command, he sprang out of his crouch and skirted to the right as Nina went left. His back was against the peeling paint of the garage wall within forty-five seconds.

He tapped his comm unit to indicate he was in position, then heard Nina do the same.

"I'm going in," Dana said.

Ben exhaled his breath slowly.

"I have her covered," Clay said softly.

He heard Dana knock on the door. Another minute passed, then she knocked again. Finally, the door squeaked as it was opened.

"Mrs. Mifflin? I'm Dana Jacobs. You called about a delivery of materials that concerned you?"

"Yes. I came home from walking my middle son to school and a truck was here, unloading bags into the garage. I told them to take them back, that I wouldn't sign for anything. He said I didn't have to." The woman's voice rose in agitation as she spoke. "I told him I couldn't pay for it either. He said it was already paid for. I don't know what he was talking about. We don't have the money to pay for food, let alone bags of stuff we don't need. I don't know what Reggie's gotten into, but I want those bags outta my garage."

"I understand, ma'am. Do you know where Reggie is now?"

"He's supposed to be at school, but I just got a call from the truancy officer again saying he wasn't there. I tell you, Miss Jacobs. I don't know what I'm going to do with that child. He's not a bad boy, but he's lost his way."

"Do you think he's in the garage now, Mrs. Mifflin?"

"No. He only goes in there at night when his friends are around. They play music, or what they call music. I've never seen him in there during the day."

Ben again tapped his comm unit, indicating he'd received all the information he needed.

"Mrs. Mifflin, do I have your permission to go into the garage and remove the items that were delivered?"

"I'm the one who called and asked you to, so yeah. I'd say you do have my permission."

Ben spoke softly into his unit. "We're moving in now. Nina, take the back. I'll go in the front. Clay, keep your sights on Dana."

Ben gripped his firearm, pressed his back against the building, and moved silently as a cat toward the front of the structure. What had been a single-car, garage had been boarded up. Now there was a door to the right with a cracked window he couldn't see through because a dirty shade covered it.

He tried the doorknob, but it was locked.

Estimating the strength of the hinges, he made his decision, took two steps back, and charged.

He rolled as soon as he busted through the door and came up in a crouch with his weapon drawn.

Stacks of fertilizer surrounded the drums, amplifiers, and electric guitar. None of that mattered at the moment.

Ben had his attention focused on the tallest stack of fertilizer bags. Someone stood behind them, no doubt the boy, Reggie. All that Ben could make out in the dimness of the garage was a dirty AC/DC ball cap and the rifle the boy was pointing at his chest.

Twenty-nine

B en heard Nina plow through the door behind him. He held up his left hand to stay her off and continued holding his Glock in front of him with his right.

"You need to put down the weapon, kid." His voice was soft, reasonable.

The rifle wavered, as if trying to determine its target. Apparently, deciding Ben was the bigger threat, the boy corrected his aim slightly.

"Set it on the ground and no one gets hurt." Ben brought his left hand down to his side slowly. He could feel Nina behind him, frozen in place.

"Easy for you to say, holding that Glock." The boy's voice was still changing, couldn't settle on a pitch.

"Tell you what, kid. You let Nina back out, and I'll put the Glock on the floor." Sweat ran down Ben's face, though the morning was still cool. "We got a deal?"

"She'll shoot me through the window."

"Nah. She'll leave her gun in here. Won't you, Nina?"

Nina's Glock hit the garage cement and slid past Ben's feet. The sound broke the stillness like a rocket tearing through a clear, blue sky.

"She's going to back out now, Reggie. Just like she came in. Soon as she does, I'll put my firearm down beside hers."

The only response was a slight nod of the AC/DC cap.

There was the almost imperceptible sound of Nina's footsteps, backing slowly away. Her shadow crossed the place where light filtered between the door and Ben, throwing the room into darkness.

Ben knew it was when he should have pounced. But he didn't. Some instinct told him not to.

"All right, Reggie. I'm setting mine down. Real easy." Ben squatted and placed the Glock gently on the floor, never taking his eyes off the boy.

"How'd you know my name?"

"Your mom, Reggie. She told us."

Sunlight glinted on metal as the boy's finger twitched on the trigger. "You're lying. She's at work."

"Not yet. She came home from walking your brother to school. That's when she saw the delivery truck. She thought they had the wrong house. Then she got scared and called us."

An eye appeared from behind the rifle. "You don't look like a cop."

"I'm not a cop, Reggie. I'm a guy trying to help, but first I need you to put the rifle down."

"So you can cart me off to juvie? I've heard how it is there, and I ain't going. I'll run away first."

"Why would we take you to juvie, Reggie? For ordering some fertilizer?"

A brown hand came up, tugged on the ball cap. "We both know it's more than that."

"Put the rifle down. We'll talk about it—just two guys. That's all I'm asking."

Reggie again adjusted the cap, this time moving it up to get a better look at him. "You ain't taking me in?"

"No, Reggie. You have my word we're only going to talk."

"He said you'd make promises. If you ever caught me." The boy readjusted the rifle. "My dad made promises too. Never kept a one. You'll double-cross me the first chance you get."

"I'm not your dad, Reggie. If I'd wanted to double-cross you, I could have done it when Nina was leaving. Remember when it got dark for a second? That's when I should have shot you, Reggie." Ben had been holding the same position for too long. He felt the muscles in his left leg begin to quiver from the stress and adrenaline. "That's what they taught us in the Army. How to take out the enemy. But you're not the enemy, Reggie. So put down the rifle. Let's go in the house and talk this out."

Reggie stood straighter behind the stack of fertilizer sacks. Ben wondered for a split second if the boy meant to raise the rifle to his shoulder and shoot him, but then he threw it out on the shorter stack of fertilizer bags next to him.

It lay there, discarded like so many other unwanted things in the old barn.

Ben waited as the boy shuffled over to him. He was clearly part Apache, though the mother had sounded Caucasian.

When he came within a few feet of Ben, he stopped and stared at his feet, apparently waiting to be cuffed.

Finally, he looked up, and for a moment it was as if Ben were looking at Joe Tafoya. Reggie's eyes were the same deep black, his cheekbones high and rising up to meet the dark circles, which proved he hadn't slept much. But in this boy's eyes there was no laughter and certainly no hope.

Ben held out his hand and waited for the boy to shake it.

"Ben Marshall," he said when Reggie finally pulled his hand from his ragged blue-jeans pocket and offered him a halfhearted shake.

"I'm Reggie. Reggie Mifflin, but you already know my name."

"Yeah. Guess I do." Ben picked up his Glock off the floor, saw Reggie flinch as he did so. "My boss gets mad if I leave this anywhere."

He stuck it into the paddle holster at the back of his pants, then motioned for Reggie to lead the way out of the barn.

Nina stood waiting, four feet away, her backup weapon drawn.

"You won't need that, Nina."

She looked uncertainly from Ben to Reggie. After a second's hesitation, she holstered her firearm, then moved inside to pick up her Glock.

Dana and Mrs. Mifflin stood at the back door of the house. Reggie's mom was thin like Dana, but there any similarity stopped. Her red hair was chopped in a short haircut, one she'd probably done herself. Though she couldn't have been older than forty, the stress of raising three boys had permanently etched lines on her face—lines that temporarily softened when she saw Reggie walk from the barn.

The teenager didn't look at anyone as he walked into the kitchen.

Ben noticed how clean the room was. A scarred Formica-topped table sat to one side, and chairs with cracked seats had been covered with white plastic.

No one spoke for a moment, then Ben sat, leaned forward, and waited for Reggie to meet his gaze. When he did, Ben said, "Reggie, we need you to tell us everything about him."

Thirty

F ifteen minutes later, Dana waited with Mrs. Mifflin in the front living room while Ben spoke with Reggie in the kitchen. Clay continued to watch the front of the house in case their perp did plan an attack, and Nina guarded the garage.

Dana attempted to calm Mrs. Mifflin while she monitored Ben and Reggie's conversation through her comm unit.

They had learned very little.

The man went by Edmond Jones, no doubt an alias. He'd contacted Reggie when their grunge band had advertised online for a new bass guitarist. Over the last three months, he'd woven quite a web of deceit around the boy.

"You're sure he didn't say what the ammonium nitrate was for?" Ben's voice was soft, relaxed.

Dana wanted to smile. Clay would have throttled the teen by now.

"No. He kept saying we'd get even."

"Get even for what?"

"Never really said. Mostly how it wasn't fair some folks had so much while we barely got by."

"Times have been tough, I guess."

"Yeah. My mom works hard, but you know. There's four of us, and my old man never comes around."

Dana looked at Mrs. Mifflin who sat staring across the living room. She'd put the youngest boy, Frankie, down for a morning nap after calling into work and telling them she wouldn't be in today. How had she handled raising three boys alone? She couldn't make much more than minimum wage at the hotel where she cleaned rooms.

Ben's voice came back over her comm unit. "He ever help you out?"

"Sometimes."

"Cash?"

"Once in a while. Then he gave me a credit card and had me order the stuff."

"And this was the card?"

"Yeah."

"You didn't use it for anything else?"

"Once or twice." Reggie's voice grew softer, though he'd shown no indication he realized the communication system was broadcasting their conversation. "I bought some groceries on it a couple times when my mom couldn't work. And once we blew an amp, so I went down to Radio Shack and got a new one."

"He ever say anything?"

"Yeah. He said he'd take it out of my pay."

"What was your pay, Reggie?"

"He wasn't ever really clear. Said it would depend on what they paid him. Said it would be *enough*. More than I make sacking groceries, but I kept sacking anyway. I kind of knew it wasn't going to pay out."

"Did he ever threaten you, Reggie?"

Dana leaned forward, wishing she could see the expression on the boy's face as he answered. Mrs. Mifflin stood and paced back and forth in front of the window, chewing her thumbnail. Dana was afraid if she left the woman, even for a few seconds, she'd fly to pieces.

"Yeah. A few times. He said I'd be sorry if I ratted him out. Said…" Reggie's voice shook, then stopped all together.

"Whatever it was, we won't let him do it. But we need to know what his plans are, if he has any."

Reggie drew in a deep breath. "Said my little brothers were real cute. Said he wouldn't mind taking them away for a while." Silence again filled the comm unit. "That's when I knew I was in over my head. Knew I couldn't just walk away."

"Your brothers are safe, son. We won't let anything happen to them."

Reggie coughed. There was the sound of a chair squeaking as someone stood up and walked across the room.

"Did he ever hit you?"

"Once or twice. No worse than my old man did."

Dana heard Ben sigh. When he didn't follow up with another question, she decided it was time to end the interview. They'd been at it for nearly thirty minutes. She'd have to get a crew in to sweep for fingerprints, move the fertilizer, and possibly relocate the family.

Her mind had slipped to those follow-up steps, which is why the next few seconds didn't immediately make sense.

Mrs. Mifflin had murmured she was going to check on Frankie in the next room. The next thing Dana knew, the woman was screaming, frantic because she couldn't find little Frank.

Reggie hollered something about a tree house near the garage.

Clay was on the comm unit, reporting movement at the back of the property, and Ben was ordering everyone to get out of the house.

"To the street, Dana." He busted through the living room door, pushing Reggie in front of him. "Take them both to the street."

Before she could argue, Ben had fled out the back door, toward the garage, toward the wall that had burst into flames.

Thirty-one

Ben ran toward the garage, calculating the amount of time it would take the ammonium nitrate to detonate.

And it would detonate. The blaze had started at the back of the garage, but the perp had used an accelerant. Even as he ran, the flames consumed the dry wood of the garage. The roof collapsed with a sigh, and the fire leapt higher into the clear, blue sky.

Any evidence they might have recovered was lost.

All he could hope now was to save the boy. Ben realized he didn't have minutes to do it. He had seconds.

Two trees towered over either side of the garage. A cottonwood to the east, and an elm to the west. The elm had branches low enough for hands and footholds.

Ben didn't slow down until he stood underneath it.

Even as he gazed up into the face of the raven-haired child, he could feel the heat from the fire. He prayed with every ounce of his soul for God to give them ten more seconds.

Looking up at the boy he shouted, "Jump, son."

The child squinted down through the growing smoke, glanced back at the fire, then peered doubtfully at Ben's outstretched arms. Making his choice, he flew into the air like a kite, falling in the sudden absence of wind.

Ben staggered back two steps. Clutching the boy to him, he plunged toward the street. He nearly made it to the southwest corner of the house.

The blast from the secondary explosion lifted him into the air and propelled him past the kitchen window. Ben instinctively curved his body around the boy.

The next instant they hit the ground and rolled. Fortunately, he took most of the impact on his left shoulder and hip. The child whimpered, but continued to cling to him.

Heat seared his back as the flames from the garage shot outward. Magnified by the fertilizer, the blaze caught in the trees. The intensity of the fire created a wind of its own, sucking items past them, over them, raking their bodies with sticks, discarded toys, and trash.

Ben squeezed his eyes shut against the smoke. When the boy coughed, he pushed his head down further into the cave he was trying to make with his body.

With one part of his mind, Ben listened for additional explosions, counting for ten seconds, then twenty. He heard the emergency vehicles, screaming across the streets of Taos.

Another part of his brain noted the boy's thin shoulders, the way he shook like a cowed pup, the broken sounds he continued to make.

After another minute, he was reasonably sure there wouldn't be any additional explosions. The boy had begun pulling in deep, ragged breaths and coughing harshly against

Ben's chest. He had to take the risk and get him out of the thickening smoke.

Ben bowed his head so the boy could hear him over the roar of the fire. "Put your arms around my neck. I'll carry you out."

The smallest of nods confirmed the boy had understood him. Ben felt two little arms, snaking up, finding his shoulders, then clasping around his neck. The boy kept his head buried, as if he could wish away the terror around him.

Ben visualized the west side of the house, then opened his eyes. The smoke immediately stung like a horde of wasps. He resisted the urge to wipe at the burning. Tears ran freely down his face, working to push out the toxins.

Ben peered resolutely through the haze, adjusted the boy's weight with his left arm, and pulled his firearm with his right.

He wouldn't put it past their madman to be waiting in the smoke.

Then he walked steadily toward the flashing red lights of the emergency vehicles. Barely visible, they provided enough of a beacon to lead him in the right direction.

Thirty-two

I t took every ounce of Dana's training not to plunge into the smoke. Ben was in there. A child was in there, and she should be as well.

Captain Covey's hand came down on her shoulder. "My men have the fire surrounded. It's still too hot to put water on, Dana. Maybe another five minutes."

She nodded once, then turned and looked him full in the face. "No one's seen them?"

"We're trying to get in closer, but after the second explosion…" The big man wiped the smoke from his face with a handkerchief. "I had to pull my men back."

She looked back toward the house so he wouldn't see her tears. Agents in charge did not tear up on the scene. What was wrong with her?

Paramedics were attending to Mrs. Mifflin. She continued to scream uncontrollably, crying out for her son. Reggie sat by his mother in the ambulance, watching his home being engulfed in the black cloud of smoke. Dana felt a tug of regret as she watched the family. She should have taken them from the home earlier, taken them into the office where they would have been safe.

The rest of Dana's crew had the surrounding block under surveillance. Her mind insisted on replaying Clay's message—the perp was on the property, he was near the garage, he had disappeared past the wall of flame. He had been here, and she didn't catch him. But she would. It might be today. It might be tomorrow. Before this was over, she would catch him.

As her thoughts flitted from concerns over Ben and Frankie to ideas for retribution, a form appeared from the west side of the house. Her heart skipped a beat, and she moved to run toward him.

Captain Covey put a hand in front of her. "Dana, it's still not safe."

She pushed past him, ran toward Ben.

Reached him at the same moment Reggie did.

Ben carried his firearm in one hand, which he holstered as he walked toward them, and the child in his other.

His face was nearly black from smoke and dirt. Blood ran from a wound on his left shoulder, and he was limping. The curly hair she'd found so attractive had been badly singed along the back of his neck, which was a bright red and had already begun to blister.

But it was his face that nearly did her in.

Smudged black from the smoke, tears had streaked two trails down his cheeks. Those beautiful mocha eyes sought hers, found hers, and held. Walking through the barricade of emergency personnel, the smile she needed to see finally broke across his face.

He grabbed Dana in a one-armed hug, the child caught between them since he refused to let go of Ben's neck.

"I was worried you didn't get out in time," he whispered into her hair.

She stepped back and smiled up at him. "You were worried about me, Marshall? You need a mirror."

"You're okay, Frankie." Reggie moved behind Ben so he could get a better look at his brother. "You scared us, man."

"Iron Man saved me." Frankie's eyes opened wide as he stared at his brother, but he continued to cling to Ben's neck.

"We better take him to his mother." Dana nodded toward the ambulance, which Mrs. Mifflin had been moved into.

Ben walked in the direction she indicated, Reggie and Dana following close in his wake.

"Any luck spotting him?" Ben asked her quietly.

"Only briefly, but we're not giving up."

At the sight of Frankie, Mrs. Mifflin fought her way out of the ambulance. Frankie immediately traded his newfound hero for his mother.

If there were days Dana wondered whether her job was worth the cost, moments like these banished all doubt.

"Mama. There was a big fire, and then Iron Man came. I jumped, and he caught me. And we *flew*."

"Frankie. Oh, thank you, Jesus. Frank, I was so scared. You scared the life out of me. I knew the Lord would save you."

"But Mama. Iron Man saved me. We flew, and the fire didn't get us."

"You were supposed to be napping." Mrs. Mifflin wiped

at the tears on her face. Unable to put any real energy into her scolding, she clutched the boy to her. "I put you in your room. And I checked. You were asleep."

"I was pretending, Mama. I counted to one hundred and then I went up to the tree house. I do it every day. After the fire, I couldn't climb back down. Then Iron Man came."

Reggie reached out and ruffled his brother's hair. "Iron Man, huh? Where's his suit?"

"Iron Man doesn't wear his suit all the time. And you should have seen him catch me. Fire shooting up through his feet, and he stood there, Mama. Just stood there and caught me like I was a baseball coming out of the sky."

Dana looked at Ben, who laughed, but looked pleased at the praise nonetheless.

"All right, Iron Man. Let's get a paramedic to look you and Frankie over." Dana signaled to the two medics closest to her.

The boy started to resist, but when he saw Ben submitting, he bravely stuck out his chin and endured.

After checking for injuries and confirming his vitals were good, it was decided Frankie could get by with a little oxygen. As long as he could continue to watch what was happening to Ben and remain in his mother's lap, the boy was content to breathe into the mask.

The medic cut away Ben's sleeve and set about cleaning the abrasions on his left arm. The skin had turned an ugly purple. Dana would have liked to think Ben was hamming it up when he hollered at the first touch of antiseptic, but the scowl on his face told her otherwise.

Frankie didn't see the look.

In fact, Frankie's peal of laughter caused his oxygen

mask to slip off as he flopped back on his mother. "Iron Man doesn't like the medicine either."

"He was kidding, Frankie." His mother pushed the mask back on the boy's face.

"Yeah, Frankie." Dana tapped Ben's knee and directed her attention to the boy. "Look at Mr. Marshall, err, Iron Man now. He's smiling while the medic takes care of him."

Ben clenched his jaw, but offered up a smile for Frankie. The moment would have been a lighthearted one had it not been for the madman who had escaped through the smoke and the sound of the roof caving in behind them. The house was now totally consumed by flames.

"I can't believe it spread to the house. This is all my fault." Reggie slumped as he spoke, the weight of his family's homelessness on his shoulders.

Ben stood as the medic finished applying cream to the back of his neck. After slapping gauze on it and reminding him he'd need a haircut now, the medic moved on to check a fireman with smoke inhalation.

Ben rubbed the top of his head as he surveyed the house, then looked back at the teen. "It's not your fault, Reggie. Don't take credit for what bad people do, and the man who got you into this is the very worst kind."

Dana watched him interact with the teen. Instead of plowing on, he waited for Reggie to raise his head and meet his gaze. The mother seemed to be coming out of shock as she continued to hold Frankie, but she, too, waited as Ben and Reggie worked through what had happened.

"We didn't have much," Reggie said, "but all we had was in there. If I had never gotten involved with him, this wouldn't have happened."

Ben looked at Mrs. Mifflin.

"Reggie's right. Everything we owned was in that house."

Dana pushed her hair back out of her face. "Did you own the home, Mrs. Mifflin?"

"No. We rented it." Her voice dropped as the enormity of the destruction in front of her seeped in. "I can't pay for that house burning down."

"The owner's insurance will pay for the structure," Dana assured her. "I'll have someone at my office work out the details with the owner."

"Where will we stay?" Reggie whispered. "It's my fault we don't have a home now."

Ben put his hand on the boy's shoulder. "You made a mistake, Reg. Everyone makes them. I want you to look long and hard at the type of destruction fires can cause though."

Firemen encircled the perimeter of the home, spraying water onto the structure. Smoke billowed over the lot like a cloud from some ancient volcano.

"*You* did not do that. The person we're hunting did. Your mistake was in trusting someone who was deceitful. If your family can forgive you for that, you need to forgive yourself."

Reggie looked to his mom. The hope and need written on his face recalled such an ache in Dana's heart, she had to turn away. When she did, Ben tugged on her arm.

"Let's give them a minute," he suggested.

As they walked a few yards away, Dana called for updates from her team. Clay had relayed the description Reggie gave of their perpetrator to the local police, but there had been no sightings of him—only the evidence he had been

VANNETTA CHAPMAN

there. Another note, very much like the one they had found in the backpack. This one again contained one word—BURN.

Nina was coordinating with the fire department. It would be hours before they could move into the site and search for clues. Even then, given the intensity of the blaze, the fire chief wasn't optimistic about their chances of learning much.

Lastly, Dana checked in with Captain at the office and confirmed all was quiet there.

She relayed a condensed version of the information to Ben.

"I'm worried about the family," Dana admitted.

"I have an idea."

"Why am I not surprised, Marshall?"

He looked over to where Reggie was now encircled in his mother's arms. "I think the father was Apache."

"The children certainly look as if they have some native ancestry."

"I want to move them to the reservation."

"What? Ben, you can't—"

"Hang on. Remember, I told you about Joe? His father still lives there. In fact, he was on the council for years."

Dana shook her head, her mind so filled with all the reasons his plan wouldn't work she barely heard his next words.

"Do you really think he was trying to destroy evidence, Dana? What evidence? He doesn't leave any on the notes, and I doubt he left any in that garage. He somehow knew Reggie was talking to us, and he decided to kill him. The Jicarilla Apache Indian Reservation might be the only place the family will be safe. It might be the one place that this maniac can't reach them."

164

Thirty-three

B en drove the department's Humvee north on Highway 522 toward the town of Costilla on the Colorado border. Red sat next to him, Glock loaded, ready, and looking like a play toy in the big man's hands.

Behind them, Frankie perched on the middle seat. It was a good thing his seatbelt held him in place, because the boy fairly vibrated with excitement. His face glowed. He looked right, then left, then right, then left. But as warned he said nothing. He was caught up in the throes of his dark hero's story.

Perhaps it was good that to the four-year-old the night's dangers were happening to Iron Man and not to him. Maybe it was his young mind's way of coping, or so Ben thought as he glanced back and smiled at the kid. Frankie remained convinced his life had, in fact, become a comic book story.

Mrs. Mifflin had readily agreed with relocating to the reservation. Mifflin was actually her maiden name. The boys' father had been raised on the reservation, but ran away at fourteen and never returned.

"You're sure Mr. Tafoya said we'd be welcome?" She leaned forward and peered through the darkness at Ben.

"The Apache take care of their own, Mrs. Mifflin." Ben met her gaze in the rearview mirror. "He'll be waiting for us."

She nodded once and leaned back against the seat. "Stop playing with that, Tommy."

"Mama, I wasn't hurting nothing." The nine-year-old's voice was a whisper as he pushed the buttons on the rear, video monitor.

Ben had disabled its feed from the main computer. There was nothing the boy could harm, but he didn't think he should interrupt the family's private discussion. Though the ride was taking place in a bullet-proof, military vehicle on a covert mission in the middle of the night, they sounded like any other family out for a drive.

"I said stop it and close your eyes. It's past your bedtime."

Reggie snorted. "Don't think they're going to sleep anytime soon."

"We'll transfer cars in another five minutes. Then it'll be a straight drive." Ben looked to Red who monitored Dana and Clay's progress on the GPS board.

"The tunnel is 3.8 miles ahead," Red confirmed.

"Everyone remember what they're supposed to do?" Ben asked.

"Roger," Frankie said.

"Ten four." Tommy sat up straighter.

Reggie tugged nervously at his AC/DC ball cap, but when Ben looked to him for confirmation, he nodded.

Construction lights flashed as they entered the south side of the tunnel, exactly as the governor had promised. Dana did have some useful connections.

A construction board indicated the road was closed for maintenance. Ben slowed enough for the worker to make out his plate number. Signaling to another man further down the line, two men stepped forward and moved the barricade in their lane, allowing them to pass through.

Glancing again in his mirror, Ben confirmed the barricade was quickly replaced. He also saw his taillights reflect briefly against the weapon stowed in the worker's holster as the man bent to reposition the barricade.

It was good to know they had a little extra protection while they were making the transfer.

Once into the tunnel, Ben sped up until he was even with the nondescript Jeep Cherokee. They stopped parallel with one another. Sitting in the Cherokee were Dana, Clay, George and Nina. Four adults, but no children. The Humvee had also held four adults—counting Ben, Red, Reggie, and Mrs. Mifflin, plus the two smaller children.

Doors flew open, and all four of the Mifflins moved to the backseat of the Cherokee. Red stood with his forearms resting on the roof of the Humvee, weapon drawn and ready, eyes alert and scanning.

Ben and Clay met at the front of the two vehicles and exchanged keys. In the darkness, he supposed they might look alike. Truth was, after less than two weeks, he respected the man in front of him tremendously and felt he knew him well.

"Watch your back," Ben said.

"I always do, Marshall." The smallest of smiles played on Clay's face. It was a first, and it certainly couldn't be misconstrued for outright friendliness. Ben wondered briefly if Clay had ever loved Dana, then he pushed the thought aside. He needed to focus on getting this family safely tucked away.

They both turned to look at their respective vehicles.

Dana remained in the front seat of the Cherokee. Of the four Mifflins sitting in the back, only the mother and Reggie were visible. The two younger boys now lay down where they couldn't be seen. The vehicle would look exactly the same exiting the tunnel as it had coming in, if no one looked too closely at the driver.

Clay would drive out with Red beside him, which hopefully would be all anyone would ever get close enough to see. For one thing, the side and back windows of the Humvee were darkly tinted. To be safe though, they'd gone with the same number of adults. George sat in the backseat, wore a ball cap, and was roughly the same height as Reggie. Nina would pass for Mrs. Mifflin at a distance, but if anyone came close the charade would be up.

As for the children, the idea was they had fallen asleep.

"Our two minutes is up," Red called.

Clay hesitated and finally settled on "Good luck."

Ben slapped him on the shoulder and continued around the front of the Jeep. The headlights created dancing shadows on the tunnel walls.

Driving back in the direction they'd come from moments before, he stole a look over at Dana. He was fully aware they'd just sent four of their team members into harm's way, but he had no doubt they could handle it.

At the staff meeting, there had nearly been a fight over who would volunteer.

Dana had to step in and remind everyone she determined assignments and she would choose who would go. Ben had wanted to laugh at the look of frustration on her face. She had to realize the issue was her staff's dedication, and that was a good problem to have.

He glanced at her again as he made his way out of the tunnel and continued south into the darkness. Her face was a mask of concentration while she monitored the comm frequencies and kept an eye on the GPS board. He longed to reach over and massage the stress from her shoulders, but the backseat full of passengers stopped him.

The sounds of yawns and deep breathing told him the younger boys had settled in to the more normal ride and were beginning to drift off. Mrs. Mifflin stared off into the dark shadows of the night. Reggie alone sought his gaze in the rearview mirror.

They had spent six hours at the office, pouring over pictures of felons.

It was Nina who had found their man and brought the picture up on the screen for Reggie to identify.

He didn't have a record, at least not a federal one.

He didn't have any aliases—even the one he'd given Reggie didn't appear anywhere. He wasn't on any watch list they could find.

But his family had lost their ranch to a land reclamation project when he was a boy—over forty-five years ago. The family had been given the fair market value, according to the State of New Mexico.

They had appealed the ruling and lost.

When the father had refused to leave, the family had been forcibly removed and the home of three generations bulldozed. There had been two stories in the local newspaper about it. Both on the front page.

After the dam was built and the land flooded, the state had considered the case closed.

Chance Drogan had not.

When Nina placed five men's pictures on the screen, Reggie had immediately identified him.

It took them another twenty minutes to learn Drogan had served two tours in Vietnam as an explosives expert.

Thirty-four

D ana looked at the family gathered around the old Apache gentleman and assured herself it was okay to leave.

If Ben trusted him, she should too.

Mr. Tafoya seemed to sense her doubts. He walked with her back to the Jeep and opened the passenger door.

"You're welcome to come out anytime, Miss Jacobs. I assure you no harm will come to this family here. I regret I did not know about their situation earlier. We would have intervened on their behalf."

"Thank you, for everything." Dana peered into the face that was a mass of wrinkles. "And I don't mean to offend you, but…"

Ben joined them, grasping Tafoya's hand once again. "What my boss wants to say, but is too polite to spit out, is she's afraid you can't keep them safe."

Dana didn't deny Ben's words. Her cheeks warmed in the cool, night air at his bluntness. "Drogan has been one step ahead of us from the beginning. Even if he followed the decoy north, he'll eventually realize where we gave him the slip. Then he'll backtrack."

"Unless Clay catches him, or kills him," Ben pointed out.

"We can hope." Dana looked at the two men beside her and the family waiting a few feet away in Tafoya's truck. "They didn't deserve to be caught in this. I want them safe."

Tafoya's smile split the wrinkled lines of his face. He reminded her of Ben in many ways. She wondered if Ben had a few drops of Apache in his own bloodline.

"My people have dealt with warriors for hundreds of years—both those that are honorable and those that are not." Tafoya looked up at the night sky. "Many nights, under these same stars, we have had to protect our women and children. God has given us the skill and cunning to do so. Men like Drogan are not new to me or the Apache Nation. They are like the old coyote—wily and dangerous at times, but not to be feared."

Dana nodded as if she understood, even though she didn't.

Tafoya held his arms out to the night, as if to catch the wind in them. "If you come looking for the Mifflins, you will not find them nor will anyone have heard of them."

At Dana's look of alarm, he placed a hand the color of the earth on her arm. "Come to me, and I will take you to them. They will be close. They will be well."

With those words, the old man crossed to his truck. His worn, leather boots crackled against the gravel road. As he drove away, Reggie turned and looked back, finally raised one hand in farewell.

Dana felt a lump in her throat and wondered if perhaps she needed a vacation when this case was over.

"It's harder when there are kids involved," Ben murmured. Instead of walking to his side of the car, he moved behind her, wrapped his arms around her waist, and rested his chin on her head.

Though she knew they needed to be on their way, she leaned back against him and allowed him to support her weight for a moment.

"Long day, boss."

"Yeah."

"We're closer than we were twenty-four hours ago."

"I suppose we are."

Then Ben surprised her again. Instead of continuing to talk, he simply held her. They both looked out at the billions of stars—the same stars Tafoya had drawn their attention to. She allowed the peacefulness of the night to seep into her soul, to minister to her spirit.

She wouldn't get a lot of sleep, and she would still have more to do tomorrow than she could possibly accomplish. But she would have this moment to cherish.

Maybe it would be enough to get her through what lay ahead.

Something told her she would need every bit of help she could find to struggle through the next few days, possibly weeks—including the man standing next to her.

No, make that especially the man standing next to her.

Thirty-five

B en had once seen St. Elmo's fire. He'd been shipping across to Iraq at the time. They were still three days off the coast, and the men's moods had gone from a slight twitch to a constant itch. By the evening of the second night of misconduct, the captain had slapped them all with extra duty cycles. Undoubtedly, he'd hoped to work the restless energy out of them.

Ben was on the deck, scrubbing the walls by the light of the aft lights at 1900 hours. The sky was dark as pitch, and no one was talking. It was unusual for a crew. He was accustomed to camaraderie wherever he served. It was how you survived the long days and endless nights.

He remembered glancing over his shoulder several times, as if expecting to see something. There was nothing to see though except the blackness of the sea. Even the stars had been blotted out by the clouds that had plagued them for days.

Suddenly, every hair on his arms, neck, even scalp had stood straight up. He'd thought he must look like a cartoon character. He started to turn to the guy scrubbing six meters down from him when a blue ball of fire ran down the flagpole of the ship and shot out across the water.

It was followed immediately by an eerie greenish glow, which lasted no more than five seconds, and then the rain started. It fell in sheets.

Ben stood there, soaked to the bone, grateful what had hit them wasn't a bomb.

Relieved the itch that had plagued him for two days was finally gone.

Able finally to draw in a deep breath as the electricity that had built up around the ship finally dissipated.

Weather reports later confirmed it was St. Elmo's fire.

Looking around the department room two days after leaving the Mifflin family with Mr. Tafoya, it occurred to Ben they could use a ball of St. Elmo's fire. Not likely in the middle of an office in Taos, New Mexico on a sunny day. Not entirely impossible.

For one thing, the itch was about to kill them all.

Clay stalked around the office as if he could force Drogan into another encounter.

Captain refused to let anyone else near the radios.

Red had broken Nina's chair when he plopped down in it in disgust. Nina, for her part, kept her counsel to herself. She spent every spare moment reading Steinbeck's *Grapes of Wrath*, as if some secret from Drogan's plan might be embedded there.

But worst of all was the haunted expression on Dana's face. She looked as if she hadn't slept since he dropped her off late Tuesday evening. Even though it was now Friday afternoon, he was willing to bet the few bucks in his wallet she was not taking off the weekend.

He'd tried twice to distract her with offers of dinner. Both times she'd flatly refused him.

St. Elmo's fire would spark up this group quite a bit in his opinion.

Ben stood and tossed the stress ball he'd been abusing to Red. The ball hit him in the shoulder, but he never looked up from the computer terminal he was staring at. Ben sighed and crossed to Dana's office. He knew she would turn him down, but he might as well try before he left.

Knocking once, he waited for her to look up. She never did, though she did answer. "Come in, Ben."

He walked in, but didn't take a seat. She was intent on watching four separate Internet windows. He couldn't make out the contents, but he could see the headers. Three were spybot cams. The fourth was the ID photo of Chance Drogan.

"Why do the bad guys always look so harmless?" Ben asked.

Dana sat back in her chair and tapped her bottom lip with two fingers. "They practice blending in. Look at him."

She leaned forward, used her mouse to switch to the full body view, and zoomed out. "The man is sixty years old, but still he managed to look like a teenager on the school's security video."

Ben walked around to stand behind her and study the screen. "He's stayed in good physical condition—five ten, one seventy tops, put a backpack and a baseball cap on him, and you can't tell his age unless..." He reached forward, drew a box with the mouse, and zoomed back in, "you look closely at his hands."

Dana shook her head, rotated the picture, zoomed out, and looked again at his profile. "The man is bald, Ben."

"True, which is probably why baseball caps were invented—to hide male baldness."

"Beady, little, blue eyes. They're set too close together. Don't you think? He looks like a rat." She minimized the profile and went back to the spybots.

Ben returned to the far side of the desk and sat in one of the chairs.

"This one has been hovering around his last known residence. No one has entered or exited the building, but if you look closely, you can see a reflection or something in the window. Here. In the southeast corner." She tapped the screen with the eraser end of her pencil. "Maybe he's in there. He could have enough supplies so he doesn't need to come out."

"Dana—"

"I know what you're going to say. The spybots have infrared cameras, but what if he had some sort of coating on the inside of his doors, walls, and windows? Or maybe he's artificially lowered his temperature." She chewed on the eraser and leaned closer to the screen. "He could be in a bunker underneath the house. Would that show up?"

She finally turned and looked at him, hope lighting her tired features.

"How long have you been sitting here?"

"I don't see how that has any relevance." She scowled, then dismissed him with a wave. "Never mind. If you were checking in before you left, there's no need."

"Dana, the spybots have remote pilots. They are well trained and have flown many missions in every conceivable scenario. Let them do their job."

"And what am I supposed to do, Ben?" She turned her frustration on him full force, slapping the desk as she spoke. "Do I sit here and wait to see where he strikes next? Swoop in and clean up another mess?"

Clay stopped what he was doing in the room outside her window. He made eye contact with Ben, but Ben could only shrug. As far he was concerned, it would do their boss good to let off some steam.

Fortunately for them both, Dana missed the exchange.

"Don't sit there and stare at me. I don't have the patience this afternoon for your... patience." Apparently realizing how absurd she sounded, Dana collapsed back into her chair. She pushed her hair away from her face and stared at Ben who still hadn't uttered another word. "You scared to speak, Marshall?"

"No, ma'am."

Dana stared at the ceiling for a moment. "All right. Let's start over. Why did you walk in here?"

"Sure wasn't to invite you rock climbing."

"Afraid I'd beat you to the top?"

"I'm more afraid you'd push me off once we got there." Ben steepled his fingers and studied her while the smallest of smiles tugged at the corner of her mouth. "We're all frustrated, Dana. Waiting is the hardest."

"It's not my first operation." The quarrel was back in her tone.

"I know it's not, but maybe if you got out of the office they would relax a little." He nodded toward the crew working in the large room outside her door. "Maybe if you left for more than four hours, they would follow your example and get some rest. And don't deck me for saying what you know is the truth."

Dana glared at him across the desk.

Ben waited and kept his mouth shut.

"Do you think I haven't tried?"

He had to strain to hear her.

"I can't sleep because I see Frankie and you walking out of those flames. I come to work and all I find is more dead ends. I know about waiting, Ben. But this is more like a hurricane, brewing on my doorstep. I should be doing something."

Instead of arguing, he nodded. "I was thinking the same thing. How about we head west at first light? Go see Drogan's homestead?"

Dana shook her head. "The one he lost?"

"Sure. We know where it is."

"That's crazy. It's under water, or didn't you get that memo? They built a dam, flooded the entire valley." When Ben didn't contradict her, she asked, "What do you expect to see?"

He stood and stretched, felt the vertebrae in his back pop. "I'm not sure, boss. It's a hunch. And like you, I need to do something. Plus tomorrow's my day off. Want me to pick you up?"

Dana shook her head, eyes wide and disbelieving.

Ben shrugged and walked to the door. He hadn't really expected her to agree to go.

He had one foot across the threshold when she called him back. "I don't know how you manage to make a bad idea sound credible, Marshall."

When he turned to look at her she still looked exhausted, but some of the frustration had fled. "What time?"

"I want to get an early start."

"Of course you do."

"Five?"

"I'll be ready." She was already turning back to the spybots.

"See you then, boss."

He slapped Clay on the back on the way out. Could have been his imagination, but the tension in the room seemed to have dissipated a bit.

He doubted a ball of St. Elmo's fire had come through, but there was always tomorrow.

Thirty-six

D ana stood outside her front door at ten minutes before five the next morning and wondered if she should have worn gloves. Though her calendar plainly declared the date to be Saturday, May 24, a chill hung in the air and the temperature read a crisp 39 degrees.

She clutched her coffee mug and squinted at the Chevy truck, making its way down her street.

Ben had barely pulled into the driveway before she was yanking open the passenger door.

"You're more eager than I thought you'd be."

"I'm freezing, Marshall."

"So water skiing is out." He handed her a bag of donuts and pushed the stick shift on the steering wheel into reverse.

"Water skiing is out. Rock climbing is out." Dana picked a cinnamon sugar donut from the bag. "But these are definitely in."

"A smile like that can sure ease a man's disappointment. Guess you don't need this coffee I brought."

"Nope. I have my own. Thank you, though." Dana took a bite and let the cinnamon melt on her tongue. She'd need to jog an extra mile, but it would be worth every step.

"I would talk, but you look as if you're having a moment over there."

"I am. These are delicious. I never buy donuts."

"You should. They agree with you."

Dana shot him a sideways look, but didn't rise to the bait. Instead, she kept her focus on the road. "So what gives, Marshall? Abiquiu Lake is no more than an hour away. Why the early start?"

"I'm not sure." Ben reached into the bag and pulled out a chocolate-covered, cake donut. "I'm an early riser, and you said you couldn't sleep."

Dana rubbed her forehead and fought the urge to stomp her feet like a child. "Tell me you had a better reason for getting me up at 4:00 a.m. than that."

"So you *can* sleep?"

"I have trouble *going* to sleep. When I finally manage to get there, I don't want to wake up unless someone has a very good reason. Now stop toying with me. Where are we headed so early?"

"We know the dam was completed in 1963."

"Drogan was fifteen years old at the time." Dana stared at the bag of donuts, but interlaced both hands firmly around her mug.

"Right. The same age Reggie is now."

Dana sipped her coffee. "You're going to tell me that is not a coincidence."

182

Ben shrugged as he accelerated onto the main road west out of town, signaling to pass a truck pulling a boat. "By then the negotiations had been going on for over five years."

"Right. All legal petitions were filed by his father."

Ben looked at her, glanced down at the bag, and pushed it back her way. "So Chance Drogan grew up under the shadow of Abiquiu Reservoir. His entire life was colored by the building of the lake and the loss of their land."

Dana stared down into the bag of donuts. The chocolate one had looked awfully tasty when Ben ate his. She decided life was short and chose a chocolate twist. "What must that have been like? Did they live nearby after their home was bulldozed, or move away?"

"Exactly. The family drops off the record books. Probably disappeared after the appeal was lost." Ben opened the second container of milk he'd brought.

The small, cardboard carton reminded Dana of endless lunch trays and how she'd always sat by Erin, always made sure she'd drank her milk. Some things stayed the same—across the miles, across the years.

"We're a long way from 1963, but we might be able to find someone who knew the family." He looked over at Dana and smiled as he wiped away his milk mustache.

"How do you plan to do that?"

"I was thinking we'd start with the old-timers."

"And they'll be at the coffee shops."

"Yeah. We should get there about the time they're into their second cup. I called around. Here's the list of the oldest diners. Only the first was open in '63."

Dana studied the sheet he handed her. On it was a map of the Abiquiu Lake area with three locations labeled and routes marked.

"Not bad." She folded up the donut bag and pushed it back to his side of the seat. "I think I'm going to be too full to eat though."

Ben hung one hand over the wheel, which looked like it belonged on a ship. Why did they make steering wheels so large in the old days? His other arm rested across the back of the seat. She thought about calling him on it, but she suddenly felt drowsy from the load of sugar she'd dumped in her system.

A little nap wouldn't hurt. Glancing at her watch, she estimated they had another forty minutes before reaching the first diner.

"Wake me up before we get there," she mumbled.

"Sure thing, boss."

Her eyes had no sooner closed than she was dreaming about a teenage boy, walking along the Abiquiu Lake bed as the waters slowly began to rise.

Thirty-seven

B en stopped Dana before they walked into the diner that said simply, COFFEE SHOP. "We probably need a cover story."

"Huh?"

"A cover story. You know, something to say in case people ask what we're doing here."

Dana tapped her foot. "Why would we need a cover story?"

"Well, we could tell them we're with the Department of Homeland Security, but folks tend to clam up when you say you're with the government. Or wait, I could just pull out my firearm. It's pretty effective early on a Saturday morning with a bunch of old-timers."

Ben smiled and waited for her to catch up.

"You think because you plied me with donuts you can be sarcastic." She squinted her eyes and held her hand up to block the morning sun. "You're spunkier since you had your hair singed off—military cut, military attitude. Maybe you should pretend I'm your commanding officer."

Ben put a hand to the back of his neck and grinned. "Want to run your fingers through it?"

Dana laughed outright. "There's nothing left to run my fingers through."

"I still have some curls up here. You can play with the top part."

She shook her head. "Stop distracting me. What's our cover story? I know you already have one."

"Sure. We're married and stopping in before a day on the lake."

"Won't work."

Ben had known she would argue.

Dana wiggled the fingers on her left hand. "No rings."

"Oh. I forgot." Ben felt around in his blue-jeans pocket. "Nope. No extra rings there."

She punched his right arm. He was grateful she chose his right. His left was still sore and a rather cool shade of purple.

"How about this?" Dana tapped her fingers against her lips. "We're dating. We both live in Taos, and we've never managed to get this far west."

"Hmm. Simpler, and it makes sense."

Dana turned and walked into the shop while he was still reveling in the fact she had agreed to pretend to be dating him. Possibly, it was a new low in his social life.

He hurried into the diner after his new girlfriend, nearly bumping into her in the process. It took a good ten seconds for his eyes to adjust to the dim light after the brightness of the New Mexico morning. When he could see, he thought they'd stepped back into 1963.

A counter ran along one wall. In front of it red bar stools were filled with men of all shapes and sizes. Each one wore either a baseball cap or a cowboy hat.

Along the front wall was a cash register that no one tended. A hand-penned sign proclaimed CASH OR CHECK ONLY, NO CREDIT CARDS. Plate-glass windows covered the entire west wall. They were spotless and gave a view of all the happenings on Main Street, which at the moment was dead.

The booths and tables were a hubbub of activity. Old men sat in groups of twos, threes, and fours, sipping coffee and telling tales. More than a few of them stopped to eye his boss, err, his girlfriend.

"Come on, honey. Let's find a table." He nodded at another sign near the front, which read, SEAT YOURSELF, I'M BUSY.

Smiling down at her, he wrapped an arm around her waist and walked her to the one open booth.

Scooting into the far side of the booth, he snagged her when she started toward the opposite side. "Sit next to me, sweetheart. I miss you when you're so far away."

"You're enjoying this, Marshall. Entirely too much." But she allowed herself to be pulled down into the crook of his arm.

A waitress with bright red lipstick and short, gray hair breezed by long enough to beam at them and confirm they both wanted coffee.

While Ben studied the one-page, laminated menu, Dana looked around the room.

"Ben, I'm the only woman in here."

"Not if you count the waitresses."

"I wasn't."

"Then you're the only woman in here."

"Why is that?"

Ben dropped the menu and smiled at her. "In Montana we have a diner exactly like this. I think every town does. The old codgers all wake up early, and the women are mostly glad to get them out of the house for an hour or two. This is their hangout."

The waitress reappeared with two, steaming, mugs of coffee.

"You two ready to order?"

"Yes, ma'am. I'll take the fisherman's special."

"That would be our biggest and best."

Dana picked up the menu and slid her finger down it until she found the item Ben had ordered. "Three eggs, fried trout, hash browns, biscuits, and gravy." She slid away from Ben and stared at him in mock horror.

"Ben Marshall. You are not going to eat all that."

"Sure am."

The waitress tapped her pen against her pad. "Now, honey. He looks like a growing boy. Probably about to spend a day on the lake."

"How did you know?" Ben smiled up at the waitress.

"I almost always guess right." The plump woman beamed back at him, then cocked her head at Dana. "Now what can I get you?"

"Do you have bagels?"

"Nope. We don't go for that fancy stuff. How about a side of biscuits? We have the lightest buttermilk biscuits around."

"Oh. All right. Well. I'll take some biscuits and a bowl of fruit then."

"Coming right up. I'm LuAnn. You all holler if you need anything."

Dana waited until LuAnn had moved away before turning on him. "Did you need to order all that food?"

"Absolutely. I'm hungry."

When she continued to stare at him in disbelief, he added, "And it would look suspicious if we only ordered coffee."

Dana shook her head, causing her ponytail to bob back and forth. He reached a hand out and tugged at it playfully.

"What are you doing?"

"I like how you're wearing your hair today, sweetheart. Looks nice and perky."

It sounded like she muttered something about shooting practice and extra ammo, but he wasn't sure. She'd stuck her face into the oversized mug of coffee LuAnn had poured.

LuAnn returned with the fruit and biscuits.

"I haven't seen biscuits this size since I was home." Ben pulled one out of the basket and held it in his hand. It was the size of his palm, and he was surprised it didn't float away into the air.

LuAnn smiled and rested her coffeepot on the table. "Sounds like you should visit home more often. I'll bet your mama misses you."

"Yes, ma'am. She understands though. I stayed for a few weeks when I was first discharged, then came to work in Taos."

LuAnn's face softened like the butter Ben had placed inside his biscuit.

"What branch were you in?"

"Army," Ben said around the bite he'd taken. "Oh, my. I better not tell Mama about these. She'll think I like someone's cooking better than hers."

LuAnn's smile grew even larger, and she picked up the coffeepot. "I'll check on your food."

She turned to Dana as she left. "Honey, try one of those biscuits. You're going to need more than a little fruit once you get out in the sun."

Ben felt Dana staring at him as he took the last bite. "What?"

"You are playing her like a fiddle, Ben. You should be ashamed."

"I'm being friendly. Watch and learn." He sat back and sipped from the coffee, thinking he was going to have to get moving after consuming all these calories.

He saw LuAnn stop to talk at a table of old geezers, nod their way, and then pick up a large plate of food from the kitchen pass-through and walk toward their table.

"I told Harold about you serving in the Army. Now he's probably going to talk your ear off, but he does like to thank any of our military boys. I hope you don't mind."

"Not at all. This looks fantastic."

"That trout is fresh. We have some kids who catch it after school, and they brought in a whole mess yesterday."

LuAnn refilled their coffee. "I'll check back with you two in a minute."

The smell of pan-fried trout had him sitting up straighter. He had only thought he was full. Grabbing the salt and pepper, he doctored the fish, then the eggs. It wasn't until he'd picked up his knife and fork that he noticed Dana had squirreled her nose in disgust.

"Try a bite," he coaxed. When she shook her head, he placed a forkful in his mouth, closed his eyes, and groaned. "Now that is the best breakfast meat on earth."

Dana's laughter surprised them both.

"What?"

"You should have seen the look on your face. Like a kid at Christmas."

"Ah come on, darlin'. One bite and you'll see why."

"No, Ben."

"One bite, and I'll leave you alone."

"But—"

"One bite. I won't say another word. I'll even go sit across the room so you don't have to watch me."

"Promise?" She scowled at him as the fork of trout came closer.

"Open wide, sweetheart." He dropped the trout in and watched her expression change. "Uh-huh. What did I tell you? I guess you won't be so quick to hassle me now."

"That's amazing." Dana swallowed. "Seriously."

She scooched closer in the booth. "One more bite."

"Yeah. You like it now." He speared more trout on to his fork and plopped it into her mouth, touching her chin softly with his other hand as he did so.

Dana opened her eyes and stared into his. Suddenly, he found he could barely swallow the hash browns in his mouth. She was as beautiful and fresh as the New Mexico morning outside their window. The need to take her in his arms nearly overwhelmed him. He thought about kissing her, moved his hand from her face to the back of her neck.

She didn't move, didn't back away.

Was it a charade? Or did she feel the same thing that was coursing through his veins, through his heart?

Before he could ask, before he could taste her lips, someone coughed.

Dana pulled away, and the moment was over as quickly as it had begun.

Ben looked up to see two men, older than his father, standing beside their booth. He wondered how long they'd been waiting and what they wanted.

Thirty-eight

D ana was at first disappointed, then relieved when the two old guys stopped whatever was happening between her and Ben. What had been happening? One minute she was eating trout for breakfast, the next she'd been drowning in Ben's brown eyes.

Unable and unwilling to look away, her heart had begun to hammer, as if she'd been chased and caught. Captured by his gaze, she felt pulled toward a future she'd lost sight of long ago.

"Scuse us, son. Hope we're not interrupting."

"Course we're interrupting, Harold. Even someone as blind as you could see he was about to kiss her."

"There was a time we'd a been home with our missus, doing some kissing ourselves, Johnson."

Ben stood and shook hands with Harold, who might have been blind but was plenty agile enough. Then he turned to Johnson, a man bent over in the way of the very old, though apparently still able to see everything.

"I'm Ben, and this is Dana."

Dana instinctively stood and shook hands with both men. To give them credit, they took her hand and shook it, though they grinned at each other, as if this would be a story to tell tomorrow morning.

"Wanted to thank you for serving." Harold nodded in LuAnn's direction. "Lu told us."

He hesitated as he glanced at Dana. "Course she didn't say whether your missus…"

Ben and Dana exchanged a quick glance.

"No, sir. I haven't been in the military, and I'm not—"

"Dana and I are dating. We're not married." Ben placed his arm around her waist, pulled her closer. "Yet."

Harold cackled. "Better not wait too long, sonny. Not with a woman as pretty as she is."

"Don't I know it. I was just telling Dana how beautiful she looks today."

Dana gouged him lightly in the ribs with her elbow, so Ben quickly changed the subject. "Say would you two like to sit down?"

"Can't." Johnson said. "We're old, but we're busy."

"Don't have to be rude." Harold drew himself up to his full height. "This man fought in the military while you and I were sitting here sipping coffee. Least we could do is give him ten minutes of our time."

"Well, they looked like they were pretty happy alone, Harold. I think Ben was being polite."

"We'd be happy for you to join us. We were about to ask LuAnn for some more coffee."

Harold nearly knocked Johnson over, pushing him into the booth. "As long as you keep eating, we'll sit. Where'd you serve, son? How long you been back?"

"I was in the desert," Ben replied vaguely as he dug into his food. Dana noticed he looked directly at the two older gents as he spoke. "I guess you two know what I mean, but I can't really name the exact places I was deployed."

"Army?" Johnson asked.

"Yes, sir."

"Thought so." Johnson turned to Harold. "Told you he looks like army."

Dana was relieved when Ben jumped in before Harold could pick up the argument.

"They're a good group of men. I was proud to serve with them. I expect you two served during your time."

LuAnn appeared at their table with her coffeepot. Dana noticed she placed Harold's cup into his hands where he could easily find it. Apparently, the old guy was nearly blind.

"Don't get them started telling war stories unless you want to eat lunch here too." With a wink at Dana, she cleared the empty fruit bowl and biscuit basket, then hurried off to take orders from two new groups of middle-aged men.

"We both served in the Air Force," Harold said.

"WWII," Johnson added.

They stared into their coffee cups, memories passing between them like water flowing from the river to the sea.

"Lu's right though." Harold cast a glance at his friend. "Get Johnson started remembering, and by the time you're free to go, you'll be too old to marry. Besides, you all didn't come here for old war stories. What brings you out to Lake Abiquiu?"

Ben's hand moved up and down Dana's arm, gently rubbing the skin with the tips of his fingers. She ignored the goose bumps that danced down her arm and hoped he wouldn't notice. After all, this was their cover story. She was simply playing her part well.

"Wanted to take my girl out on the water," Ben said, pushing his plate away. "Give her a day to relax."

Johnson grunted. "Wouldn't mind a day out fishing myself."

"And how would you get in the boat?" Harold demanded.

"At least I could see the water."

"You might be able to see it, but if you fell in you'd fall to the bottom like a snail all curved up like you are."

"Oh, yeah? How 'bout we go out there and see who falls to the bottom."

Dana looked to Ben who had moved his attention to playing with her hair. She scowled at him, and he cleared his throat, interrupting Harold and Johnson's apparently oft-repeated barbs.

"Big lake, right?"

"You bet it is." Harold tapped his cup with fingertips yellowed by time. He stared off at the far wall of the diner. "Over five-thousand surface acres of water."

"And fifty-one miles of shoreline," Johnson added. "Plenty of places to fish."

"Some of the best fishing in northern New Mexico."

The two men looked at each other and nodded, for once at a loss for how to argue with each other.

"What else is there to do?" Dana asked. "Other than fish."

"There's swimming," Harold said. "Or you can water ski if you brought a boat."

"No boat today." Ben ducked his head, as if the admission shamed him. "Maybe someday."

The three men sat in silence, sipping their coffee, as thoughts of boats clouded their brains. It occurred to Dana that Ben fit in pretty well here. She didn't know if the knowledge pleased or frightened her.

"Guess the lake was a big boon to the local economy." Dana twirled her coffee cup.

"Yeah. It's helped bring in lots of visitors," Harold allowed.

"People come and buy trinkets in the shops in downtown Abiquiu." Johnson looked around the diner. "That's why we stay out here."

"Don't need any trinkets and don't need any espresso either." Harold said the words with obvious contempt.

Ben sipped his now cold coffee and nodded, as if he'd never touch a trinket, let alone a cup of espresso. Dana felt his knee jerk under the table as he angled in for the kill. "So everybody's happy. Folks downtown have their trinkets. Everyone else has... this."

Harold shrugged, waved his hand over his head for LuAnn to bring one more refill. "Most folks are happy now. Wasn't always that way though."

"No, sir," Johnson agreed.

"Time was a few people didn't even want the lake built."

"Or the dam."

Dana felt all the hairs on her arms stand up. Ben's hand froze where he'd been massaging the back of her neck.

"Why would anyone be against a lake?" she asked.

Johnson held his cup out as LuAnn bustled over to the table. "Well, if you live around the shoreline, then it's a pretty good idea. But if you live where the water's going—"

"Not such a good idea," Harold finished.

"You two telling that story?" LuAnn frowned. "It's too pretty a day for such sadness, and these two lovebirds don't need to hear about tragedy and heartbreak."

She glanced around the diner. Things had settled down in the last few minutes, so she pulled a chair over to the end of the booth and set her coffeepot on the table. "Course the story of the Drogans is one that's hard to forget. And maybe there's a lesson there for anyone willing to listen."

Thirty-nine

B en didn't realize he was gripping Dana's neck until she let out a yelp.

"Problem, Miss?" Johnson looked up sharply.

"No. I bit my tongue is all." She eased away from Ben ever so slightly as she reached for her glass of water.

Ben grasped his coffee mug with both hands as LuAnn refilled it.

"I should bite *my* tongue. We all should, talking about those poor people's misfortune."

"They brought it on their self, and you know it, Lu." Harold squinted toward the end of the table. "Folks couldn't stop that dam or that lake. Drogan was a fool for trying."

"Maybe so," LuAnn agreed. "Mind you I wasn't old enough to know the old man. The boy, Chance, he was a few years older than me in school. In fact, he was in the same grade as my cousin, Angela. She's the one who told us most of what happened."

"Most of what happened was in the paper," Johnson pointed out.

"The lawsuit and the appeal, but not everything that went on afterwards." LuAnn leaned forward, ready to share her secret. Then two groups of men came through the front door. "I better go and help those folks. I'll be back."

Ben stared after her. He only remembered Johnson and Harold were still sitting at the table when Dana began speaking to them.

"So this Drogan, he didn't want the lake to be built?"

"That's an understatement. He did everything he could to stop it," Harold said. "Both legal and illegal."

"Now you don't know that." Johnson banged his coffee cup against the table. "You can't know that for sure."

"Guess I can't prove it, but folks know."

"Why was he set against it? If the lake helped the area so much?" Ben tried to sound casual, but his heart rate was kicked up a notch—either from the coffee, from Dana's closeness, or from the answers hovering so close.

"The Drogans owned land in the middle of the lake bed, that's why."

"Land wasn't that good," Harold interrupted.

"Land doesn't have to be good. If it's yours, if it's been yours and your family's, then land matters. Drogan didn't want to let go. Government came in offering fair market value." Johnson leaned forward, caught up in the story, in a different time. "How do you put a fair value on an acre of land worked by your father and your father's father? Can't dig up memories and move them somewhere else."

The four at the table fell silent, the only sounds were those from nearby tables.

LuAnn sat back down with a groan, resting the coffeepot on the table. "My dogs are tired, and I haven't had a break since coming on at five. Folks needs to get their own coffee refills." She looked around the table. "Someone die while I was gone?"

"Not while you was gone, but someone died all right." Harold reached out and patted her hand. "You tell that part."

"Oh, yeah, the Drogans." LuAnn leaned forward, her cherry-red lips forming a pout. "My, but those were dark times round here. Chance's pa lost his appeal. Course I guess these fellas told you they paid him for the land. Near 'bout made him crazy though. He took to drinking, and he was mean to begin with."

LuAnn turned the pot of coffee and stared into its murky depths. "My cousin, Angela, was supposed to meet Chance the night it happened."

LuAnn stopped and stared curiously at Dana for a moment. "She looked a little like you, come to think of it. Course that was a long time ago. Could be she was just young and pretty." Sighing she went on with her story. "They were supposed to go to the movies, but her pa wouldn't let her go. Everyone was upset about all that had gone on. Can't blame my uncle for not wanting her in the middle of it. She was just a girl. Chance Drogan took it hard though."

LuAnn looked out the window, as if she were seeing into yesterday. "I think Angela blamed herself for what happened next. She wanted to explain to Chance why she didn't show, but he never called again. He... they..."

She tried a third time to finish the story. Someone behind her called out for coffee. LuAnn called out, "Hold your horses," and accepted the napkin Dana handed her.

Ben found Dana's hand under the table, entwined his fingers in hers.

"No one really knows what happened," Johnson said quietly. "Found both his parents dead up on top of the dam. Could have been an accident. Could have been a double homicide."

"I better go make some fresh coffee." LuAnn moved her chair back to the adjacent table, checking her makeup in the mirror over the counter before moving to warm-up coffee cups.

"What happened to the boy?" Ben asked.

"He was supposed to go into foster care, being as he was in high school at the time. Town would have took him in, but he ran off before anyone could offer." Johnson pushed his mug away, attempted to sit up straight.

"Went on to serve in Nam," Harold said. "Terrible war. Seemed to mess the boy up more."

"So he came back?" Dana asked. Ben noticed her fingers were ice cold against his.

"He'd stop in every few years." Johnson said.

"He even bought a place at the end of Old Crown Road," Harold added. "But I haven't seen him in years."

"You haven't seen anything in years."

"I can see you, and some days that's more than a person ought to have to look at."

Johnson grinned, happy they were back on comfortable ground.

Ben glanced at his watch, then reached for his wallet. "Nearly eight. I better take this pretty lady out to the lake before the day gets away from us."

Dana slid to the end of the bench and stood.

As they walked to the register, Harold and Johnson made their way back to their table.

"You two enjoy the sunshine," Harold called as they turned to go.

"And enjoy your youth. It slips away while you're doing other things." Johnson maneuvered awkwardly to scoot back into his chair.

Dana turned to Ben. "I'll be right back. Wait for me?"

"Course I will."

With a teasing smile, she turned and walked to Harold and Johnson's table. Ben couldn't hear what she said, but he saw Harold put his head back and laugh, and Johnson blushed when she kissed him lightly on the cheek.

As they walked into the sunshine, he couldn't help asking. "You going to tell me what you said to them?"

"Nope."

"Then I guess we're off to Old Crown Road."

"Yeah. I guess we are."

It seemed appropriate that in an otherwise clear, morning sky, a single cloud chose that moment to pass over the sun, obscuring the light.

Forty

T hey drove to the dam and bought a map that included county roads. Walking back to the truck, Dana lowered her glasses and gave Ben her best supervisor's glare.

"It's none of your business what I told Harold and Johnson."

"But we're dating. As sweethearts, we shouldn't keep secrets from each other."

"That was our cover story, Marshall. *Was*." She pushed her glasses back up, grateful for their reflective tint, and waited beside the truck.

Ben spread the map out on the hood.

"I'll trade," he said.

"Trade what?"

"A ride back to Taos. Now tell me what you said to those two old geezers."

Dana laughed and took a drink of the bottled water he'd pulled from the cooler. "You can't stand it."

"Can't stand what?"

"Not knowing everything."

"Guilty. Whatever you said though, it took the sadness out of their expressions for a few minutes. It was a kind thing to do."

His look flustered her more than his words. "Oh, all right. I was a little worried we'd been too interested in their story. So I asked the tall guy—"

"Harold."

"Yes, Harold. I asked Harold what type of boat I should buy you for a, err, wedding present." She felt the color mounting up her neck into her cheeks.

"A wedding present? Wow. I'll get on my knees now if I'm going to score a boat out of the deal."

She made a swipe for his arm, but he ducked out of the way in the nick of time.

"He named off a few kinds, engine sizes, etc. I don't remember the details."

"That's it?" Ben had stopped studying the map.

Dana tried to ignore the way the sun bounced off his skin, the way he looked as natural standing on the dam of Abiquiu Lake as he did working in her office.

"I said if you were going to spend more time with the boat than with me, maybe I should think of something else."

"Must be when he started laughing."

"I guess." Dana fiddled with the label on her water bottle. "I wanted to, you know…"

"Distract them."

"Right."

Ben turned and leaned back against the truck, still holding the map. "All right, Miss Jacobs. What about

Johnson? I distinctly remember you kissing him on the cheek. Was that a distraction as well?"

Dana looked out over the lake, a place that for at least one family had caused so much pain. "I felt bad for him. It must be terribly difficult for him to get through each day. To not be able to walk straight, or sit down easily. And you can tell he feels like he's lost his dignity."

Ben nodded, but didn't interrupt her.

"I thanked him. That's all. Told them we'd stop by again if we were ever out this way."

She stared out at the lake a little longer, took another swig of water, then cleared her throat. "So do you think we can find this road?"

"Sure. Only so many roads around a lake. I'll study the east side of the map. You take the west."

They stood there in the sunshine, studying the map on the hood of Ben's Chevy truck. Neither felt a need to talk more. Dana did her best to ignore the nearness of him, the way his arm brushed against hers as he followed a line on the map, the delicious shiver when his hand would casually touch hers.

She was acting like a teenager and she knew it, except her adolescent years had never approached normal. She had nothing to compare this to, no way to know if it was a schoolgirl crush or something more.

Twenty minutes later, they were driving around the west side of the lake. Old Crown Road did, in fact, dead end back in the woods overlooking the lake. When they first turned on the road, there had been an occasional fisherman's lodge. Ten miles down the road, the places spread out until they disappeared.

The forest grew denser, blocking out the summer sky completely. And then the road simply ended.

There was no gate. No sign saying STAY OFF or PRIVATE PROPERTY. Nothing to indicate anyone had ever been or was currently living there.

Which, of course, is exactly what Dana would expect from someone like Chance Drogan. Not the child who'd been left an orphan. Not the boy who didn't keep a date with LuAnn's cousin. She could feel pity for either of those boys that Chance had been. This is what she would expect from the man Chance Drogan had become.

She couldn't feel anything for the person who had pulled Reggie Mifflin into a man's game, a criminal's war. And she despised someone who would put a family at risk, an entire community in danger.

While Ben secured their vehicle and unloaded Kevlar vests and extra ammo, she called into the office. She apprised Cheryl of their location and made sure they could receive the GPS tracking signal from her cell phone.

"Ready?" Ben asked.

"As I'll ever be."

With weapons drawn, they walked into the darkness of the forest. A overgrown trail led to the northeast—whether it had been made by wildlife or Drogan was hard to tell.

Thirty minutes later, they came in sight of the cabin.

Forty-one

One of the things Ben respected most about his boss was her ability to let the most experienced man lead. In this situation, he was the most experienced, and they both knew it.

Odds were, the cabin was rigged to blow.

They walked through the woods, each carrying a pack. Ben held his rifle in his left hand. Both were armed with pistols and wearing Kevlar vests. Ben motioned for Dana to stay six feet back. He was looking for trip wires. He didn't see any, but that meant nothing. Anyone who had served in Nam could hide a trip wire no one would find until it was too late.

He pulled a pair of binoculars out of his pack and focused in on the cabin. Starting at the bottom west corner, he moved slowly—south to north, bottom to top. He saw no wires, no motion sensors, nothing suspicious. Reaching down, he picked up a stick.

He looked back for Dana's approval. She shrugged, then flattened her back against a tree. He threw, hitting the east wall of the cabin. Still no explosions.

Ben pointed at Dana and pointed at his tree. She was at his side in seconds.

"Might be the wrong cabin," she whispered.

"I don't think so. This is definitely the end of the road. Anyone else would have NO TRESPASSING signs posted at the property line. Not Drogan though. He'd play it cool and hope everyone would go away."

"Looks like it worked. I think the place is deserted."

Ben glanced around the tree. "Maybe. One way to find out."

"We could wait. Call in some drones." She looked at him, the familiar worry lines pulling between her eyebrows.

"Or I could go first."

"Sounds dangerous."

"You're so sweet. We've only been dating a few hours and already you're concerned about my welfare." When she didn't so much as crack a smile, he changed tactics. "You're right. Drones would be the smart way to go, but it would take six hours to fly them up here by the time we get approval and send our location to the regional boys."

Ben glanced around the tree. "Doesn't look like he's home right now. I say we go on in. I'll go first. If nothing explodes, you come after me."

Dana sucked her bottom lip in and worried it between her teeth. "What if you get blown up?"

"Call for backup."

"Seriously, Ben."

"We've circled this entire cabin. I haven't seen any signs it's rigged. Course he could have buried the wires. That's why I want to go first." He cinched the backpack up on his shoulders. "I don't know. I get this itchy feeling when something isn't right, and I don't have it right now."

"Not a real technical reason."

"I think we're good."

"Okay." She still looked worried. Actually, she looked like she wanted to kiss him. She'd been glancing at him oddly since they'd traced their route around the dam. Possibly, she was experiencing heat exhaustion though. He wasn't very experienced with women.

She didn't kiss him. Instead, she reached up and brushed some leaves off his shoulder. "Be careful."

"I'll whistle when it's clear for you to follow. In the meantime, keep your back against this tree. Just in case."

Forty-two

D ana watched Ben move into the clearing. When he turned to look at her, she ducked behind the tree as instructed.

Why did she let him talk her into these things?

Then again, what kind of maniac set his own cabin to blow? Surely Drogan wasn't completely insane.

She peeked around the tree in time to see Ben cautiously climbing the steps of the porch. Closing her eyes, she tried to picture a summer beach or the view from The Block Head, but it was no use. The only image she could see was the wall in her office and three framed pictures.

Wrenching her eyes open, she stared at the trees in front of her. A cardinal hopped from a higher branch to a lower one, cocked its head at her, then flew away. Maybe it was a sign. Perhaps the bird knew they should run.

She was about to tell Ben to scrap the plan when she heard his whistle—two shorts and a long. Breathing deeply, she turned from the tree to see him standing in the open door of the cabin.

He waved to her, indicating she should retrace his route in the dew-moistened leaves.

Once she gained the steps, she noticed a look of disgust on his face. As soon as she crossed the doorway into the cabin she learned why.

"Tell me that odor is not a body."

"Spoiled food. Bodies smell worse." Ben walked in front of her as they covered the perimeter of the single room. A bathroom had been partitioned off at the back and there were two additional doors, one which led to a closet and another which exited toward the back of the property. Ben set his rifle near the front door.

"This surprises me," Ben admitted. "Explosives guys are normally neat freaks."

"Maybe we do have the wrong place then." Dana found herself wishing she had gloves on. The place made her skin itch. There were dirty blankets and sheets on the unmade bed in one corner. A fireplace in another corner was apparently the only source of heat. Some animal had tracked ashes across the floor.

The end of the room which housed the kitchen was even dirtier and definitely the origin of the foul odor.

"What is that smell?" Dana held her sleeve up to cover her nose as she crossed the room to stand in front of the two-person table.

"Fridge. Looks like the power went out some time ago. Probably Drogan stopped paying his bills. Want me to open it?"

"I guess we should. Just to be sure... well, you know."

Ben opened the fridge, scowled, and shut it quickly. "Definitely where the perfume is coming from all right."

"Oh, my gosh." Dana turned to the open door, stepped out on the porch, and drew several deep gulps of fresh air.

"You okay, boss?"

"I'm fine. What was it?"

"I'm not really sure, but I think it was game he caught and froze. Then the power went out." Ben stuck his head out the door and grinned at her. "Sure you're all right?"

"Yes." Dana lifted her head, determined to have as tough a stomach as he apparently did. "What kind of game?"

"Maybe squirrel? Something small."

"That is disgusting."

Ben shrugged. "A guy has to eat. Long way to town from here, and I have a feeling Drogan wasn't real sociable."

Ben disappeared back into the cabin.

Dana preferred the porch, but if there were any clues to Drogan's plans or whereabouts, she doubted they were carved on the front steps. Pulling back her shoulders, she stepped inside.

Which was when she saw Ben pull his Glock and signal for her to do the same.

Forty-three

B en knew something was wrong the minute he opened the pantry door. The small room's dimensions were all wrong.

Holding his firearm in his right hand, he signaled to Dana with his left. She pulled her own pistol and crouched in the doorway, aiming toward the bathroom at the back of the cabin.

He'd cleared that area when he first walked in, so he knew Drogan wasn't there. But he hadn't realized there was a space in between the bathroom and the pantry.

Creeping silently toward the back of the cabin, he stopped half way to the back wall. The cabin made an L shape, as if the area containing the bathroom and pantry had been added on as an afterthought. He had assumed the pantry backed up to the bathroom, and he'd cleared it as he had the rest of the cabin.

Only later, when he was searching for any clue as to where Drogan might have gone, did it occur to him the dimensions were all wrong.

Standing across from the bathroom, he couldn't see anything to indicate a door or secret room. He was about to signal to Dana that he was going outside when she raised her left hand like some schoolyard crossing guard.

Her pistol remained steady in her right hand. Her left palm faced toward herself. She crooked her index finger—once, twice, three times. When he'd moved three paces toward her, she turned her hand and pushed it forward—the universal symbol to stop.

A smile spread across her face, and she pointed at the wall directly across from him.

At first he didn't see it, then the light coming through the dirty windows shifted. Suddenly, in front of him was a barely perceptible seam in the smooth logs of the wall.

Ben ran his hand over the entire outline of the hidden door, which was as clear as the big dipper in the night sky once someone points it out to you. Once he was as sure as he could be that it wasn't rigged with explosives, he rested his palm against the place the handle should have been and pushed.

The door opened without a sound, revealing a set of stairs leading down into darkness.

Dana moved beside him.

She nodded once, confirming she was ready for whatever the next few minutes might bring. He took in a steadying breath, one filled with prayer for her safety and a plea that his aim would be true if need be. Then he plunged into the darkness.

Light from the room above showed stairs built to be sturdy, each one lined with rubber matting. His vision adjusted quickly. Although the room below was large, essentially the same dimensions as the cabin, he knew immediately it was empty.

"Throw me down a light, Dana."

"Can I come down?"

"Let me check for wires first."

She pitched him the flashlight from their pack. He ran it along the ceiling, across the floor, even behind the workbenches.

"We're clear," he said, flipping on the wall switch as she made her way down.

"Explain this to me." She still had her weapon raised and in front of her, as if Drogan might appear out of thin air. "I thought the power was out."

"We were supposed to think that, and it is out upstairs. He apparently bypassed the main box when he ran the lines to this room."

Dana continued to grip her firearm, looking around in amazement.

"I think you can holster that, boss. We're all alone down here." He surveyed the high-tech equipment and contemporary furniture. It was minimal, but efficient. "Not quite what you'd expect underneath a hunter's cabin."

"I didn't expect anything," Dana admitted. She holstered her weapon, but seemed somewhat reluctant to do so.

"Probably this was a root cellar to begin with. He spent an impressive amount of money to turn it into his command center."

"I'll say. What's the point though? I don't understand why he bothered. This must have taken years, and what has he accomplished?" She remained in the middle of the room, slowly turning, trying to take in everything she saw.

"We don't know what he's accomplished or planned," Ben agreed. "There are probably a lot of clues down here."

"I'll have to call in a crew to go over this entire room. Of course, if he comes back, any activity will scare him off. Maybe it would be better to post a patrol, sit back, and watch."

"Turn around a second." Ben unzipped her pack and pulled out two pairs of plastic gloves. "Doesn't hurt to look a little while we're here."

He snapped on a pair and walked to the first worktable. Over it sat a map of the Abiquiu Lake. "No surprise here."

Dana had stopped in front of the computer terminal. "Should we try?"

"I wouldn't. It will be password protected, and it might have a remote alarm that alerts him when it's been turned on—much like a LoJac. You can purchase tracking devices on the Internet now and have them alert your cell phone if someone accesses your computer."

Dana scowled at him. "You're not applying for a transfer to the cyber-crimes division are you?"

"And miss Saturday hikes in the woods with my boss? No way." Ben laughed when Dana actually blushed, then turned to the next worktable. Above it was a map of Taos. "You might want to take a picture of this."

Forty-four

D ana snapped on her own pair of gloves, then pulled the digital camera from her pocket and began snapping pictures of the map. On it were several marked positions. Some were obvious locations, such as the school and their office. Others she couldn't assign any obvious logic to.

She was leaning in, trying to figure out why Drogan would have stuck a pin in what she was sure was the Bucket-o-Chicken location. Suddenly, she heard Ben suck in his breath. Turning around she saw his back had gone completely rigid.

He had opened what looked like a dartboard case, but his body fully blocked what was inside.

"Ben?"

He didn't answer immediately, frightening her more with his silence than with anything he could have said.

She moved toward him, reached out to touch his back, and caught a glimpse of her own face. Was it a mirror?

"What is it?"

"Back away, Dana."

His voice suddenly sounded very far away. There was a sound like the waves of Puget Sound, crashing against the rocks. She tried to draw a breath, but couldn't.

Putting her hand against his shoulder, she attempted to push him out of the way.

He turned and caught her by the arms. "Don't look at it, Dana."

"What do you mean, don't look at it? *It* is me." She knew she was shouting, heard her voice rise to a frantic pitch. She tried to push past him, clawed at his arm when he barred her way.

Ben remained rooted, immovable. "Stop it. Dana, stop. Look at me."

"What kind of freak is he? What kind of freak does that?"

He was backing her up, moving her across the room and away from the unimaginable. She momentarily calmed, and his hands went from her arms to her face.

It was less than a split second, but it was enough.

She shot past him, drawn to the collage of pictures like a magnet.

While the rest of the room was as orderly and clean as any surgical operating suite, this cabinet seemed to contain the heart of the madman they sought. Inside its felt-lined doors, Dana gazed in horror at a myriad of pictures of herself.

Not merely pictures, but Picasso-like dissections.

Many had been carefully dismembered so they looked as if she were viewing herself through the mirrors of a circus fun house. Except there was nothing fun about the words and blood spilled there. She knew without a doubt it was real blood—hopefully his blood and not someone or something else's.

She felt the trembling start in her arms and spread until she was sure her legs wouldn't hold her.

"You've seen enough, honey." Ben reached around her and closed the doors to block the messages, but he couldn't take away the images seared in her mind. "Let's go upstairs. Come on."

Shaking, she only nodded. He gathered their things, turned out the lights. When they reached the top of the stairs, the stench greeted them, reminding her again of what she'd seen, what Drogan had dreamed of doing.

She bolted for the door, down the steps, and across the clearing.

She'd finished vomiting her breakfast by the time Ben caught up with her there, kneeling in the woods.

"Take this," he said, holding back her hair.

She accepted the bandana, wiped her mouth and face. Rinsing her mouth with the water from their bottle should have cleaned it of the putrid taste, but it didn't.

When Ben touched her shoulder, she began to shake again.

"I don't understand," she whispered.

He sighed as he sat there, kneeling beside her in the leaves. "I don't either. Maybe you remind him of someone. LuAnn said you looked a little like her cousin. We can do some checking. You're sure he's never made contact?"

Dana shook her head. "I would remember." She drew a deep breath and stiffened her spine. "I've had people shoot at me before, try to kill me. But I've never had anyone obsess over me, think of doing *those* things before."

Ben stared out through the trees. Maybe he was questioning her ability to continue to lead this op. He didn't understand what it felt like to be a woman, to be soiled in such a fundamental way. He certainly didn't know about her childhood and how this attack against her personally somehow brought those memories to the surface.

"He's obviously a very sick person, Dana. Once we get analysts to look over it, maybe they can figure out some pattern—"

"No analyst will ever see those pictures." Dana stood and marched back toward the porch where their pack lay.

Ben hurried behind her. "What are you talking about?"

"You heard me."

"I heard you, but I don't understand what you said."

Dana turned to face him, both hands on her hips. "I said no analyst will ever see what is in that cabinet."

"That's crazy. There might be something important there."

"Important? You think my house, my face, my body as I jog in the morning is important? How about those photos of me sitting on my back porch?" She stepped closer until she had to look up to glare at him. "I'll tell you what's important. Catching this maniac, and no one has to go into his cabinet to do that."

"But—"

"No. Don't contradict me. This isn't a discussion."

"So we ignore this place because you're embarrassed?"

His words were like a slap in her face. She took a step back, nearly choked on the sudden rush of fury she felt.

"I am not embarrassed, Ben. I am violated. If you don't

know the difference…well, maybe you don't know me very well."

She bent down, grabbed the pack, and walked to the end of the clearing.

Ben closed up the cabin, removed any traces of their having been there, then met her where the shadows were long and the sunlight didn't quite penetrate. He had shouldered the heavier of the two packs and carried his rifle in his left hand and her pack in his right.

"How am I supposed to do this, Dana? Tell me what the rules are."

She knew she'd unfairly lashed out at him, but she felt as if a bubble had descended around her. One which kept her from reaching out to him and kept him from being able to cross over to her.

She had calmed while he was working. It was an icy, numb feeling. The mosaic Drogan had created continued to play through her mind like some terrible horror flick.

"Bring Clay or Red back tomorrow." She took her pack from him. "Set up a perimeter around the clearing and at the entry points. We can requisition a drone to watch the place. But no one is going inside that cabin."

Ben didn't look as if he agreed with her decision, but neither did he argue.

So she turned, and she walked back the way they had come. But not exactly the way they'd come. Her mind was torn between all they'd done and all they would need to do. Her heart was hurting from what she'd seen.

And so she forgot to let Ben lead them out of the forest.

She didn't think to retrace their steps.

She was careless as to where she placed each foot.

Forty-five

B en knew he and Clay would have to go back into the cabin. There was no way he was bringing Sayeed. The man should still be on leave in his opinion. He definitely did not belong in the field. Of course, he did know more about explosives and combat than Clay, so perhaps they could set up a live feed. Sayeed couldn't risk another injury this soon though.

No, he would need to bring Clay. And they would have to go back into the basement, gather as much evidence as possible, and look for clues as to where Drogan was and what he had planned next. They'd also have to set up a twenty-four hour guard around Dana, or move her. From the tongue lashing he'd received and the way she'd pulled rank, he knew she wasn't going to easily accept either recommendation from him.

His mind was so completely preoccupied with all he would need to do, he slipped and forgot his current duties. Or that's what he would tell himself later. He should have never let Dana lead, not knowing Drogan was an explosives expert.

The instant he heard her foot contact the mine trigger, he recognized it for what it was.

Launching himself through the air, he knocked her to the ground and rolled, covering her body with as much of his own as possible. The explosion in the clearing behind them sent a low rumbling through the ground beneath them.

Ben felt her heartbeat beneath him as he held her tight. Tendrils of smoke filled the air, stinging his eyes. But there were no flames, no secondary explosions.

Pulling back slightly, he dusted the leaves and dirt from her hair. He tried to see her face, but she was cowered in the fetal position.

"It's over, Dana. Are you okay?"

She lowered her hands slowly and stared up at him with an expression that would haunt him as long as he lived, even if he lived to see his great-grandchildren. She didn't speak, but she sat up with his help, nodded her head, and looked around as if dazed.

"Did I hurt you?" he asked.

"No, no. I don't think so."

He pulled the pack off her back, found the water bottle, and uncapped it.

"Is he here?" She'd begun shaking and couldn't hold the water when he offered it to her.

"I don't think so. Here, drink this." He held it to her lips, pressed her hand to the bottle. Recapping it, he knelt in front of her and rubbed her arms. "You stepped on a mine, Dana. It was a remote detonator. I'm surprised we didn't hit it on the way in. He's not here."

She looked at him in disbelief.

"Do you understand me? If he were here, he would have ambushed us. He wouldn't have blown up his own place."

She nodded slowly, relief flooding into her face.

"I'm going to go back and look."

He started to pull away from her, but she staggered to her feet.

"I'm coming with you."

"Are you sure?"

"Yeah. I was… rattled a little. I'm better now."

Ben walked over and picked up his rifle from where he'd thrown it, inspected the stock and firing mechanism, then chambered a round. "We're good." He shouldered his pack and led the way back into the clearing.

What had been a cabin was now a pile of logs. One part of Ben's mind wanted to give Drogan credit, for there were no flames escaping from the structure, only smoke from the settling debris.

Dana moved a step closer until her arm brushed against his. "What if we had been inside when that happened?"

Ben turned and looked in her eyes, saw the fear and exhaustion there. Setting his weapon on the ground, he pulled her into his arms.

"I am so sorry." Her words tumbled out as the shaking once again consumed her body. "You were right. I was thinking of myself. I have to think of what he could do to the Mifflins, to the town."

She pulled back and stared up at him, tears running down her cheeks. "I was so scared, Ben. When I saw those pictures and realized he'd been watching me. For years. Now all that evidence is gone."

Throwing herself against his chest, she clutched him to her, as if he might disappear like the smoke was dissipating in the early afternoon air. Ben brushed her hair back from her face. Rubbing the tears that had escaped with his thumbs, he tilted her face, forced her to look at him.

"Anyone would have been upset to see what was downstairs, Dana. Please don't be so hard on yourself."

She finally met his gaze, and he read there her insecurity, her need.

"We're going to make it through this, sweetheart. Together, we will. Okay?"

"Yeah." She sounded doubtful, but managed a weak smile.

So there in front of the smoldering ruins, he dipped his head and kissed her gently.

"Do you believe me?"

"Yeah." Stronger this time.

Switching the rifle to his left hand, he laced his fingers with hers. "Let's go home then."

Forty-six

D ana slept most of the way back to Taos. She woke with a start, imagining she was trapped in Drogan's dungeon. Ben's hand on hers calmed her, brought her back to the warm sun, filtering through the Chevy's windows.

She smiled at him, pulled out her phone, and called the office. An hour later she'd showered, changed clothes, and was back at work. The emergency meeting she'd called included Ben, Clay, Cheryl, Sayeed, and Red. She would have included everyone, but it was Saturday. The strain was beginning to show on her staff.

She saw the surprise on Ben's face when she told them everything. Also saw approval, and finally understood how much it meant to her. The realization sent a shiver down her spine.

Once she had to stop and reach for her glass of water, but she never broke down. She didn't leave out a single detail. In the end, she'd recognized the wisdom of Ben's words.

The most important thing was catching Chance Drogan before he hurt someone. Her pride, any violation she had suffered personally, was secondary.

Clay's face had grown redder as she spoke. By the time she finished describing all they had found, she could tell he was struggling to contain his anger.

"Where will you stay until we catch him?" Clay asked.

Dana reached again for her glass of water, drank more than half of it to buy herself time, then set it down carefully. "I'll stay in my home."

"That's not acceptable." Clay turned to Ben. "You were there. How would you assess the situation?"

Everyone turned to Ben. Dana had to fight the urge to rebuke Clay, to remind him she was in charge. Instead, she decided to trust this man who had now saved her life twice.

"I'm not comfortable with Drogan's fixation on Dana, and I wish we could have retrieved more evidence from his bunker. As it is, we only have a few photos of the maps and workbench." He paused, looked directly into her waiting eyes as she sat at the head of the conference table. "If Dana feels safe staying in her home, I'd say it's her call."

Dana let out the breath she didn't realize she'd been holding.

"I don't believe this," Clay muttered.

"Are you sure, Dana?" Cheryl had been sitting back silently, but now she leaned forward.

Red continued stroking his beard.

Ben had to raise his voice to be heard over the group. "If it's okay with Dana, I recommend we install a perimeter security system around her house and another field around her lot. I also want to do a sweep of her car twice a day."

Everyone turned to stare at him. Dana wanted to reach for her glass of water, but suddenly, she didn't trust herself. She had known the danger was real. Hearing Ben's ideas emphasized how real and immediate the danger was.

"We should also follow up on this lead about LuAnn's cousin, Angela. Maybe Drogan is confusing Dana with this person from his past." Clay started a list on his laptop.

"Dana." Red placed his hands on the table in front of him. She hadn't noticed before how large they were, but he splayed them out and stared at them, as if they might hold the answers. When he looked up at her, she read a fatherly look in his gaze that made the lump in her throat grow again.

She hadn't thought she could cry any more today, and she didn't want to—not here. Not now.

"I know you value your privacy, and you're an independent and capable woman. Would you mind though if we kept someone with you at all times? Except when you're home, of course, then you'd have Ben's security system. You're an astute person, but one pair of eyes can't see everything. We can't risk losing you. We need you around here."

"It wouldn't be forever." Cheryl's voice was soft, reasonable. "Just until we catch him."

Dana swallowed past the lump in her voice. "Everything you've recommended sounds reasonable."

Clay's face relaxed, but only marginally.

He and Ben left to design and implement the security system. Cheryl went to work on the photos they'd brought back. Red volunteered to send encrypted messages to the rest of the staff, updating them on what had happened.

Dana sat in the empty conference room and knew she was near a breaking point. Each time she teetered on the edge, Ben was there to pull her back. But she couldn't always depend on Ben Marshall. She had to find a way to handle the curves life threw at her on her own.

Her thoughts, as usual, drifted to Erin. She longed to call her sister, hear her voice, but it was already past midnight in Texas. Better to wait until morning.

On second thought, maybe she'd wait until this little mess was cleared up completely. They had long ago made a vow not to lie to each other, and Erin was bound to ask questions she didn't want to answer right now.

A small voice in her heart whispered, "What if you don't have that long?"

But she pushed it away, rose from the table, and went back to work.

Forty-seven

D ana was surprised how quickly it became routine.
She would rise in the morning, take her shower, and
phone the office to tell them she was leaving. They would
disarm her alarm system remotely. Backing out of her
driveway, it never took her long to spy her bodyguard.

Usually, it was Sayeed, but some days it would be Red
or Cheryl. Once she'd been surprised to look in her rearview
and see Captain's customary scowl. Rarely was it Ben, but
then he saw her home each evening—no matter how late she
worked.

The rest of her staff rotated three-hour shifts during the
night.

As she pulled into the parking lot on Wednesday
morning, Ben waited beside his Chevy.

"Morning, boss."

"Marshall." Stepping out of her Honda, she straightened
her white blouse. Looking up, she saw Ben hadn't moved. In
fact, he was still staring at her, goofy grin firmly in place.

"Well. Are you going to..." She waved her hand at the car.

"Huh?" He pulled his attention away from her and stared at the car, as if trying to figure out what was wrong with it.

"The wand? You're supposed to wand the car."

"Right. I'm on it, boss." He immediately began to walk around the car, glancing up and grinning at her every few steps.

"If I didn't know better, I'd say you enjoy this."

"Can't deny a man his toys." He winked at her as he moved toward the front of the vehicle.

"How do you think Drogan would have gotten within a hundred feet of my car? I can't get near it without permission from one of your goons." She leaned against the driver's door and crossed her arms, doing her best to look pouty.

Ben pretended to wand her, then placed one arm on either side of her. "You seem more magnetic than usual, Miss Jacobs. Want to confess now?"

Dana slapped him in the stomach with the back of her hand as Cheryl walked out the back door of the office.

"Is Marshall giving you trouble again?"

"As a matter of fact he is." Dana glanced back over her shoulder as she walked away from the car. "Someone needs to take that wand away from him."

"We caught him using it on the copier machine earlier. The man's passionate about his work."

"That's one word for it."

"I can hear you," Ben called from under Dana's car.

"We were hoping you could," Dana hollered back. "Cheryl, tell me some good news, like you found Drogan eating donuts at the local shop."

"Sorry, no. We did find something interesting in those photos though."

Dana followed Cheryl back inside, discussing what progress the night shift had made. Sayeed had been the one to discover the places designated on the map created a path across the town. Perhaps the locations weren't important in and of themselves, but the route could be a key. The locations might even be used as drop-off or pick-up points.

Sayeed met her as soon as she walked into the main room. He looked exhausted, but pleased with the work they'd done.

"We didn't notice it at first because there are so many locations, and they appear quite random," Sayeed explained. "Plus our greatest fear was they might be targets."

"But who would target a chicken place?" Ben had joined them by this point and was sitting on top of the back table, staring at the mock-up of the map they'd created.

"Exactly." Sayeed adjusted the sling his arm rested in. "It occurred to me last night to consider a different scenario. Where he might be using the points as a grid across Taos."

"Fallback positions?" Dana accepted the mug of coffee Red pushed into her hands.

"Possibly. Or prearranged spots to store things." Sayeed studied the map. "We can't really know."

"But we could set up cams." Ben stood and paced in front of the map. "It would take some work, but it's not unrealistic."

Dana looked at the board, then at her small, early morning group. "There are over one hundred locations on this board."

"True, but this is the first time we have been ahead of

him," Cheryl pointed out.

"Not necessarily. He knows we were in the cabin if he knows it blew up." Dana sipped the coffee, even though her stomach was already tumbling.

"Possibly. But remember how hard a time we had finding that door? I think Drogan considers himself to be a pretty smart guy." Ben hopped off the table, paced back and forth in front of the board, and finally plopped into a chair, interlacing his fingers behind his head. "I think there's a good chance he'll believe kids or hunters set off that explosion. And on the off chance he thinks it was us, he'll doubt we were smart enough to find the secret basement. In fact, we almost didn't find it. I might not have if you hadn't spotted the recessed door."

Dana felt her cheeks warm at his praise. "We do have a limited budget. And we haven't proven Drogan is still a threat to the area, but I'll petition to regional for the extra supplies to put in detection devices at all locations."

She looked at Sayeed and Ben. "How long would it take you to install them?"

The two men ducked their heads together and scribbled figures on a pad.

"If we went in full force, we could do it in thirty-six hours," Sayeed said.

Ben sat up straighter and gave her a long look. "I think it would be better to slow down a little in case he's watching. After all, he can't be everywhere, and a man has to eat."

Dana set down her cup, then cocked her head at him. Perhaps he had used that wand a bit too much.

"What I mean is, make it look as if we're casually walking into these places. Pick up a piece of chicken, order a burger, have some pizza. It might add another day to the installation process, but it lowers the odds of Drogan realizing we're on to him."

Dana stood up. "I should have your answer by noon. In the meantime, draw up plans to move forward with this."

She went to her office, shut the door, and closed the blinds. She intended to immediately write the e-mail to regional.

Then her tremors started.

She stared at her left hand as if it belonged to someone else. Placing her palm firmly down against the coolness of her desk, she rubbed it with her right hand. Why was this happening? She was sleeping. Things were going reasonably well. She felt confident they would catch Drogan— eventually.

And there was the rub.

How long would it take?

How many nights would she have to be put to bed by one of her staff?

How many mornings until she could jog again?

And what if he found a way through the layers of security?

She was no safer than she'd been as a child.

Pushing the thought away, she pulled her wireless keyboard toward her. Resolutely, she opened a new message, determined to do whatever was necessary to keep up the calm demeanor everyone needed to see from her.

But her hand continued to betray her, refusing to cooperate with the keys. She tucked it under her leg to still the shaking and pecked out the message with her right fingers.

Forty-eight

B en had realized he was in over his head the moment he threw himself on top of Dana in the woods. Had she been killed, had she died on his watch, he wasn't sure how he would have forgiven himself.

Over the last three days, he'd come to accept his need to see her smile each morning. This morning's embarrassing scene in the back lot was a prime example. He kept tabs on all the feeds each night and knew she was fine, but seeing her drive in healthy and whole—well, it gave him a sense of satisfaction like he'd never experienced before. He felt as if he could breathe again when he saw firsthand that she was safe. Monitors and audio feeds didn't provide the same reassurance.

Calling her each night before she went to sleep was above and beyond. He'd finally admitted to himself and his family that his concerns weren't about the job.

"I can't fall in love this fast," he'd argued. "I've only known her three weeks."

"You don't get to choose, Son." His mother's voice was gentle but firm.

Watching Dana this morning, he'd known in his heart he was past the point of infatuation. How was he to explain that to her though? She already thought he was daft, and he really didn't blame her.

Maybe it was better to focus on the job. Let their feelings sort themselves out over time. If they had time.

Ben studied his half of Drogan's grid and concentrated on plotting cam locations. The best way to help Dana was to catch Drogan. Then he could date her like a normal person.

Dana received approval for the equipment before noon.

Immediately, Ben had more volunteers than he knew what to do with. He sent four people as far away as Santa Fe to purchase the cams. He could have found all the equipment in Taos, but he didn't want to be so obvious. There was no telling who Drogan had on his side.

Then the fun began.

Red claimed to frequent the chicken place often.

Captain swore he used the Squeaky Clean Laundromat at least once a week.

Cheryl was suddenly dying to see the new flick at Taos Cinema.

Setting up a receiving center was Clay's job. One he took seriously.

"Monitoring over a hundred feeds won't be easy," Ben observed. "What's your plan?"

"Ten screens, split into ten pictures each." Clay had the flat screens lined up and stacked. They covered an entire wall of the conference room and would have made any man's testosterone level jump.

"But how do you watch a hundred scenes? I mean, visually you can't possibly take in that many images at a time." Ben could watch two, even three baseball games at a time, but this was beyond him.

"Actually, no one has to watch them. The computer will." Clay had wired the screens together. He handed the central cable to Ben. "Hold this while I crawl under here."

"The computer is going to watch a hundred live feeds?"

"Sure. We'll put a person in here, too, but I've fed Drogan's profile to the computer's facial recognition program. It will scan continuously, and an alarm will sound if he crosses a cam."

Ben stared at the screens as the feeds came on line one-by-one. "You're not kidding me?"

"I wouldn't do that, Marshall."

"And I wouldn't want you looking for me, Clay."

"Then don't do anything wrong."

Ben was grateful the man smiled when he said it. At least he thought it was a smile. "Roger that."

He turned and glanced once more at the screens. They made him feel like a hundred eyes were watching him. "I'll go tell Dana everything is set up." He fled the room, grateful to be away from so many cameras.

He nearly ran into Dana as she walked out of her office.

"Clay has all the live feeds up."

"Great." She didn't look quite as relieved as he thought she would.

"Did he tell you about the facial recognition software?"

"Sure. It's something we've used a few times before, never on this scale, of course."

"Gives me the creeps." Ben rubbed the back of his neck. "Say, you want to get out of here? Go for a walk or something?"

She looked at him skeptically. "You mean I'm allowed?"

He stood up straighter, crossed his arms behind his back. "I guess this has been tough on you."

"A little."

"We could go rock climbing." The thought instantly relaxed the tension in his neck. Was it really just four days since they'd been out near Lake Abiquiu? It felt like they'd worked a month straight.

Dana was already shaking her head. "No. I can't. There's too much to do here."

"Nothing your staff can't handle."

"It took us what—three, four hours by the time we drove out there and back."

Red walked past them, a bucket of chicken in his right hand. "It would do you good to get out of here for a while."

"Why is everyone in my business?" Dana asked.

Ben only shrugged.

Suddenly, she clasped her left hand under her right arm, as if she had a sharp pain in her side.

"What's wrong?"

"Nothing." She turned away from him toward the windows. "It does look nice outside."

Ben moved closer. "Seventy-two and sunny." She looked at him as if he'd lost his mind. "What? I happened to check the weather at lunch."

"And why would you do that, Marshall?"

"Fishing forecast," Captain said, as he passed them on his way to the copier. "Checks that fishing forecast on his work terminal every day."

"The man enjoys ratting me out."

Dana smiled, but Ben noticed she was still clutching her left hand.

"All right. I have been missing my jog. How about four-thirty? If you think you can keep up."

"You're on, boss. You need to go by your house?"

"No. I have a gym bag in the Honda."

"Good deal. Four-thirty then."

Two hours later, they were jogging through the Fred Baca Park. Ben wore a fanny pack with his Glock tucked safely inside. He didn't tell Dana he had Red parked at the north end and George parked at the south. What she didn't know at this point might help her relax.

He'd caught her twice clutching her left hand to her side, and once he was sure he saw it shaking.

After five miles, he begged off.

"What's wrong, Marshall? Out of shape?"

"Maybe I'm not used to this mountain air." He walked to a water fountain at the side of the path. "Ladies first?"

Shaking her head yes, she stepped in front of him, reaching to thumb the water on with her left hand. When she did, he again noticed the tremor. She tried to tuck the hand away, but he placed his hand over it and helped her push the button.

She drank slowly, then wiped the water from her mouth. "Thanks."

"You're welcome."

Taking a long drink himself, he turned and found her standing with her back to him, arm clutched against her side.

He walked up to her, pulled the hand away from her side, and held it between his own. "Let's walk a little," he said.

She met his eyes and nodded.

As they walked, he massaged her hand, her wrist, even the lower part of her arm. She didn't seem to want to talk about it, so he didn't bring it up.

It occurred to him that maybe that's what love does at times. Maybe it lets some things slide.

Forty-nine

D ana wasn't sure when it happened, at what point she let Ben under her guard. It might have been on the path in the park when he noticed her tremor, saw her vulnerability, and never said a word.

It might have been during one of their late-night talks.

They began as a way for him to check in, remind her to set the alarms from the inside of her home, assure her they'd set the outer perimeter security.

But over the course of the last week, those conversations had turned into something else. She found herself hurrying through dinner, watching the clock, knowing he would call after she'd been home an hour.

He always did. Some nights they would talk only a few minutes. More often though, their conversations would last well past midnight. She'd curl up in the red leather chair, pull an old afghan over her—more for comfort than for warmth— and listen to him talk of his days growing up in Montana.

Two nights after their jog, she found herself asking him about the tremor. The fact he hadn't brought it up impressed her tremendously. The truth was it embarrassed her, and she worked hard to hide it from everyone else.

"What do you think is causing it?" she finally asked him.

"It's hard to say. I'm not a doctor, Dana." She heard the sound of him walking out the front door of his apartment. He often talked to her as he sat on the small patio that led down to the stairs. "Are you having any numbness in your fingers?"

"No. I start shaking without any warning and at the oddest times. It always starts in my hand, then travels up my arm." She tried to laugh it off, but heard the desperation in her own voice. "It's like looking at someone else's arm, Ben. I can't hold a phone or a toothbrush."

When he didn't speak, she added, "It's a little frightening. Sort of like a seizure on one side of my body."

"I had something similar once," Ben admitted.

"A seizure?"

His laughter eased the tension she'd felt building in her shoulders since broaching the subject. Maybe she was taking it all too seriously.

"No, not a seizure. A tremor. It happened after my first bombing in Iraq. I worried I'd been hit with sarin gas or some other biologic, so I went to the medic." His voice grew softer, and she knew he was thinking of his friends still half a world away. "They told me my body was experiencing something similar to PTSD—post traumatic stress disorder."

"That's been in the news a lot."

"Sure it has—the major stuff—but people react to stress in less noticeable ways also. At least that's how the doc explained it to me. He had lots of fancy words, but basically, my body was coping with what it had seen. He said it would work its way out eventually and sent me back to my assignment."

Dana thought of all that had occurred in the last month. "So you think my tremor will resolve itself over time?"

Ben sighed. She could practically see him running his hand through his hair as he tried to find the right words. "I think you've been through a lot of pressure, Dana. Life is stressful for everyone, and I believe God can help you carry that load."

She started to interrupt him, but he hurried on. "I want to help you too. I care about you."

"I know you do," she whispered.

"These conversations, the walks we take, you letting everyone have a full part in your security—it will all help to divide the stress." She heard a screen door slam as he walked back into his apartment. "But it's still hard when you're alone at night. I understand what that's like. It takes a toll on a person."

She didn't answer, wasn't sure what to say. His words tore at the wounds she struggled to keep hidden. She was afraid if she spoke, her voice would betray her emotions.

"We haven't known each other very long, but I want to be there for you, Dana. I want to ask you—"

"I can't talk about this now." She forced the words out, had to stop him before he went further. Suddenly, her pulse was pounding, and she was terrified. "Ben, I can't... I need to focus on Drogan right now. Okay?"

"We're going to catch Drogan. Don't doubt that."

"I hope it's soon."

"I do too, sweetheart."

She said good night then, pretended she was going to bed. And she was tired, so exhausted she sat there, staring into the darkness. She needed Ben and wanted him to come closer. At the same time, she was so afraid of what would happen if he did.

And what of his god? Obviously Ben's faith was an important part of who he was, but staring into the darkness, Dana knew the truth. She didn't have the courage to believe again. Once Ben accepted that, he wouldn't want her any more than her father had.

Fifty

T wo days later was Dana's day off. She worked from home all day, but at least she stayed away from the office. On Sunday afternoon, Ben called her and talked her into taking a short hike at Cimarron Canyon. The fresh air had brought some of the color back into her face. After five miles of hiking, she actually seemed more rested than when they'd started.

Coming around the corner of the trailhead, the parking area came into sight. Theirs were the only two cars left. He reached for her hand as they walked slowly across the gravel lot. "Why do you have to go in?"

"I want to be there at shift change. See if they've made any progress on Drogan's location."

"George would have called you." He said the words softly while rubbing his thumb over the back of her hand.

"I know." She tucked her hair behind her ear and smiled up at him. The tenderness in her gaze took his breath away—

felt like a punch to his gut. He would do anything to keep it on her face. "I'm used to stopping by."

"You can get used to root canals. I wouldn't recommend having one on a Sunday."

Ben ducked in time to miss the well-aimed swipe she took at his head.

"I'm trying to limit my hours. I didn't go in yesterday."

"And folks were still talking about it at lunch." Ben laughed, pulling her toward his truck when she started to walk away. They'd reached their cars parked at the beginning of the trailhead. He lowered the tailgate on the truck and sat on it. "Stay long enough to enjoy the sunset."

He watched her battle between what she wanted to do and her sense of duty. He could pressure her, but knew it would be a bigger victory if she won it on her own.

"Until sunset," she agreed.

They sat there as the day cooled, legs swinging, and Ben thought of how some things were the same no matter where you were. No doubt a few of the guys in Iraq were seeing the same sunrise, and his family in Montana was probably sitting in the old porch swing, watching it set.

He'd like for Dana to experience a sunset from the homestead in Montana. It truly was like no place on earth. The thought caused him to realize he knew very little about her.

"What?" she asked. "Do I have dirt on my face?"

"No."

"Then why are you staring at me?"

"I was thinking about the sunset." Ben glanced out over the mountains in front of them, then looked back at Dana. She was the prettier view.

"You're staring again. I can't relax when you do that." She pushed him, and he nearly toppled off the tailgate.

Instead, he grabbed her arm to steady himself. Deciding holding her was an even better idea, he tugged her closer, leaned against the bed of the truck, and wrapped his arms around her.

With his chin resting against the top of her head, they both gazed out at the red, purple, and orange colors splashed across the sky.

"I was thinking how beautiful the sunset is," he admitted. "My folks are probably doing the same thing in Montana at this very minute. We have this old swing off the back porch. Most nights they go out before dinner, sit, and watch the day play out."

"Do you miss them?" Dana's voice was small, a whisper in the dying light.

"I sure miss my mom's cooking." Ben laughed when Dana elbowed him. "Yes, I miss everyone, but I talk to them once a week. They know my job takes me away."

She nodded but didn't speak.

"Thinking of home made me realize I don't know anything about you, and I want to." He felt her stiffen beneath his arms. "Don't take it wrong. I think you're amazing, but I only know about your life here. Your sister lives in Texas, so I guess you grew up there. What was it like?"

Dana pulled away from him. "I have to go."

"Wait. What's wrong?"

"This is wrong. Everything is wrong." She walked away from the truck and stood looking out at the sky now losing its color.

"Whoa. Hang on, beautiful. What did I say?" He took her by the shoulders and turned her toward him, waited for her to meet his gaze. "I didn't mean you had to tell me your darkest secrets, Dana. I was thinking about family, and I realized I'd never heard you talk about yours—except for Erin. What about your mother and father?"

She wrenched herself from his hands, walked to her car, and unlocked it, but she didn't get in. He watched her in amazement, wondering what he'd torn open. In the near darkness, she turned toward him.

"I'm not like you, Ben."

"How are you not like me?" He longed to go to her, to wrap his arms around her as the first chill of the evening blew through the air. Something told him even one step toward her would send her fleeing into the night. So instead, he steadied his heart rate and softened his voice. "Talk to me, Dana."

"You never stop. It's as if I'm an onion, and you won't stop until you've sliced through every stinking layer."

Her hands clinched into fists at her side. She stared past him into the gathering dusk, forced her hands open, and walked back to him. It was like watching an android walk. It was like seeing the woman he'd first met so many weeks ago. He ached for how much ground they'd lost in the last three minutes.

She came within a few inches, but was careful not to touch him. Peering up into his face, she spoke softly, her voice completely empty of emotion. "You want to know about my parents? You really think it's important to know me that well? My father killed my mother."

There were no tears, and her voice never rose. She might as well have been giving a briefing to the staff. "He's serving a life sentence in Huntsville State Prison. He killed her when I was ten. My sister and I were raised by foster parents, always afraid he might be paroled."

She turned and walked back to her car.

"Dana, I'm—"

"Do not…" Finally, her voice broke, and her head dropped. He moved toward her, but she put her hand up to stop him. "Do not say you're sorry, Ben. If you care about me at all, please. Don't say anything."

She drew a deep, steadying breath, then looked up at him. What he saw in the twilight was a woman so wounded he wondered how she managed to walk through each day.

"I don't need your pity, and I don't want it."

"Is that what you think? That I pity you? Dana, I love you, and God can—"

"Do not speak to me about your god. He wasn't there for me eighteen years ago. Do not tell me he was there the night I held my mother, the night she died."

A lone tear slid down her cheek. She stared down at the ground for a moment. He could barely make out her next words.

"God turned away from me a long time ago."

"No. He didn't."

"You weren't there." The words were a screech, torn from her heart. "You were not there. You didn't hold her. You didn't wait for someone to come and save you."

She looked out past him. His need to go to her was a physical ache in his chest. She stood poised to run. And he feared she'd never come back.

"I'm bad luck, Ben. Figure it out now. And we are not the same. My parents never sat in a swing and watched the sunset." She looked up, steeled herself. "That's fine. I'm fine. I can do this alone. I don't need your faith. I don't need a family either."

"Dana, everyone needs someone."

"No." Her voice was a whisper again, softer than the call of the night birds. "Some of us do it alone every single day." Then she climbed into her car, and she drove away.

Watching her taillights, Ben stared out into the blackness of the night and wondered what he should have said, what he should have done differently.

Fifty-one

B en called her twenty minutes later to confirm she'd made it safely into the office. She didn't answer her cell. He wasn't surprised.

He thought of driving over to the office, but didn't trust his temper. Dana was scared and hurting. Now was not the time for him to push. He punched in the main number. Clay answered the phone.

"Is Dana there?"

"Yes."

"Put me through to her, please."

He waited for a good three minutes, much longer than it took to transfer a call. When Clay came back on the line, he had to resist the temptation to pitch his phone into the darkness.

"She's busy."

"In other words she refused to talk to me."

"Correct."

Ben sighed and rubbed his forehead where the pounding

was beginning with a vengeance. "Make sure someone follows her home."

"Of course."

"I'll take the 4:00 a.m. shift."

"Copy that."

Ben dropped the phone beside him on the seat. Starting the Chevy truck, he drove toward his apartment. He could go into work. Might as well, since he knew he wouldn't sleep. But work was her refuge, her only shelter at this point. He wouldn't deny her what comfort she could find there.

No, he would go home, if the one-room apartment could be called that. Suddenly, he missed the camaraderie of his unit. Not nearly as much as he missed Dana though, and she'd only been gone thirty minutes. Something told him the scars she was struggling with were going to keep her away longer than a half hour.

Pulling into his parking lot, he picked up the phone and called his parents. He'd hoped to reach his dad, but his granddad picked up.

"Benjamin. How are you, Son?"

"I'm all right, Granddad. How's the fishing?"

The old man cackled. "Caught six trout this morning. Your mother fixed them for lunch. Wish you'd been here."

"Me too."

Silence stretched between them. Ben ran his hand over the black, steering wheel, envisioning the miles it had covered. Thought of the things his granddad had seen.

"You want to tell me about her, Son?"

Ben didn't answer right away. He considered all the ways to describe Dana, but they all seemed inadequate. "You remember the spring I was a kid and we found that fawn?"

"Sure. You were ten. We heard some shots early on a Saturday morning."

"Right. It was poachers I guess."

"Never did find them." He could hear his granddad rocking in the old swing. "You were sure taken with that fawn though. Insisted on bringing it home. Thought you could raise it like a dog."

"You told me a deer was a wild animal. Course I wouldn't listen."

"Benjamin, you've had a stubborn streak from the moment you were born. Your mother says that's why you were born breech—too stubborn to turn around."

Ben stared out the front window of the truck, but he was seeing the enclosure he'd built for the deer. The one he'd thought was high enough to keep her in.

"Nearly broke your heart the morning you walked out and found the fawn gone. Deer aren't meant to be domestic animals though. You did a good thing, helping her through those first few weeks."

"I can still see her eyes." Ben said.

"We talking about the deer, Son?"

Ben laughed. "Maybe not, Granddad. Dana reminds me a lot of that fawn."

"Dana's a beautiful name. Be patient, Ben. It's not easy for a man, but it's possible."

Ben thought back on what Dana had told him, what had been piercing his heart for the last hour. "Do you think when something hasn't had the nurturing of a mother it can ever be whole again?"

"Your girl has had a difficult time."

Ben flinched at the possessive pronoun. "Yes, sir."

"Well, I think God's grace can heal anything, even the absence of a parent."

"Regardless of what caused the absence?"

He heard the old guy draw in a deep breath. When he finally spoke, his voice sounded older and gentler than the wind in the trees outside Ben's window. "God's bigger than that, Son. Can't put limits on him like you would a river or a person. He can do anything."

The creaking of the old swing resumed. "Sometimes we can accept God did the tremendous things—like create those stars you're staring at. Then we try to believe He can heal a fawn, or a person, and we stumble. Our belief falters. God can take care of your Dana. Don't ever doubt it."

"Thank you, Granddad."

"Sure, Benjamin."

"Don't catch all the fish."

"I'll leave some in the river for you."

Ben hung up, more hopeful than he'd been when he'd driven into the parking lot. And quite a bit humbled by a man who at the age of eighty-five had trouble walking the banks of a river.

He didn't know what he was supposed to do, but it wasn't the first time he'd been at a loss for direction. Granddad was right though. He could trust God to know what to do. Patience was something he'd never claimed to be good at, but maybe it wouldn't take very long.

He smiled, walking up the stairs in the darkness, realizing how impatient his thoughts were. He definitely had a lot of learning to do.

Fifty-two

D ana wanted to change the work schedule so she wouldn't have to look at Ben the next day. She'd never told anyone about her parents. She was mortified.

Now he knew she was a freak.

So she was fairly surprised when she pulled out of her driveway and he was parked at the corner. After ignoring his calls last night, she'd expected him to hand the assignment off to someone else.

He gave her his usual one-handed wave, then pulled in half a block behind her. She still wasn't ready to talk to him though. When her cell phone rang and his number showed on the display, she ignored it and turned up the radio.

Cowardly, but effective—for a few miles anyway.

When they pulled into the parking lot behind the office, she had decided how to hide her embarrassment. She wouldn't give him a chance to break it off with her— whatever *it* was. Had they been dating?

Regardless of what they called it, obviously their relationship was over after last night. She wasn't like him. She'd never be like him. In fact, she wasn't like most people. Most people had families and knew how to deal with relationships.

She wasn't most people, which was why she was so good at keeping folks at a distance. Starting today, Ben Marshall would stay where he was supposed to—out of her personal life.

Grabbing her purse, she shoved her sunglasses on and hopped out of the Honda, slamming the door a little harder than necessary. She turned around and nearly walked right into Ben.

"Cell phone broken?"

"Pardon?"

"I was wondering if your cell phone was broken since you didn't pick up when I called this morning. Or last night for that matter."

She raised her chin even higher, grateful he couldn't see through her sunglasses. "I guess I had the ringer off. Besides, I was busy on the drive over."

"Busy?"

"Yes." She walked away from the car, ignoring his closeness as he followed her toward the building.

"Busy as in reading briefs while you were driving? Or maybe there was someone in your car I couldn't see that you were having a conference with."

She turned on him like a guard dog on attack. "It's none of your business what I was doing, Ben. I didn't have time to answer your call. If you need something, talk to Clay or send me an e-mail."

Satisfied that he was momentarily speechless, she turned and fled into the building. Of course, she had to clutch her left hand across her ribs as she did so to still the tremors, but it seemed a small price to pay.

With Ben Marshall and all personal matters out of the way, she could focus on her day.

Which was exactly what she did, in spite of the fact she caught him glaring at her several times. Let him glare. He'd figure out she was serious and then back off. She'd meant what she said last night. He was better off without her. The truth was painful, but accurate.

"Surveillance program is running at 100 percent," Clay reported at the Monday morning staff meeting. "No sign of Drogan, but I've added a program that looks for and identifies repeat visitors."

"Wouldn't most people be repeat visitors?" Dana asked.

"I'm telling you I only go to the chicken place twice a week," Red declared. "Three times at the most."

Everyone laughed except Ben who continued studying her.

"You're right," Clay said. "Most people do visit the same place repeatedly. They have a routine. The program catalogues them, checks them against the federal database, then discards them as a person of interest if they're not found."

"Drogan wouldn't have appeared on any federal databases," Ben pointed out.

"True. One of the persons he used to put the surveillance bugs in place here had a federal record. The other did not. So we know sometimes he uses people without a record." Clay shrugged. "It's a long shot. The program slips the discarded repeats into a file so we can look at them later manually. If anyone can't sleep at night and wants extra work, see me after the meeting."

Several people groaned, but Dana sensed it was good-natured. Overall, they seemed to have adjusted to the increased stress.

"Any additional status reports?"

"That call we had from the motel," Nina said. "Someone had skipped their bill and left a note claiming anthrax was in the room. Tests came back from the state lab. As we suspected, it was Johnson's Baby Powder."

Red lurched backward in his chair, causing it to groan. "What?"

"Cornstarch with aloe vera," Nina continued. "And vitamin E."

"I put on a hazmat suit for baby powder?" Red buried his head in his hands.

Nina looked up from her notes. "I walked into the hotel room without the hazmat."

"Yes, I remember that you did." Red sat up straighter. "I bet you have softer hands now."

"I didn't touch the stuff, Red." Nina looked at him solemnly, while the rest of the staff snickered.

Everyone except Ben. He continued to watch Dana, and when her hand began to tremble, when she tucked it safely under the table, she looked up and met his gaze. Of course, he had noticed.

She didn't see him the rest of the day, and she didn't ask why.

Instead, she focused on her work, cleaned all the files off her desk, and managed to complete the two personnel reviews that were a month overdue.

Every time there was a knock on her door, she expected to see his face and his smile.

Each time her heart skipped a beat.

And each time she was disappointed.

Fifty-three

B en followed in his truck up into her driveway at nine o'clock that evening. It was well past dark. He waited in front of his truck as she parked her Honda in the garage, walked slowly to the back, and stood looking at him.

"What are you doing here, Ben?"

"I want to talk."

"You could have called."

"Would you have answered?"

She looked past him. "Probably not."

"I want to come inside."

"No." Now she did look at him. The expression on her face was hard, set. She clutched her left arm under her ribs.

"I see your arm's still bothering you," he said softly.

"Cheap shot, Ben."

He walked away from the truck, into the darkness of her yard, then back again. "Can we sit on the porch for a minute?"

She shook her head.

"Please."

"No," she whispered.

"Why, Dana?"

Instead of answering, she turned away and started up the walk. He was at her side in three long strides. She didn't resist when he turned her toward him. She only looked at him, eyes as big as that fawn's. He read her answer there, knew she'd already decided.

But he had to try.

He couldn't make himself leave without trying to reach her through the barriers she'd built around her heart.

"Dana, sweetheart. Don't you know I love you?"

"Stop."

"Can't you tell? Do you think I'd lie to you?"

"Please stop."

He moved his hands up her shoulders, framed her face, brought his lips to hers, brushed them ever so gently. It was like kissing a statue.

"Dana, please don't do this." He brushed the hair back from her face, tried to read her expression in the near darkness of the landscape lighting.

"You should go." Then she turned and walked into her house.

He stood there awhile, maybe a few minutes, maybe longer. Finally, he walked to his Chevy and found the strength to drive away.

He'd been so sure if he could see her away from the office, he could make it right. What had made him think it would be that easy?

Fifty-four

D ana believed her week couldn't get any worse.
It was past three when she fell asleep Monday night. Her mind insisted on replaying those moments with Ben. She couldn't help wondering what would have happened if she'd melted in his arms like she'd wanted to.

They'd only be back at square one, and they'd have to face this morning all over again farther down the road.

She looked out her kitchen window Tuesday morning and knew she'd done the right thing. He fancied himself in love with her, but he didn't understand the extent of her damage. Even if she could somehow hide the broken parts from him, he would want children. How could she be a mother? She had no idea where to begin caring for a child.

Yes, she'd practically raised Erin, but that was different. As they'd grown older, Erin had become the mother hen of the two. Dana smiled at the thought of the animal ark her sister ran. It would seem one of them had grown to adulthood unscathed.

Rinsing out her coffee cup, she set it in the dishwasher and picked up her shoulder bag for work. As she turned, the light through the window caught on the toaster, creating a sort of rainbow.

Arks and rainbows. She remembered the biblical story from her days in Sunday school—before her mother had died. Back when she'd been naïve enough to believe in such things. God had promised Noah safe passage. As a young girl, she had been foolish enough to believe such promises applied to her as well. So the teacher had told her.

Life had taught her differently though.

God might have kept His promise to Noah, but He didn't seem to keep the promises He made her.

Which was one other reason she needed to stand firm against Ben Marshall. He was a man of faith, and she respected his beliefs. But faith was something she didn't possess.

Marching to her car, she pulled the note from her windshield, recognized his handwriting, and ripped it to shreds. Tucking the pieces into her bag, she backed out of the driveway and headed into work. Already she could tell it was going to be a long day.

Fifty-five

"You're sure she tore it up?"

"I'm sorry, Ben." Sayeed spoke into the phone as he followed Dana into the office. "I saw it with my own eyes. She tore it up and stuffed the pieces in her bag."

"At least she didn't cast it to the wind," he muttered.

"Dana is not one to litter," Sayeed said. Ben could make out the sounds of early morning traffic in the background. "You sound desperate, my friend. In my country we would go to a woman's family and ask for permission to wed. We do this here as well. It is a sign of respect."

Ben sighed. "Different culture, man. Thanks anyway." He disconnected and stared at his desk, thinking the situation might be hopeless enough that he'd give Sayeed's idea a try—if Dana had any family.

The thought clicked so loudly in his head he looked around to see if someone had dropped a book on the floor. Dana did have family. Her sister Erin lived in Texas. Surely he could find her phone number. Of course, Dana would kill him if she found out, but since she wasn't speaking to him anyway, he didn't have much to risk.

"Dana's pulling in, Marshall." Captain looked at him with his usual unreadable expression.

"Right. Got it. Thanks."

"You want some advice?" Captain adjusted the headphones so they were slightly askew. He rubbed one eyebrow as he spoke, not bothering to wait for Ben's response. "Don't give up on her. The ones you have to work the hardest for, they're the ones worth having."

Ben had expected criticism, sarcasm, even outright hostility. He hadn't expected support. "Thanks, Cap."

"Don't mention it." He readjusted the headphones. "You're late."

"Right." Ben grabbed the wand and jogged out the back door, which is how he nearly collided with Dana. "Morning."

"Ben." She didn't smile or look at him, just marched on through like a commander to battle. He realized then that's what she was. Each day she headed into combat, forced to battle anew her fears and her ghosts. Every morning she had to put aside the things from her past, which wouldn't remain buried. Now her fears and insecurities had taken on an additional form in Drogan.

He stood staring after her, seeing clearly what he'd done wrong over the last two days. He hadn't made it one bit easier for her. Instead, he had applied more pressure.

He stared down at the wand in his hand. The urge to rap himself on the head with it was almost overpowering.

"Have you forgotten how to use that?" Sayeed had walked in behind Dana and stood staring at him.

"It's not the wand I've forgotten how to use." Ben moved past him, slapped him on the shoulder. "It's my brain."

He walked out to the parking lot, whistling as he stepped into the sunshine. As he checked her Honda, he thought back over every conversation they'd had since the night at Cimarron Canyon. How could he have been so stupid?

Even the talk with his granddad had done absolutely no good. He'd been about as patient as a three-year-old on Christmas morning.

Dana was scared, exhausted, and under extreme pressure. She'd told him so in a dozen different ways. He'd responded by scaring her more, wearing her out, and cranking up the pressure. *Way to go, ace.*

Funny thing was, it had taken an old codger like Captain to make him see the truth.

He headed back inside, intent on a new path.

Today he would stick to doing his job, doing it better than he had.

He would find extra ways to help her, but he'd be subtle about it. He'd be patient. As granddad had reminded him, it wasn't easy for a man, but it was possible.

He walked back inside, went to the workroom, and decided to take another look at the forensic evidence from the semi-truck Drogan had blown up. He had no doubt the two incidents were related. If he could find a common denominator between the explosion at the cabin and the explosion with the semi, he'd begin to lay the groundwork for a criminal trial. He might also find a clue as to where Drogan purchased his materials.

Both would aid Dana in closing this case. It was time he started helping her and quit being a thorn in her side.

Three hours later he was surprised when she walked into his workroom. Pulling off his goggles, he smiled at her. The look seemed to catch her off guard.

"I'd like you to come and look at something Nina's found."

"Absolutely." He set the goggles on the table, washed his hands so he wouldn't taint anything with explosive residue, and followed her back into the main room.

Though her shoulders were still rigid with tension, she seemed to relax when he started talking to her about the work he was doing.

"I think Drogan might be mixing some of his own materials. I'm finding tiny particles of a unique mineral. I'm not sure why he'd put it in the compound. I still need to do some testing, but why it's there is less important than where it's from. If I can narrow down the where, we might be able to locate his other base. Sayeed thinks it could be from the Enchanted Circle area."

Dana stopped and stared at him as they reached Nina's desk. "Nice work, Ben. Thank you."

"You're welcome." He plopped down in the chair across from Nina's desk. "So what's up?"

Nina looked to Dana for approval.

"Tell him," Dana said, moving her left arm behind her back.

Ben pretended not to notice, crossed his legs at the ankle, and grinned at them both. "You two must have a really terrible job you want me to do."

"Why would you say that?" Nina asked, her solemn expression not giving away a thing.

"You're ganging up on me. Dana would normally just order it done."

"She knows you'd say no," Captain piped in.

"Uh-oh. Even Cap'n knows. Now I'm intrigued." Ben crossed his arms and pretended to look put upon. "Can't leave a man alone with his explosives. That would be too simple."

"Give him the book, Nina." Dana used her right hand to wave at something Nina was holding.

Nina reached into her workspace cabinet and pulled out an old, blue book. It didn't look like a bestseller.

"That? That's what you want me to do?"

"This is what was in the backpack—*The Grapes of Wrath.*" Nina pushed the book across the desk toward Ben. "It's not the same book. The one Drogan had has been sent to the regional lab, but it's… identical."

"I don't want it." He pushed it back.

"Told you he wouldn't do it," Captain said.

"Come on, Ben. There could be some clue to Drogan's plans here." Dana didn't smile at him exactly, but she had stopped scowling. "You've figured out Drogan better than any of us. We need you to read it."

"Look how big this is. It's bigger than some of the military manuals I had to digest."

"Plainly, he's not a reader." Captain leaned back triumphantly, as if he'd predicted Ben's illiteracy.

Ben picked up the book, felt its weight, and set it back on the desk. "Give it to Captain to read."

Nina shook her head. "He's read it already. We want your take on it."

Red passed through the room, carrying yet another bucket of chicken.

"Give it to Red then. He needs something to do while he's eating all that chicken." Ben opened the book and actually did feel a small surge of panic. "Look how small this print is. What was wrong with publishers back then? There wasn't even a paper shortage."

"Ben, Nina thinks Drogan may be identifying with one of the main characters, actually the family the story is about. If you read it, even just the tabbed portions she's marked, maybe something will stand out to you."

Nina nodded, but didn't voice her own opinions.

"Want to tell me what you're thinking, Nina?" Ben drummed his fingers against the cover of the book.

"I'd rather wait until you've finished it."

"Were you planning on retiring from this office?"

Captain's laughter surprised them all. Ben picked up the book and trudged back to his workroom. He'd agreed to be patient. He'd even made progress all morning. Now this. It seemed no good deed went unpunished—something he needed to remember for future reference.

Fifty-six

D ana sat in her office and tried to puzzle out the change in Ben. He'd definitely been unhappy about his new assignment, but something else was going on. She traced back through the day, running the images through her mind like the pages of a flip book.

He'd scowled at her when she'd walked in, obviously still hurt about last night. She'd expected as much, which is why she'd barreled right past him. She distinctly remembered being able to feel his gaze boring a hole through her back.

Before she'd walked into her office, Sayeed had asked Ben if he'd forgotten how to use the wand. She'd heard his reply. It had struck her as odd at the time, but she'd been so intent on escaping into her inner domain that she'd slammed the door shut and forgotten it.

What had he said? She replayed the scene again in her mind. Something about it was his brain he'd forgotten how to use. That was it!

A pretty strange thing to say, even for Ben.

She hadn't seen him all morning, which was unusual. Yesterday, he'd passed her window at least once an hour and scowled at her.

Then she'd gone into his workshop. She had put it off, dreading being alone with him, expecting him to bring up last night. Instead, he'd been genuinely excited about the progress he'd made on Drogan's case.

She looked up at her wall of honor. They were good men, all three of them. Ben Marshall was as well. She'd known it the moment she'd met him. His shot on the semi, the way he'd worked with the Mifflin family, even the way he'd accepted Nina's book, all indicated how dedicated he was to his job.

He'd been no happier about the reading assignment than a high school student forced to study during summer break.

The look on his face had made her want to laugh out loud. On the one hand, he'd looked generally aghast, but she hadn't doubted for a moment he would do it. Something told her he was playing the clown—trying to ease the tension in the room.

Maybe that was the difference she had sensed. He'd taken the focus off their relationship and put it back on the mission. She didn't know why, but she was grateful. Her neck felt slightly less stiff than it had when she'd arrived this morning.

Now if they could make a break with this case.

Her personal life, she could ignore.

Or so she told herself.

Then Clay appeared at her door. "Tafoya's on line 2."

"For me?"

"Yeah. He says it's about Drogan."

Fifty-seven

T wenty minutes later, Dana hung up the phone and went in search of Ben. She'd barely stepped out of her office when she walked into Sayeed—literally.

One glance at his face told her the day was snowballing into disaster.

"There's something you need to see. I want to show you first, but I think you're going to want to share it with the entire staff."

"All right. Should I come to your work station?"

"It might be better if we have some privacy." Sayeed searched her face. "It is rather startling, but I believe it's a step forward in our investigation."

Without another word, Dana ushered him back into her office.

"I can access the files from your terminal." Sayeed waited for her permission.

When she nodded, he sat down behind her desk, entered his own pass code, and pulled up three files. Though she felt dread growing in her stomach like a monstrous ache, she stepped behind him.

"This first picture is of Angela Dixon. She is the cousin of LuAnn."

"Our waitress at the diner?"

"Correct. She is the same age as Mr. Drogan and attended the same high school. I found the picture through one of the Internet services that allows you to contact lost classmates."

Dana reached for her desk as her legs began to tremble.

"Finding the old picture was simple enough. Discovering her current whereabouts proved impossible. I finally resorted to contacting LuAnn and telling her you might be in danger. She gave me Mrs. Dixon's current name and address as well as a picture."

Sayeed clicked on the second file and a photo of a pleasant, middle-aged woman appeared. "This picture is of Mrs. Dixon now. She has moved to Canada and is fifty-eight years old. This picture isn't particularly relevant, but I was able to speak with her. I've sent you a file with a transcription of our conversation."

Dana backed slowly around her desk and sank into the chair. She watched as he pulled up the last file, though it didn't surprise her a bit. She didn't think anything would ever surprise her again. She saw the third photo come up, as if she were watching it from a great distance. Of course, she knew that picture. She remembered having it taken and attaching it to her paperwork when she'd come to work for the Taos office.

"This is your picture, Dana." Sayeed turned to look at her, his black eyes sorrowful. "I wasn't here when you first came to work in this office—"

"Five years ago." Her voice seemed to come from somewhere else. The first and last pictures might have been the same person, especially if viewed from a distance. Dixon had a better nose, in Dana's opinion. She'd never really liked her own nose—it was a tad too large. But their eyes, jawline, and cheekbones were all identical.

"Your hair was shorter then, like Angela's. When I modified your picture to black and white, as hers is, the similarities are even more apparent."

Dana stared at the screen as if it would change, then turned again to Sayeed.

"Drogan thinks I'm related to Angela Dixon?"

Sayeed leaned forward on her desk. "Mrs. Dixon couldn't tell me exactly what Drogan thinks, of course. She hasn't heard from him in over thirty years since he came back from Vietnam."

"She spoke with him then?"

Sayeed looked down at his hands, then back up at her. "Yes. He asked her to go away with him. When she refused, he became irrational. She was already married with children, but he wouldn't accept that her life had moved on while he was gone. He began stalking her."

"There's nothing in the court records about this. Drogan has no criminal file." Dana stood and paced around her office.

"No. She never filed any formal charges, though she did speak with the local authorities. She couldn't prove it was

Drogan, but she was certain nonetheless. I put it all in the file." He turned back to her computer, signed off, and stood.

"So you think five years ago Drogan transferred his obsession to me?"

"I don't know, Dana. We need to share this information with the rest of the team. Maybe they can reach a consensus. I believe it's possible he is confused. Perhaps for Drogan time froze in 1978. He may think you *are* Angela Dixon. The last time they spoke, he swore to kill her if she ever returned to the Taos area."

"So she moved to Canada?" Dana's voice squeaked in spite of herself.

"Her husband was offered a transfer with his multinational firm. It seemed expedient to accept the offer."

Dana stood and walked to her door, forcing her gaze away from the wall of honor as she passed it. "Thank you, Sayeed. I can't say I like what you found, but it may answer some questions."

"Unfortunately, it makes your situation more uncomfortable. Should I forward this information to the rest of the staff, or will you go over it at tomorrow's briefing?"

She tried to pull all the pieces together—a seventy-year-old book, Tafoya's call, now this.

"Dana?" Sayeed reached out and touched her arm.

"Please forward the files to everyone, explaining it exactly as you did to me."

Sayeed nodded and left without another word.

Dana closed her door, unsure now about seeking out Ben. Once he learned of this development, he would want to encase her in a bubble. A part of her actually liked the idea. Somewhere cozy and safe.

The grown-up Dana knew there were no such places.

So she stood and gathered her things, then went in search of the people she would need to continue the investigation. But when it was time to leave the building, Dana didn't complain about her bodyguards.

Fifty-eight

B en threw his pack into the backseat of Dana's Honda the next morning, then climbed into the passenger seat. He wasn't happy with the fact that Dana insisted on traveling while Drogan was apparently lying in wait around some corner, but his every argument had been shot down— all via e-mail since she still wouldn't resume their nightly phone calls.

He considered the e-mails a step forward in their relationship. He wasn't delusional though. He was riding shotgun because Tafoya had asked for him. Dana had told him as much in her e-mail the night before, but she wouldn't reveal anything else about the meeting.

"Sure you don't mind driving?" Ben asked.

She shook her head, causing her brown hair to slip forward. "I'm surprised you're not arguing more. Men always want to drive." She pushed her sunglasses up and pulled out into the early morning traffic.

Ben tapped the book he'd dropped in his lap as he was buckling his seatbelt. "Thought I'd get in a little reading on the way to the reservation."

Dana lowered her sunglasses and peered at him over the top. "Seriously?"

"Yes. This is actually pretty interesting, and I think I see where Nina was headed." He opened midway through the book and found his spot.

"You read half the book yesterday?"

"Uh-huh."

"I'm not buying it, Marshall."

"Wouldn't lie to you, boss."

She maneuvered the car into the westbound lane, then set it on cruise. "Any idea what Tafoya wants?"

"Nope. I haven't talked to him since Sunday."

"Why did you talk to him then?"

Ben placed his finger at the spot he was reading and looked up at her. "I went out there in the morning to attend services."

"Services?"

"Right. Services."

"What kind of services?"

"Church."

Dana tapped her hand against the wheel, seemingly preoccupied with the road.

Thinking he'd answered her questions, Ben went back to the problems of the Joad family in Steinbeck's book. He was pretty sure Drogan saw himself as Tom, the main character. He was anxious to return to the office and talk to Nina about it.

"Apache church?" Dana asked.

"Huh?" Ben turned the page, engrossed in the descriptions of the government camps during the Great Depression.

"Could you put the book down for a minute, Ben?"

At the note of aggravation in her voice, he snapped it shut, then remembered he'd forgotten to mark his place. Jerking the book back open, he scanned for the spot he'd been reading.

"Ben!"

"Right. Closing it." He set the book on the floorboard and turned to give her his full attention. Even though she looked utterly exhausted—he'd glimpsed dark circles under her eyes before she'd rammed the sunglasses back on—she was more beautiful than ever. She wore her customary white blouse and had added a white scarf to her hair to keep it out of her face.

He thought of telling her how nice she looked, but stopped himself in time. Patience.

"Why would you go to an Apache church service?"

"I didn't."

She pushed her hair back over her shoulder. "But you said you went to church with Tafoya on Sunday."

"Mr. Tafoya is a Christian. So was Joe. I've visited with Mr. Tafoya a few times since I've been here, and he invited me to join him on a Sunday when I had a day off. I thought it might be a good time to check on the Mifflin family as well."

Dana studied the road as she digested all he'd said. "I assumed Apaches followed their tribal beliefs."

"He respects his tribal beliefs, but he's dedicated his life to God."

Dana rubbed her left hand.

"If your hand is bothering you, I'd be happy to drive."
Ben didn't look away when she scowled at him. There was
no use pretending he hadn't seen the tremor.

"No." Dana sighed. "It doesn't last long."

He reached down and picked up his book.

"Tafoya didn't tell me what he wanted to meet about,"
Dana admitted.

"He can be rather… guarded at times."

Dana reached for her mug of coffee, waving at his book
as she did so. "You don't have to talk to me the entire way.
Read."

Ben smiled, sank back into his seat, and did as his boss
commanded. Which was more difficult than he expected. The
smell of her filled the car. She must have been wearing a
light lemony scent. It reminded him of their run through the
park in the sunshine. He wanted to reach across the space
between them, rub his hand up and down her arm. Loosen the
scarf and run his fingers through her hair. Knead the tension
from her shoulders.

Instead, he sank into Steinbeck's world. Read it as if he
were fifteen and watching his father fight a hopeless battle
with the government and lose his land to a water reclamation
project and forfeit his family to a madness that would
consume them all.

Fifty-nine

"**B**en?"

He snapped the book shut and looked up. "Yeah. Did you say something?"

"I said we're here." Dana pulled in behind Tafoya's truck and turned off the Honda.

"He brought Reggie," she murmured.

Ben met them halfway between the cars.

Dana thought the three looked natural together, though with his brown, curly hair it was plain Ben had no Apache blood. Tafoya and Reggie could have been related though. The boy looked healthier than he had two weeks ago. He still wore the ragged AC/DC cap, but his skin had lost its pale look.

He greeted Ben with a firm handshake and seemed completely comfortable with Tafoya.

"How are you, Reggie?" Dana removed her sunglasses as she spoke to the boy.

"I'm all right." He looked embarrassed as they all focused their attention on him. "It's nice to be out of school."

"And the rest your family?" Dana asked. "How are they doing?"

"Good. Frankie and Tommy like it out here. Mom has found work already."

"I'm happy to hear that." Dana looked to Mr. Tafoya.

He motioned to the piñon tree his truck was parked under. "Perhaps we should talk in the shade." They walked the few feet in silence. He lowered the tailgate, and Ben took a seat.

No one spoke, but Tafoya reached out to the boy and put his hand on his shoulder. Some unspoken thing passed between them. Reggie nodded, stood straighter, then turned to Dana.

"I have a way to contact Drogan. I should have told you earlier, but I was afraid to. I'm sorry." When she didn't respond, he rushed on. "It has to be from my phone though, or he'll know. And I think it has to be my voice too."

Dana glanced at Ben, then back at Reggie. "Has Drogan contacted you since you've been here?"

"I've had a couple of calls that showed on the display as *unknown*, but they didn't leave a message. I didn't answer them." He looked down, kicked at the dirt, then drew in a deep breath. "I didn't want to mess this up. You know? It seemed like my family was finally safe, and I didn't want to ruin it for them. I'd messed up everything before."

He looked past them, out across the mesa. "But as I listened to the elders talk about community, and I heard the pastor talk about God's grace, I knew I needed to do something."

When he returned his gaze to them, Dana saw he'd already made his decision. She feared then, whether she agreed to his plan or not, he would find a way to accomplish it.

"I want to do this, Miss Jacobs. I need to do it. You're still trying to catch him, right?"

Dana shook her head. It was tempting, but she couldn't allow it. "I'm sorry, Reggie. We can't involve a civilian, let alone a minor."

"What difference does it make how old I am?"

"You know Drogan is dangerous." She pushed her hair back, folded her arms across her waist.

"I do know. I met with him once a week for two, three months. You think I don't understand what I'm saying?" Reggie sat down beside Ben on the tailgate. "I'd rather never hear the guy's voice so long as I live. But if I call him, then you could get a fix on his location. You have some kind of tracking software, don't you?"

Dana shook her head and fought to push away the beginnings of a headache. Maybe Ben could convince Reggie to give up the phone and the number. Of course, she could try and obtain a warrant for it, but since he was on a reservation it would take a few days.

"We might be able to get a fix on his location, but Drogan apparently knows our capabilities. If he thought we were listening, he'd keep the call short. Then we wouldn't get anything."

"So I'd set up a meeting with him. You could nab him then."

"Absolutely not." Dana's palm came down on the tailgate of the truck, causing everyone to stare at her.

"Reggie, we cannot put you in harm's way. It's not going to happen."

"You don't think I'm in harm's way now?" Reggie was off the truck and in her face in seconds.

It was all Dana could do to hold her ground against a scrawny, teenaged kid.

"Do you think I'm going to stay here the rest of my life? Never leave? I like it and all, but what if I want to see the rest of the world, Miss Jacobs? Maybe travel to the East Coast or head up north? What then? Are you going to babysit me? Or maybe you can send Ben? What happens when my little brothers get older or my ma decides to marry again?"

"Reggie, it's not going to take us that long to catch him."

"So you're closer."

"Yes. No. Sort of." The boy's intensity reminded her of Ben. In fact, he made Ben appear relaxed. "Give me the phone and the number, Reggie. We'll take care of it."

"Like you took care of my house?"

"Reggie, I'm ordering you to give me the phone."

"You're not my parent, and I don't see a warrant." He stormed off toward the piñon tree. "Should have known you wouldn't listen to me."

Dana turned and walked to the front of the truck. Frustrated and angry, she remained there, wondering about the best way to proceed. She had no experience with sullen teenagers. She was still trying to cool off when Ben showed up beside her.

"Were you like that?" she asked.

"Absolutely." He grinned, as if he were proud of the fact.

"I didn't mean it as a compliment, Marshall. He's strong-willed and hard-headed, not to mention stubborn—"

"All of those things are beside my name in my high school yearbook." He put his hands against the truck's hood. "You're not going to win this one, Dana. He didn't bring the phone, and he won't tell anyone where it is."

"How do you know that?"

"He's a smart kid, he's still a little scared, and I asked him."

Dana sighed and leaned against the front of the truck. "I don't know how to do this. I can manage a staff of thirty, but I don't know what to do with one fifteen-year-old." She laughed at herself. "Any ideas?"

"Me? Nope, but I have a feeling Tafoya might."

Turned out Tafoya did. He'd bring Reggie with him when he left the reservation to pick up casino supplies. The boy would be hidden in the back of the truck. Dana would have a person waiting to transfer him to one of their vehicles.

They would take him to an undisclosed location to make the call. If they couldn't tag a location, they'd set up a meeting. Only as a last resort.

"Your mother must approve this plan first, Reggie."

The boy pulled a sheet of paper from his back, blue-jeans pocket. Dana shouldn't have been surprised to see it was notarized, but she was.

"Where did you learn this stuff?"

"TV." Reggie actually grinned as Ben slapped him on the shoulder.

"See you, kid."

Tafoya drove off in a cloud of dust. The entire meeting had lasted less than forty minutes, but it had completely drained Dana. This time when Ben offered to drive, she didn't argue. He could read his book later.

Besides, if she kept her sunglasses on, she could sneak glances at him as he drove. Since she'd made it plain there could be no relationship between them, she didn't feel bad about allowing her imagination to wander. Knowing nothing would ever come of her dreams allowed her a measure of freedom.

Sixty

B en stared at the slip of paper in his hand.
He'd gone back and forth all evening. If he waited any longer, it would be too late.

Picking up his cell phone, he punched in the Texas area code, questioned his sanity, and hit TALK.

The number had been frighteningly easy to find.

Erin Jacobs.

Livingston, Texas.

Animal Rescue Center.

Given the power of Google and those three pieces of information, he had her number in milliseconds. He'd had it for two days. Had it and hadn't used it.

But when Dana had slept all the way back from the reservation, he'd become concerned. On one level she seemed to be pulling herself together. On another, he wasn't so sure.

A woman answered on the fourth ring.

"Noah's Ark."

"Huh?"

"Noah's Ark Animal Shelter." The woman pronounced each word slowly, as if Ben had recently learned to speak and shouldn't be rushed.

"Oh, right. Yeah. I'm looking for Erin Jacobs."

"You got her. What can I do for you?"

This was Dana's sister? She sounded impossibly chirpy. Why had he expected another wounded, reserved woman? Perhaps she'd been too young to be affected by the tragedy in her family.

"You still there, mister?"

"Yeah. It's just that, well…"

"Spit it out. You can't surprise me."

He heard the sound of barking in the background and possibly the grunt of a pig.

"I've heard it all, even at this hour. Make that especially at this hour."

"It's not. I mean, I don't." Ben switched the phone to his other hand and tried to think of how to start.

"Cats, dogs, hamsters, guineas, snakes, horses. I'm serious, you cannot surprise me. Few weeks ago, someone gave me a pig. Whatcha got?"

"Let me start over. I'm in Taos, New Mexico, and I'm calling about your sister, Dana."

There was complete silence on the line, so that he wondered if the call had been dropped. He checked the display to be sure they were still connected, then held it back against his ear in time to hear a screen door slam.

"Is she okay? Tell me what's happened. I can be on the next flight out of Houston."

"No. I'm so sorry. I'm doing this very badly. Nothing's wrong. I mean, maybe something is. That's why I'm calling, but she's fine." Ben let out a long breath, tried to roll his shoulders. "I'm Ben Marshall, and I work with Dana."

"You're Ben?"

"Yeah." He waited a moment, wondering what her question meant. When she didn't elaborate, he went on. "I was assigned to the Taos office a month ago and—"

"She told me."

"Told you what?"

"Enough. Dana and I are very close. Only siblings."

"Oh." Ben stood up and paced around the room. Talking to Erin was like trying to talk to one of his younger cousins. He was never sure if they were even on the same subject.

"What's wrong with Dana?" Erin asked.

"I don't know," Ben admitted. "I'm worried about her, but I'm not even sure if I should be. She's under a lot of stress."

Erin snorted. "My sister thrives on stress. How do you think she got that job?"

When Ben didn't answer, she added, "This is different though."

"Yeah. I think it is."

"What can you tell me?"

Ben had promised himself he wouldn't betray Dana's confidences. He kept his descriptions vague, but gave Erin enough details to get the general idea across.

"Has she had the tremor thing?"

"Tremor thing?" Ben nearly dropped the glass of iced tea he was holding.

"Yeah. She had it once in high school. I don't know if she even remembers. We laughed about it at the time, but I think it really bothered her. Dana really wanted out of Livingston, out of Texas in general. I don't know how much she's told you—"

"Enough."

"Well, if she said anything you must have won her confidence. Most people don't know about her Texas side." Erin laughed, but it seemed more of a nervous laugh than one with any humor in it. "She was taking her SATs. They would get her into college—hopefully Rice University—and college would buy her ticket out of here."

"A lot of pressure."

"Right. Except for Dana, it wasn't only pressure for her. She needed to make it so she could provide for me, or so she told herself. Which was not exactly true, because we were with a good foster family at that point. They were providing well for both of us—at least the basic food and clothing."

Ben tried to picture a younger Dana, but he couldn't.

"So the week before the SAT exams, she shows me her hand. It was shaking like a leaf. We thought it was funny at first. When it didn't stop, I came up with all these crazy scenarios to try and help her lighten up."

"Like what?" Ben stretched out on his cot, trying to imagine the two sisters growing up together.

"Oh, you know. We'd put her in the freak show in the circus, and I'd stand outside and take tickets. Or we'd be like the Bronte sisters and have to live together the rest of our lives so I could take care of her." Erin's voice faded away, lost in the memories of all those years ago.

"Did she go to Rice?"

"Yeah. Full scholarship. As far as I know she never had the tremors again. She even worked an extra job during the academic year so she could send money home to her kid sister."

Ben thought of all Erin had told him. He still didn't know how to help Dana deal with the stress of tomorrow, but he did have a better picture of who she was.

"I'm glad I called you, Erin."

"Me too. I'm sort of relieved you don't have any animal to rescue though. Already have all the boys and girls in bed around here. They get riled up when there's a new arrival."

He promised to call her if he needed anything. Unspoken between them was the fact Dana didn't need to know about the call. As he was about to disconnect, he heard Erin's voice calling to him.

"Ben?"

"Yeah."

"Watch after her, okay?"

"I will."

"She thinks she's very tough, but even tough girls wear down."

"I'll remember that."

He went to bed and dreamt of an ark. One which held no animals. He was all alone on it. He walked from room-to-room, searching for Dana, but he couldn't find her. Throughout the wooden boat, blaring from giant speakers, ringing in his ears, he heard his promise to Erin.

Sixty-one

I n the end, Dana chose to use the rodeo grounds the next evening. Mainly because it was public, and they could see a long ways in any direction. Of course, they had all the floodlights on. If anyone asked, there was a maintenance crew, checking equipment. Drogan's chances of getting there first and rigging an explosion seemed infinitesimal. She assured herself they'd taken every precaution and then some.

"I told you, the phone can't be bugged." Reggie squirmed as Ben went over him with the wand one last time.

Dana waited for Ben's nod, then tapped her comm unit. She had a perimeter team set up around the rodeo grounds. Chance Drogan wasn't getting within a mile of Reggie Mifflin.

"Any phone can be bugged, kid." Red looked up from his table in the middle of the arena. "Nowadays phones have GPS chips in them. Drogan could have found out what your chip number is, then he'd know your location whenever you turn the phone on."

"That's only true for phones made since 2004." Reggie looked at his phone with a mixture of pride and disgust. "My phone is a relic."

"Kid knows his stuff," Ben said.

"Five minutes until contact." Dana spoke calmly into her comm unit. She didn't believe Drogan had the cell phone pegged. She also didn't expect him to answer when the boy put the call through, but since they'd had no luck finding him on their own it was worth a try.

"Okay, Reggie. You'll talk into the phone like normal." She ignored the roll of his eyes and continued. "Everything you say will be recorded here on Red's computer, and we'll be able to hear what you say and what he says. As you can see, our software will run a program to pinpoint Drogan's location. The longer you can keep him talking, the better chance we have of finding him."

"How does it work?" Reggie asked.

Dana looked to Red who combed his fingers through his beard.

"Ever use Google Earth?" When the boy nodded, Red pointed to the bottom quadrant of his screen. "It's going to look similar. We'll zoom in on him with three to six satellites."

Dana noticed the kid pulled on his AC/DC cap more when he was nervous. "You don't have to watch if it makes you anxious. You can turn the other way and pretend we're not here."

"Right, because I talk in the middle of a rodeo arena all the time."

"Two minutes." Dana offered what she hoped was a confident smile.

Ben assumed his military stance, feet spread and arms clasped behind his back, while he surveyed the south side of the arena. He looked as if he expected Drogan to charge through in a tank. Red had all four parts of his screen up and running. Reggie held the phone in his hand.

At Dana's signal, he tugged on his hat, punched in the number from memory, and pushed TALK.

Dana nearly choked when Drogan answered on the second ring. Every hair on the back of her neck stood up as adrenaline pumped through her veins.

"Reggie. It's been a long time."

"They've been keeping a close eye on me. This was the first chance I've had to call you."

Dana and Ben had gone over possible questions Drogan would have for him. Reggie actually had some improvement on the script they'd drawn up.

"And who is they, Reggie?"

"My mom, people."

"People." Drogan's voice sounded calm, normal, almost good-natured.

It made Dana's skin crawl. Made her feel dirty in a thousand different ways.

"I want my money. You promised, and you owe me."

"You blew up all my materials, Reggie. I'd say you're the one who owes me."

"I lost my house because of you." Reggie's voice rose as Drogan baited him.

Dana kept shifting her gaze from Red's screen to Reggie and back again. The computer had found a lock and was beginning to zoom in. She made a motion with her hand for Reggie to keep Drogan talking.

"We both know I couldn't leave any evidence in your jam room, Reg. You should have been more careful."

"You told me they'd deliver the goods at nine-thirty after she went to work. This is all your fault." Reggie's voice was a shriek now. There was no acting on his part. All the fury he'd been holding inside was pouring out on the grounds of the arena.

Ben walked over, stepped in front of the boy, and held up four fingers. They needed four minutes.

Reggie pulled in a shaky breath. "I want my money. My family has to start over, and we need that money."

"Aren't you a good boy, Reggie. It's possible we could arrange a transfer of funds. There is one more job I have. It's dangerous though. If you think you're man enough…"

Dana started shaking her head. When Reggie didn't seem to get her message, she waved her hands. He was not to agree to do anything for Drogan. She had been clear about that in their meeting.

"What is it?" Reggie said.

"Meet me at Elizabethtown. Have Mr. Tafoya drive you—no one else, not even Angela."

Reggie had frozen as soon as Drogan had said the name Tafoya. Ben was down to two fingers and continued to stand directly in front of him. Dana heard Drogan mention Angela, knew he must be referring to her, but she could only watch in fascination as the screen on Red's computer zoomed in on northern New Mexico.

"When?" Reggie asked.

"One hour," Drogan said. "That should give you plenty of time."

"Where at in the town?"

"It's a ghost town. I'll find you."

"All right, but bring the money."

Drogan laughed. It was a frightening sound. "One more thing, Reggie. Tell Angela I've started another mosaic. She never should have come back to Taos."

Then the line went dead.

VANNETTA CHAPMAN

Sixty-two

D ana had no reaction to Drogan's last words. None.
She heard them like you would hear music playing in the background as you shop for groceries.

One part of her mind even understood what he had said, and the inherent threat in his words. The rest of her—the blood coursing through her veins, her tongue as she bit down gently on it, even the image of Ben as he stood in front of her speaking—it all seemed sort of frozen.

Then, quickly, like falling awake from a dream, everything around her and in her came alive with rushing clarity.

The tremor began in her left arm.

Red was hollering that Drogan's location had been south in Santa Fe.

Reggie had plopped down in the dirt and was turning his cap round and round in his hand.

Ben's hands were rubbing her arms, warming her. Why was she suddenly so cold?

And she understood with perfect clarity that Drogan meant to kill her.

This time, instead of being afraid, it made her extremely angry.

She stepped away from Ben, tapped her comm unit, and spoke to Cheryl. "Get Clay on the line. I need three teams ready to go in ten minutes. I also want the Albuquerque office alerted and covering all northern roads, stopping anyone who meets Drogan's description."

She turned to Red. "Get Tafoya on the phone. I need him here—now."

Walking over to Reggie, she squatted down in the dirt. When he raised his gaze to hers, she saw the fear in his coal-black eyes. Saw his frustration and understood it. "He's not playing fair, Reggie. He never has."

Reggie shook his head and wiped at the tears she wasn't supposed to see.

"I promised your involvement in this ends here, and I hoped that was true. I don't think Drogan's going to hurt you though. It's me he wants. If you're willing to go to Elizabethtown, and if your mom agrees, I would appreciate the help."

He'd put the cap back on and was nodding before she'd finished.

"You'll have to wear a Kevlar vest, kid. Sure you're up to it?" Ben held out his hand to help the boy up.

"Long as none of my friends see me." He dusted off his pants. "I'm going to look like a total nerd."

"What are you saying?" Ben patted the front of his vest. "Women tell me I look cool in this."

"Red, get Mrs. Mifflin on the line." Dana turned at the sound of a truck and saw Tafoya driving up under the bright lights.

She met him at the entrance to the arena. "We need your help."

"Tell me what to do."

She summarized the phone call, leaving out Drogan's final comment.

"Have you been to Elizabethtown?" he asked.

"I've been through it."

"It was once seven-thousand people," Tafoya explained as they walked back to where Ben and Red were packing up the equipment. Reggie moved closer to the old man while he continued his story. "At its height, there were gold and copper mines. Plenty of outlaws too."

Dana tucked her hair behind her ears. "Now it's a tourist town, right?"

"Could call it that. Mostly, it's a ghost town like Drogan said. There are maybe seven buildings left. In the old days, the Topeka and Santa Fe Railroad used to go by there."

Dana looked to Ben.

"I'm on it, boss. Maps of the railway lines."

"What concerns me more," Tafoya admitted, "is the area has a history of evil."

"What do you mean?" Dana asked.

"Surely you've heard of the serial killer, Charles Kennedy."

Dana nodded as a shiver ran down her spine.

"The cabin he used isn't far from there."

"Say, Tafoya." Reggie pulled off his cap, creased it, and set it back on his head. "You don't think an area can be like a vortex of evil, do you?"

"No, I don't, Reggie. All of the earth is God's creation, and I believe all of it is meant for good. I'm not sure Drogan knows that though."

"We're ready here," Red said.

Dana looked at the four men around her. Reggie might as well be considered a man. She was going to depend on him to do a man's job. They were all, without exception, good men.

A part of her wanted to slip back into the frozen place where she had temporarily sought refuge. It provided numbness so she could rest for a while.

Instead, she squared her shoulders, gave them a grim smile, and said, "Let's roll out then."

Sixty-three

B en realized Dana would never stop surprising him.
She'd recovered faster than a jackrabbit could cross a road. There'd been a moment in the arena when he thought Drogan might have won. Terror doesn't have to be delivered via a bullet to incapacitate someone.

Twice Drogan had used Angela's name. Both times he'd obviously meant Dana. There was no doubt now that he intended to harm her.

But Dana had held together. She was made of tough stuff, pretty much like Erin had described to him. He smiled at her as he sped east out of Taos.

"Why are you smiling, Marshall?" She was studying the maps of the railway lines.

They'd been closed for years. He had marked the spots Drogan might try to use.

"I think Drogan ought to be scared. He doesn't know what he's up against."

Dana peered over at him in the darkness of his truck. They'd decided it would be less obvious than the Humvee. In addition, two Humvees were speeding through Wheeler Peak Wilderness, planning to meet them from the north. Reggie rode three miles ahead in Tafoya's truck. Another Humvee was five miles further back behind them.

"You know what I can't figure?" She closed the ruggedized laptop and rested her head against the back of the seat. "Why an hour? If he was in Santa Fe—"

"He wasn't. That's my guess anyway."

"But the trace—"

"He bounced it. We saw his ability to do so with the surveillance devices he left in our office. Should have expected it with the phone." Ben ran his hand through his hair, then checked his watch. They'd make it, but it would be close.

"You think he's already there?"

Ben shrugged. "Maybe. Or maybe this is a wild goose chase. He enjoys yanking our chain, letting us know he's superior."

Dana turned her head and stared out into the night. Finally, she sighed and looked back at him. "Did Clay tell you about the disguises?"

Ben shook his head.

"There were at least two incidents on the cameras where we're fairly sure we caught Drogan, but he was wearing disguises. Clay's been working with a layering program that cuts through facial disguises."

"Like mustaches and glasses?" Ben tried to focus on the road, but he couldn't help staring at her to see if she was serious.

"No. The program would have seen through anything superficial immediately. We think he's been using prosthetic effects."

"You mean *Nutty Professor* stuff?"

"Exactly."

"Wow. What else does this guy have up his sleeve?"

Dana drummed her fingers on the laptop. "He knew we were looking for him. So he must have figured out we had been inside the cabin, inside his room."

"Because he made the comment about the mosaic."

Dana nodded. "So he also realized we'd seen his board with his drop points."

"And he was testing our programs."

"He always seems one step ahead." Dana ran her fingers through her hair, pulling it out of the clasp, closing her eyes for a moment.

Ben wanted to tell her to rest a while, but he knew they didn't have time.

"Did you ever finish the book?" Her eyes were still closed, but she obviously wasn't sleeping.

"Yeah, I did. Nina and I agreed. Drogan sees himself as the lead character, Tom."

Dana sat up, cornered herself in the truck, and stared at him. "But Tom was an admirable character if I remember correctly. How could Drogan possibly identify with him?"

"Both lost their land. Tom spent some time in prison, and Drogan knows he will go to prison if he's ever caught." Ben fidgeted under her gaze. "The connection I saw was more about the anger though. Steinbeck describes a simmering anger that ferments and grows until it can't be contained."

"You could certainly describe Drogan the same way."

Ben heard the resignation in her voice. "He's not going to win, Dana."

"How do you know that?" She turned back around in the seat and opened the computer on her lap. "It's a nice thing to say, but there's no way you can know for sure. Bad guys win sometimes."

Before she turned back to her maps, she added, "You make sure Reggie and Tafoya make it out of this alive, Ben. They are your priority. You understand me, right?"

He knew what she was telling him. He didn't like it one bit, and he fully believed he could have two priorities. No need to get in an argument now though.

"Sure, boss. I understand."

Sixty-four

T en minutes later she received her first report from Clay. "The spybots have tagged him. He's at the Hotel Mutz, and it looks like he's alone."

"There's a hotel?"

"It's a ruin," Tafoya's voice over the comm unit surprised her. The man sounded like a natural though. "Only two walls are still standing."

"Any idea why he'd choose it for his setup location?" Dana asked.

"Top of the hill," Tafoya said. "He'll see us all coming from at least five miles away."

"Any ideas, Ben?" She closed the laptop in disgust. The railway lines didn't offer any hope as far as she could tell. At least they didn't seem much of a threat either.

"Put me in the bed of Tafoya's truck. Once we pull in, I can cover them, or provide a distraction."

"What if he has night vision goggles?" Red asked.

"Then I'll have to shoot faster than he does."

Dana stared out into the darkness. "If someone has a better idea, I'm listening."

The comm unit was empty as they all hurdled toward Drogan's trap.

"All right. Tafoya pull over and let's transfer Ben. All other vehicles, maintain a distance of six miles, repeat six miles."

"I don't like it, Dana." Clay sounded angrier by the minute. "We're at ten miles now. Two of my men can hoof it in by the time you get there. He won't see us coming on foot."

"All right. Do it, but I want them in contact the entire time."

Ben had pulled the truck over behind Tafoya as she spoke with Clay. Picking up his rifle and pack from behind the seat, he smiled and tossed her the keys. "Go easy with the Chevy, boss."

"Finally, he lets me drive his truck."

The look he gave her was filled with such tenderness. As he walked past her, she had the craziest idea he intended to stop, take her in his arms, and kiss her. That thought was quickly followed by the memory of her pushing him away.

He gave her a mock salute. "See you in a few."

Then he lowered the tailgate of Tafoya's truck and climbed in, leaving the tailgate down. He waved at her once as they pulled away.

Sixty-five

C heryl's voice came over the comm unit, alerting Ben to the fact that they were coming in view of Elizabethtown. The GPS coordinates for all vehicles had been programmed into the master grid and were displayed on each vehicle's onboard panel. Dana had been able to view it on her laptop since Ben's truck wasn't exactly retrofitted with the latest technology.

Ben tapped on the cab of the truck once, indicating Tafoya should slow down so he could roll out. He'd left the tailgate down so he wouldn't have to go over the side. No doubt Drogan was watching from on top of the hill.

He'd have night vision goggles, but there was a possibility the heavy metal of the older truck would keep him from seeing the third body signature. Ben had positioned himself directly behind Tafoya, hoping to buy himself the five seconds he needed to escape detection.

His strategy was to drop out and roll while Drogan had his goggles on the truck and the road behind the truck.

No plan was perfect. What this one lacked in good common sense, it made up for in audacity.

Ben inched his way to the end of the tailgate. When he felt the truck begin to slow, he let his body fall the rest of the way to the ground. Once there, he rolled to his right.

His directions to Tafoya had been clear. "Find me a spot near a ditch."

The man hadn't disappointed him. Ben hit the nestle of weeds and lay there, waiting to hear the ring of gunshots. When he didn't, he snapped on his own night goggles and raised his head.

Drogan was alone at the top of the hill behind the only wall at the Mutz Hotel with three windows—if you could call holes with no glass windows. Since there was no roof or adjacent walls, the entire description seemed a bit of a stretch.

Ben briefly scanned the other six buildings. "Confirming Drogan is our only contact."

"Can you tell if he's armed?" Dana's voice was tense.

He knew it was agony for her to wait out-of-range.

"Negative. He's holding a cell phone and wearing night vision. Tafoya's stopped in the middle of the street, five hundred yards from the hotel." Ben set up his rifle as he spoke. "I have him in my scope."

At that moment, Drogan ducked behind the thick, brick wall.

"Take the shot, Ben."

"He stepped behind the south wall of the hotel."

"Probably why he picked it," Cheryl said. "Those walls are at least three feet thick. It would take a mortar round to pierce them."

"Reggie's phone is ringing," Dana said. "Looks like it's him. Reggie, take it slow and easy. Ben is right behind you."

"Hello."

"Reggie. I see you found me."

"I found the town, if that's what you call this place."

"Indeed, it is. And you brought Mr. Tafoya. I'd like you both to step out of the vehicle."

"Why should we? I'm done doing what you tell me. Where's my money?"

"You and I have unfinished business. You're going to do one more favor for me. Then I'll give you what I owe you. Now step out of the truck with Mr. Tafoya and walk toward the hotel."

"What's to keep you from shooting us?"

"I could shoot you now, Reggie."

Ben kept his scope trained on the last place he'd seen Drogan, but the man remained behind the brick wall. It took all of his training not to glance at Reggie and Tafoya.

"He wants us to get out of the truck," Reggie relayed to the old man.

"Let's do this and go home."

Two doors opened, then slammed shut.

Ben heard them walk forward. The spot between his shoulder blades began to itch, and he knew whatever Drogan had planned, it wasn't going to end well for someone.

"Can you still hear me, Reggie?"

"Yeah, I hear you. Can't believe there's cell service out here."

"You'd be surprised what ghost towns have. Walk ten paces more toward the hotel."

Over the comm unit, Ben heard the sound of the two doing as they were told. The town was eerily quiet. Apparently, whoever ran the two buildings that were open for tourists didn't bother staying over during evening hours. He couldn't blame them. Elizabethtown wasn't a very hospitable place.

When the boy's shuffling footsteps stopped, Drogan began speaking again. It took Ben a second to realize the sound was not coming through the cell phone and into the comm unit, but out of loudspeakers Drogan had set up around the crumbling relic of a building. The sound was so disturbingly like Ben's dream of being on the ark that he jerked away from the rifle.

When he looked back, Drogan still wasn't in any of the windows.

"Reggie, you've been a disappointment. You should have stood firm and been true to our agreement. For your failure, you must pay with your life."

"Ben, get them out of there." Dana started the Chevy, revved the engine.

Even as she did so, Ben jerked the rifle up and began to run.

"Mr. Tafoya, your people received what my family did not—their land. In order to balance the accounts, you will pay with your life."

Ben climbed on top of the shed next to the E-town museum. The elevated position allowed him to see the entire site of the Mutz Hotel and the road passing through Elizabethtown.

Tafoya had grabbed the boy and was pulling him out of the street toward the general store.

Ben saw movement in the middle window. He didn't hesitate. His first shot sent bricks flying. Before he could get a second round off, the museum behind him exploded. White hot pain shot through his left arm as he was knocked from the roof of the shed.

He rolled on the ground, bits of gravel biting into the wound on his arm.

His comm unit had been damaged in the explosion, but the sound of his truck coming up the road told him he didn't have much time. Drogan would target Dana. It was his real goal—not Reggie and certainly not Tafoya. They were bonus points. By targeting them, he'd assured himself he would get a chance at her. Dana had long been his obsession.

Ben clutched his left arm to his side, gripped the rifle with his right, and started toward the hotel. He had to get there before Dana came into view.

Sixty-six

D ana pushed Ben's truck, deciding to cut through the field rather than barrel down Main Street.

The explosion assured her she was headed in the right direction. Glancing at her open laptop, she saw Cheryl and her team were closing in from the north. They had him surrounded, if they could arrest him before he killed someone.

As she gained the south side of town, a second explosion lit up the sky. The electromagnetic pulse caused her to slam on the brakes and jerk her head down. The pain to her ears was brief but excruciating. Her laptop went black at the exact moment the truck died.

Grabbing the backup pack from behind the passenger seat, she ran from the truck. The town was completely dark except for the smoldering fire at the museum.

Tafoya's truck sat in the middle of the street, both doors wide open.

Dana pulled her Glock with one hand and tapped her comm unit with the other. Nothing. Of course, the EMP had fried it as well.

Seeing movement near the old church, she jerked up on her pistol.

Tafoya stepped out of the shadows.

"Reggie?"

"He's fine. Ben went toward the hotel."

Dana nodded. "Stay with the boy."

She knew how exposed she was as she ran, but there was nothing to hide behind. The town was, after all, a ghost town. Drogan had chosen well the scene for his final showdown.

"Dana." Ben motioned to her from the southwest side of the building, one of the few remaining corners.

She flattened herself against the south side, while he covered the west. Which was why she didn't immediately notice he was injured. It wasn't until she turned to hear what he was saying that she saw the blood running down his arm.

"You're hurt. Let me look at it."

"We don't have time. He's not here. I've cleared this ruin, but he hasn't left the area."

Her eyes sought his in the darkness. "How much blood have you lost?"

"It's a flesh wound, darlin'." He motioned toward the smoldering building. "You can look at it when we have him handcuffed. Where's Tafoya and Reggie?"

"Old Church."

"How do you want to handle this, boss?"

"Let's go back to the churchyard. Tafoya has a gun. With three of us, we have a better chance of fighting him."

"How close were the other teams when the EMP hit?"

"Three, maybe four miles."

"All right." Ben nodded toward the street. "You're first, sweetheart. I'll cover you."

Sixty-seven

T heir journey to the church was quiet—too quiet in Dana's opinion.

"Where is he?" she whispered as they crept down the side of the old building.

"He's close. The EMP fried his way out of here too."

They'd reached the end of the building. "On three," he mouthed. "One, two…"

He and Dana charged around the corner of the building at the same moment and found themselves facing the muzzle of a gun.

"Tafoya." Ben moved back a step. "Nice to see you."

Tafoya grunted and relaxed his grip on the weapon.

Dana peered past him. "Is Reggie—"

"I'm fine." The boy walked out of the darkness.

As he moved into their circle, Dana noticed he was holding a small pistol. She looked from it to Tafoya and started to protest, but he stopped her.

"I have been working with him. We knew this could happen, and he needs to be able to protect himself."

Dana realized he was right, but she still didn't like it. The thought of the boy waiting unarmed, with Drogan still loose, kept her from arguing.

"Dude, you are completely messed up." Reggie stared at the blood dripping down Ben's shirt in fascination.

Dana's heart lurched at the reminder. She dropped her pack and pulled out the emergency med kit. Knowing he wouldn't let her take time to clean the wound, she pulled out the materials to apply a compress and slow the bleeding.

"Is it a bullet?" she asked him.

Ben shook his head. "I was too close to the explosion. Something hit me." He turned to Tafoya and Reggie while she selected the roll of gauze and began to wrap his arm. "Any idea which way he went?"

"No. I saw him come up with the weapon. Reggie and I hit the ditch—"

"You yanked me into the ditch," Reggie corrected. "You totally saved me."

Tafoya blinked once, then continued. "Seconds later you fired a round."

"Only hit brick," Ben muttered, sucking in his breath as Dana tightened the end of the bandage.

"Next thing we knew there was the flare in the sky and the high-pitched sound." Tafoya pointed to the sky as he spoke.

"What was that?" Reggie asked. "It was worse than my math teacher's scream when we all failed her unit tests."

"Flex your arm, Ben. I want to be sure it's not going to bleed through." When he started to argue, she moved closer in the darkness. "Do it."

He bent his arm at the elbow two, then three times. She couldn't see any bleeding through the compress, but she knew it wouldn't hold for long. "We need to clean this wound soon, or it will become infected."

"Later." He turned to Reggie. "The flare was an electromagnetic pulse. It fries anything with a circuit board."

"Like with a nuclear bomb." Tafoya ran his hand down his long braid.

"Exactly, only we've advanced the technology. Now you can deliver an EMP from the ground up and without the messiness of a bomb—an EMP flare."

"What's the point?" Reggie asked.

"No communication and no way out." Dana sank back against the plank boards of the building.

Reggie looked down at the cell phone in his hand.

"The circuit board is fried, kid. Just like the starters in our trucks." Ben turned to Dana. "What about your laptop?"

She shook her head. "I left it open on the seat."

"How could a laptop survive an EMP thing?" Reggie asked.

"Government laptops are ruggedized—built with a special case to withstand an EMP, but I left mine open on the seat." Dana rubbed her forehead. If she had closed it, they could contact someone.

Tafoya placed a hand on her shoulder. "You remembered the most important things—to grab the pack, to get to us. The rest will take care of itself."

"Tafoya's right," Ben agreed. "We have two more units coming from the north, plus Clay's men on foot."

"And Red's unit from the south, but they have no way to contact each other." Dana looked at the three faces peering at her. "How will they communicate?"

Ben shrugged. "The old-fashioned way—instinct and common sense. They'll rally here. Tafoya, you know the most about this area. What would Drogan's plan be? He obviously hoped to kill you and Reggie."

Reggie threw his hands up in an I-don't-know gesture, then checked the paddle holster where he'd stowed the pistol.

"Drogan knew his own vehicle would be disabled at the same time ours was," Ben said, pacing the short area behind the building.

"He's back at the truck, looking for me." Dana's eyes widened. "He said he'd started another mosaic, which means he had plans for me. He knew we'd all be following. The EMP was to disable everyone in their positions."

"And once he'd killed us—" Reggie grimaced as he spat out the word.

"And blew me up," Ben added.

"Then he'd come after me, because my vehicle would be disabled." Dana stood up. "It makes sense, but what was the rest of his plan? Something tells me he wouldn't have been happy to shoot me. You saw those pictures, Ben. This guy wanted to make it last. So how would he get us out? Can you shield a vehicle from an EMP?"

"Not that I know of." Ben shifted his rifle to his left hand, ran his right through his hair. "They were experimenting with things in the military, but hadn't come up with anything foolproof. Think about the cover on the laptop.

What could you create to cover an engine block? It would need to be huge and heavy. There's nothing around here that size."

"Perhaps the answer is less rather than more complicated," Tafoya said. "Perhaps he planned to use horses."

Dana and Ben stared at each other, then began shouldering their packs. "Where are they?"

"Behind the cemetery. There's an old stable. They keep some animals there for a trail ride. Tourists can rent them."

"Stay here and wait for the other teams. Tell them we went after him." Dana paused, then walked back to Reggie. "Thank you."

She wanted to touch his face, embrace him like she would a child. Instead, she held out her hand. He shook it awkwardly. "After college, if you're interested in a career with Homeland Security—"

"I'll give you a call." His smile shone, even in the darkness.

She turned and looked at Reggie and Tafoya one last time. The boy stood close to the man. The two could have passed as father and son. It might have been the light or the way they both looked so resolute. It was an image she would hold in her mind through the long night ahead. It might have been the first time the word "father" brought her comfort instead of pain.

Sixty-eight

B en found the old stable behind the cemetery just as Tafoya had said. The corral gate was open, and all of the horses were gone, except for one.

A lone pinto stood at the fence, its lead rope wrapped around the railing.

"It's like he wants us to follow him," Dana whispered.

Dana checked for tracks while Ben saddled the animal. In five minutes, he was ready to go. "Looks like we're riding double."

She climbed on behind him. "The majority of the tracks lead north across the hills. One set goes south toward your truck."

Ben had fastened his pack on behind their saddle. His rifle rested across the front of the saddle horn. He held the reins in his left hand. His right hand rested lightly on the rifle.

"Have you ridden before?" He let the mare adjust to the feel of their weight in the darkness.

"Twice, when I was a girl."

"Hold on to me with your left. I want you to be able to shoot with your right."

"I can shoot with both," she reminded him.

"So can I, but my left is going to be slower with this bandage. A second can make all the difference, and he already has too many advantages tonight." He wished he could turn and look at her. "Dana?"

"Yeah."

"It's going to be okay."

"I know. You told me before you got shot."

"I didn't get shot."

She waved her hand, indicating he should go.

Ben smiled at her impatience. It was a good sign. Better that she be angry at him than frightened. He had a feeling there would be plenty of time for both emotions in the next few hours.

He urged the pinto into a trot, staying on the grass to muffle her hoof beats. The new moon gave them the barest of light to travel by. It was enough—too much really. The pinto's white coloring would stand out in the light. He knew it wasn't an accident Drogan had left this particular horse.

He patted the mare's neck and murmured softly to her. She was a gift, no matter her coloring or what hand had left her tied in the corral.

He slowed when he saw his truck in the distance. Handing her the reins, he slid out of the saddle. "Stay here," he whispered. "Keep her in the open, where he can't sneak up on you."

"I'm an easy target here," she hissed at him.

He reached up and touched her arm. "He can't see you. I can barely see you. His night goggles were disabled like everything else. I'll be right back."

He melted into the night, carrying nothing but his rifle. Reality slipped away, and he couldn't have said where he was. There was only the hunter and the hunted.

He reconned the truck in under two minutes and was back at her side.

"He's been there."

"And?"

Reining the mare in, he turned back the way they had come. "And he's gone."

They rode back toward the cemetery in silence.

When the old tombstones came into view, Dana asked the question he'd been stumbling against. "Why did he leave the one horse?"

"He wanted someone to follow him."

"Whoever survived."

"Right."

"So he wants a last stand."

"Yeah." Ben felt tired. What if they'd guessed wrong? What if Drogan's primary target was the boy? He could have already circled back. Perhaps they should return to the church, join up with Tafoya and Reggie, and wait for the others.

He was about to suggest as much to Dana when he saw a shadow, darker than the rest, move through the trees at the far end of the cemetery.

"Did you see that?

"I didn't see anything." Dana leaned in against him. "Which direction?"

"There, past the angel."

"Angel?"

"The statue." He stilled the mare, but for the space of a few seconds the distinct sound of clopping continued. Dana released her grip on his stomach. He felt her lean right, raise her Glock, and aim with both hands.

The shadow moved again, and she fired as their horse reared, throwing her off.

Ben tightened his hold on the reins, moving the pinto away so she wouldn't step on Dana. The sound of galloping echoed through the night.

Dana was screaming, "Hold still. I need to get back on."

"Easy girl. It's okay. Shh. Easy."

"What do you mean it's okay?" Dana continued to prance around, trying to find a way to get back on the horse. "Hold still. It's not okay."

"I'm talking to the horse, Dana. If we don't quiet her, she won't be any good to us."

The mare was throwing her head, still trying to rear on her back legs. Ben leaned forward in the saddle to counter her weight, stroking her neck and murmuring.

Out of the corner of his eye, he saw Dana had backed away, though she continued to bounce from foot-to-foot. By the time he'd finally calmed the mare, she stood looking defeated, staring off in the direction Drogan had fled.

"Good girl. That's it." Ben rubbed the mare's neck. When her trembling had stopped, he turned to Dana and held his good arm down to her. "Okay, quick."

She was behind him in a flash, waving wildly in the direction Drogan had disappeared.

"I think I hit him. I think I saw him fall backward."

Ben let the horse pick its way carefully through the cemetery. Once they reached the other side, he thought he could barely make out Drogan's form on the far side of the western field.

Then he let the horse have its head, and they flew.

Sixty-nine

T he first five miles passed quickly.

Drogan barely maintained his lead as he headed northwest across the open fields. Ben had to fight his itch to rein in the mare and pull out his rifle. He knew it would be madness in the darkness at such a distance. Without the night vision scope, he didn't have a chance of making the shot.

So he urged the mare on as the temperature dropped and deep night fell around them.

At least they had Drogan on the run.

The man would either make a mistake and they would catch him, or he would turn and fight. Ben was ready for either. Except for the fever in his left arm. He could ignore it a few more hours, then he'd have to stop and let Dana dig out the shrapnel.

He prayed for time and wisdom as they rode through the darkness.

Fifteen minutes later, Drogan entered the cover of the forest. Ben slowed the mare and followed.

Dana jerked up on her Glock when an elk passed within three feet of their right flank. He was a monstrous bull and never bothered to look their way, simply disappeared into the trees as if they didn't exist.

Dana let out her breath and lowered her gun.

They could hear Drogan's horse up ahead, neighing softly. To Ben's surprise the man called out, his voice ripping through the stillness of the night.

"You don't want to come in here, Marshall. This is my land."

Ben eased from the saddle, slipping the rifle from the front of the pack as his feet touched the ground. After softly stroking the mare's neck, he handed the reins to Dana.

"I guess you know they took my last place, so I claimed this area. Kit Carson National Forest. Nice land."

The man did not sound injured. Too bad Dana's bullet hadn't hit him in the vocal cords.

"It's been a dry year so far. One match and I could send the whole thing up in a blaze of glory. Man ought to be able to do whatever he wants with his own land. Wouldn't you agree, Mr. Marshall?"

Ben wanted Dana to back the mare slowly out to the clearing, then he'd try to get a shot off. "Take her back," he whispered. "Slowly."

Dana seemed to understand, though he could tell by her expression she didn't want to split up in the wilderness. Her expression seemed frozen in disbelief, but when he patted the mare Dana began to slowly back her in the direction they had come.

Shooting in the dark was dangerous. In the dark in a forest, doubly so. He didn't know when he'd get another chance at Drogan though. The man's rantings indicated he was getting cocky. If Drogan had been injured by Dana's first shot, he wasn't showing it.

The stiffness in his arm as he positioned the rifle convinced Ben he had to try. His wound was worsening by the minute.

"Leave Angela here, and I'll let you walk away."

Ben pinpointed the direction of Drogan's voice, crept forward, corrected his aim an inch to the left and fired. He continued firing in regular increments from left to right until he'd made a one-hundred-eighty-degree arc.

By the time he finished, his ears were ringing. He didn't hear any sounds to indicate he'd hit Drogan, but at least the man had quit talking.

He backed his way out of the woods. The pinto was chomping at the grass, apparently unfazed by the noise in the trees.

"Did you hit him?"

"No, but I shut him up for a minute." He patted the horse, looked back the way they'd come, then forward into the woods. "Maybe we should return to Elizabethtown."

"Do you have any idea where he could be headed?"

"This is national forest land. He could have a hideout in here anywhere or he could be passing through, heading up to Bobcat Pass. From the direction he's taking, I'd put my money on the latter."

"Why?"

Ben rubbed the horse between the ears. He felt a restless urge to move quickly, but he knew the mare needed a minute.

"If he's still in this forest come daylight, we'll find him. One of the teams will have a working laptop. They'll contact regional. A full-fledged manhunt by daylight, and you know what that entails. He knows it too. No, the sensible thing to do is head for Bobcat Pass and get out."

"Does Drogan strike you as a sensible guy?" Somewhere in their flight, Dana had lost whatever she was using to hold back her hair. Now it fell down past her shoulders. She pushed it away.

"Not sensible, but not necessarily suicidal."

Dana grimaced, as if she'd tasted something bitter. "All right. We keep following then. I don't want him to slip away again."

"Dana, there's one other thing."

"Your arm?"

"Yeah." Ben needed to be truthful with her, wanted her to know their odds going in. "There's fever in it. If we haven't caught up with him in another hour, two at the most, we'll have to stop so you can look at it again."

She nodded, then shook her head. "I suppose you still want to drive."

"Hold her steady," he said. Grabbing the saddle horn with his good hand, he pulled himself up behind her, then pulled the pinto's head to the left, away from the forest.

"Where are we going?"

"There's a path to the north, if I remember correctly. Joe and I only came through here once, but we should be able to find it. I don't like being in the deep forest with him." He didn't tell her Drogan's horse had never shied when he was shooting, while he could barely get off a round without risking their lives. He needed a path, some space to maneuver.

Dana rode silently in the circle of his arms for a few minutes as they skirted the woods, found the path, then began the ascent. It was a five-thousand-foot elevation gain.

He prayed the mare was up to it.

Seventy

I t seemed to Dana as if she were riding through one of her nightmares. Every muscle ached with the steady clip-clop of the horse. She wanted to sink back against the solid warmth of Ben, but then she would remember her vow to maintain a professional distance.

Why had she made that vow? There had been some compelling reason, but her mind couldn't call it up as they rode the forest trail, chasing a madman who was intent on dismembering her.

She should have called Erin before she left. Should have told her how much she loved her one more time. Her mind snatched back from the thought as her hand had from the hot stove when she was a child.

"You're okay. I've got you." Ben's soft voice in her ear did nothing to calm her. "Try to relax into the saddle."

A stream they had been listening to finally curved near the path. The horse slowed, then stopped all together.

They could still make out Drogan's horse, a distant sound far off in the night.

"She wants a drink," Ben explained. He hopped off, then helped her down.

Dana's legs didn't want to hold her weight. It was as if they'd forgotten how.

"Takes a minute." Ben held on to her arms and peered down into her face.

"I'm okay. I was just a little—"

"Disoriented."

"Yeah."

Ben pulled the rifle from his pack. "I'll go on ahead in case he doubles back. You might want to walk it off." He looked at the mare. "Let her drink her fill. She still has a long way to go."

He walked down the trail a ways.

Dana watched him go. Her vision had adjusted to the darkness of the night. By the light of the half moon she was able to make out Ben's silhouette, and she marveled at the fact he carried the weight of their survival so easily. If she had a mirror to look in, she was sure she'd find her own shoulders bowed with the thoughts of all that could and had gone wrong.

She'd walked to the stream and was watching the water play over the stones and the moonlight reflect off its surface. Rubbing her eyes, she blinked and then peered into the darkness. She refused to believe what she was seeing. Then the horse moved toward her, nudged her side, and caught the scent.

Whinnying once, it moved away.

Dana grabbed its reins before it could run. Mimicking Ben's earlier gestures, she rubbed its neck and made soothing noises. She didn't dare turn her attention away, but she heard Ben's footsteps running back to where she tried to calm the horse.

"What happened?"

"Over there, by the stream. I thought it was..." She shook her head, walked the horse farther down the path. "Go and look. The horse saw it, caught the scent or something."

Before she could find the words, Ben had moved on to the stream. Dana turned the horse where she could keep an eye on Ben. He knelt by the carcass of the coyote, studied it a minute, then walked back to them.

"You okay?"

"Yes. Of course. But what could kill an animal that way?"

"Drogan, playing games."

"But how?"

"He might have had a trap. You can catch a coyote in a trap. Put fresh meat in it. Probably the coyote was dead already when he slit its throat." Climbing up into the saddle, he positioned his rifle, then reached down for Dana. "I'd feel better with you in the back this time."

Dana readjusted her pack before climbing on behind him. As they rode, she thought of a dozen reasons why Drogan would have left the coyote near the stream. None of them were good.

Seventy-one

The next sacrifice—that was how Ben thought of them, as Drogan's sacrifices—was a fawn. He'd brought it down with an arrow, probably the day before since the carcass was stiff. Where had he stored it? How had he known they would pass this way?

He left the carcass undisturbed the way Drogan has positioned it—head to the right side of the trail and the body to the left. There was no doubt as to who had done it.

He was relieved when Dana pressed her face into his back, refusing to look. The pinto tossed its head, but kept moving forward.

Steadily, they continued climbing, the stream and meadow falling away to their left. To their right it seemed the forest sloped more gradually, but Ben could hardly tell. His vision had adjusted, but he couldn't see far.

Which is why he nearly stumbled on what Drogan left in the middle of the trail.

He should have noticed the mare's nervousness.

Instead, he pushed her on until she refused to go any further.

"Why are we stopping?"

"I'm not sure."

Ben once again pulled the rifle and slipped to the ground. Ten steps revealed a large shape in their path—twenty showed it wasn't dead yet.

Walking back to Dana, he grabbed the horse's reins and moved her farther back down the path.

"Ben, what are you doing?"

He took off his jacket and threw it over the horse's head. "I need you to stand here, hold her reins, and keep her head covered."

"But what—"

"Trust me." He touched her face and then walked toward the mountain lion.

Somehow Drogan had managed to muzzle the beast and slit open its stomach. It was slowly bleeding out. The pitiful look in its eyes made Ben want to weep. He felt an icy calm settle over him, and he knew without a doubt he could kill Drogan if he ever had him in his scope again.

Any man who could do this was no longer a sane being. More importantly, he was capable of committing terrible atrocities. He was merely the shell of a person—less than a man, certainly less than this noble beast.

Ben walked to within three yards of the mountain lion, looked through his scope, and fired.

Then he bowed his head and waited for the final breath to leave the animal's body. Slinging the rifle over his shoulder, he walked back to Dana.

"What was it? Ben, what was it?" Her voice rose, and her eyes reminded him of a wild animal. He pulled his jacket off the horse, then wrapped his arms around his boss. Cradling her there, he prayed to God for her safety.

He knew with certainty now what he had suspected for some time. This wasn't only a mission. This was a battle.

He rubbed Dana's back to quiet her trembling. "We'll go around. Come on. We'll walk the horse."

She nodded and clasped his hand as they gave the path a wide berth.

Ben paid closer attention to the horse's behavior after that. If the mare hesitated, Ben stopped and listened. If the mare hurried forward, Ben gave her leave to do so. The animal had an instinct for survival unthwarted by the past or the future.

Ben estimated they'd made it halfway up the ascent when he called for a rest. He'd tried timing how often he heard Drogan, but his watch had stopped working with the EMP. He felt confident the man was still in front of them, traveling at roughly the same speed.

"The mare is starting to tire. Let's give her five minutes." He didn't add that he'd noticed Dana nodding off. He didn't mind her resting, but he sensed they were getting closer to a standoff.

He could barely move his left arm, and he was worried Dana would have to hold the reins or do the shooting. One way or the other, he was going to need her.

He caught her as she nearly fell out of the saddle.

"Long night," he murmured.

"Yeah. Think I'll stretch my legs… if it's safe."

He nodded, and she walked up the trail a few feet. Rubbing down the mare, Ben tied her lead rope to a low branch. He wished he could let her sleep, but knew it wasn't possible. "Rest, girl."

He looked up to where Dana stood at a bend in the path. Grabbing the rifle more out of habit than any sense of real danger, he walked slowly up to where she stood.

"How's the arm?" she asked.

"Stiff."

When she continued to study him, he admitted, "More than stiff."

"Can you use your fingers?"

"Yeah, but my movement is restricted. I'm having trouble bending at the elbow."

She stepped closer, began massaging his fingers, then worked her way slowly up his arm until he winced and drew away. "We're going to need to re-wrap it."

"I know."

"And get the shrapnel out," she reminded him.

"We can't stop that long."

She stepped closer, put a hand on his chest, and looked up into his face. "Ben, the fever means infection is spreading."

"Four more hours, then you can put me in the hospital with all the IVs you want." He met her gaze, thought of how he'd give his arm, right now, if it would guarantee her surviving Drogan.

The thought had no more occurred to him than he heard the mare. Her whimper was a low, ominous sound in the night. Then it was silent.

He turned and ran back down the path.

Seventy-two

D ana sank to the ground and then turned and vomited in the trees beside her.

The horse still kicked once more, then lay still. It was clear she was dead. The blood from her wound ran down the path, down the way they had come.

Ben knelt beside the animal.

She thought for a moment he would shoot it, like he had shot whatever else was in their path earlier. Then he seemed to realize that wouldn't be necessary.

He was at her side instantly, jerking her to her feet.

"What—"

He held his fingers to his lips, pointed back the way they had come. Raising his rifle, he aimed it down the trail and motioned for her to pull her Glock.

Back-to-back, they made their way up the trail to the bend they were at when they heard the horse cry out.

"How did Drogan get behind us?" Dana whispered.

"I don't know. We need to get in the woods where he can't see us." They backed in slowly, three yards, then five, finally fifteen. With no GPS and no radio contact, Dana was terrified of becoming lost.

Then she remembered the horse, the way Drogan had slit its throat, and the tremor started in her left hand. Being lost wasn't the worst thing that could happen to them.

After they had walked for half an hour, Ben stopped her. Pulling her close, he spoke in whispers.

"We'll move closer to the trail, but stay in the cover of the trees. To the west is a drop off, so we'll keep to the east side, where the slope is more gradual."

"What if Drogan is watching?"

Ben studied the trail. "He's only a man, Dana. He can't be everywhere. If he's on the trail, he won't be able to see us. If he's in the woods, we'll hear him."

Dana nodded and bowed her head near his. "How close are we to Bobcat Pass?"

"Maybe another seven miles, ten at the most." As if reading her mind, he added. "We might be slower on foot, but it will be harder for him to track us."

Then he laced the fingers of his injured hand in hers, trusting her to shoot with her left. She smiled at his confidence, and they moved on up the slope, toward Bobcat Pass.

She thought she was merely growing more tired until she had to reach for a tree limb to pull herself up. The slope was definitely increasing.

"We need to skirt a ravine here. Do you want to double back to the trail?"

She shook her head, then leaned back and tilted her head up to eye the path. The slope rose and curved to the right around a stand of trees before crossing their path. At that point it looked like easy walking for the space of half a mile, their route running almost parallel with the hiking trail.

Ben indicated with his right arm where she should cut through the trees, cross the path, and head back into the trees directly across from them. It was the only way across the ravine.

"I'll stay here and cover you," he whispered. "Once you're across, take up position in the far trees. Then I'll cross."

"Okay." She smiled at him, tried to look confident even though her legs were shaking.

If she could make it to the clearing, she'd be fine. If anything moved in the clearing, Ben would shoot it. The trees had her worried. They were a dark, ominous place. Recollections from her childhood merged with images from the trail.

"Ready, boss?" Ben adjusted the rifle in his good arm.

"Of course." She wiped her palms on her black, camouflage pants and moved off, away from Ben.

The trees immediately closed in around her. She pushed her doubts and fears away, focused on charging through.

"Ben's behind me. Ben's behind me." The words became a mantra as she whispered them, but doubt soon overwhelmed her. What if Ben wasn't behind her? What if Drogan had already found and murdered him? She wouldn't have heard the slice of a knife.

The idea paralyzed her. She stopped, temporarily disoriented. A branch moved, and she brought up her gun.

Scanning left, then right, she saw nothing. She turned in a circle, trying to find Ben or the noise that had startled her. A night bird flew to her right, moving one branch then another. She followed its progress through the sight of her gun until she was looking at the clearing.

Lowering the weapon slightly, she continued walking, ignoring the branches that caught in her hair. Finally, she broke through and drew a deep breath.

She lowered the Glock and increased her pace. No doubt that was her mistake. She was watching the distant stand of trees, worrying she'd left Ben waiting too long. Later, she would remember looking down briefly. In an instant, she saw signs of freshly dug dirt. Evidence he'd been there. But her mind registered it all a fraction of a second too late.

She felt the ground shift, tried to grab something, but there was nothing to catch hold of. She was in a meadow.

Then the ground gave way, and she was falling.

The stars were above her, and below her was an abyss.

Seventy-three

B en was running before Dana hit the bottom of the
ravine. He had watched in horror as the ground began
to give away, tried in vain to call out to her.

He prayed as he ran.

The climb down seemed to take an eternity. When he
reached her, she was lying on her back and beginning to
come around.

"Don't move, Dana. Honey, lie still." He ran his hands
up and down her legs, wondering how she could have
survived such a fall without breaking anything, knowing it
would have been a miracle. He was checking her left arm
when she came to and gasped.

Her amber eyes were the most beautiful thing he'd ever
seen. If they were the last thing he saw, he'd die a happy
man.

"What happened?"

"You—"

"He—"

Ben tried a third time and finally gave up, the emotions too strong as he sank his head and allowed relief to wash over him.

Dana's fingers in his hair brought him back. He wiped at his face and stroked her hair.

"You look happy to see me," she whispered.

"Yeah. I guess I am."

She winced again as she leaned on her left arm.

"Let me help." He moved to her right side, supporting her as she sat up, then retrieved a bottle of water from his pack. Her pack was covered with leaves and branches, and the outer pockets were torn, but it was holding together. "I think your pack took the brunt of the fall."

"Tell my arm that." Dana bent it at the elbow, but when she tried to move her wrist, she looked at Ben and shook her head.

He ran his hand gently over it. "I can't feel a break, but you probably have a nasty sprain." Opening his pack, he pulled out an ACE bandage and fashioned a sling. Positioning it over her head, he brushed the hair out of her face. "It's a miracle—"

"I don't want to hear about your miracles." She practically spat the words at him as she holstered her weapon. She'd managed to protect it in her fall, but the cost had been the injury to her arm.

"Look at the fall you survived."

Dana shook her head, struggling to stand up as he spoke. "Look at us, Ben."

He stepped back from her anger.

"What else could go wrong tonight? All of my teams are scattered. We have mutilated animals at every turn. You're injured, and we'll be lucky if you can use your arm come sunrise."

"Luck has nothing to do with it."

"You're right, because we don't have any luck. If we did, we'd still have our horse. Instead, we're walking, which is why I stepped into his trap."

Ben's head snapped up at her last word. "The shelf looked solid. Maybe last year's rains wore away the shelf underneath."

"It was a trap. I saw the shovel marks, but I saw them too late. Somehow he knew we were going to cross there. How did he know?"

Ben stepped near her in the darkness, close enough to see past her anger to her fear. "What are you talking about?"

"Before the shelf gave way, I looked down and saw freshly dug dirt. My falling was no accident. It was a trap. This entire night is a trap."

Ben walked over to where he had dropped his rifle, picked it up, and inspected the barrel to see if he'd damaged it on his slide down.

"Let's go."

"Where?" she demanded.

"What do you mean where?"

"He made sure we'd end up in this ravine, so wherever we go is a where Drogan wants us to be. Do we want to keep following his plan?"

Dana's eyes reminded him of the mountain lion, wild and without hope.

Ben pointed to the steep banks on both sides. "Can you climb out of this with your wrist sprained? Because honestly I don't think I can with my shoulder injury. So we can sit here and wait for him to shoot us, or we can head north in this ravine and hope there's a way out."

When she still didn't move, he walked back over to where she stood. "Dana, we can't stay here and wait for him to kill us."

"Tell me why, Ben. Tell me why God allows men like him to live."

"I don't know why, but I do know this isn't over yet." He knew his answer wasn't good enough. The need to move was suddenly so strong he almost picked her up and ran with her.

"Yeah. Okay." Dana shrugged the pack over her right shoulder, refusing any help, and followed him.

She didn't ask any more questions, which was a good thing. He'd proven that he'd run out of answers.

Seventy-four

T he walls of the ravine grew steeper and more narrow as they walked, which was about what she expected. Dana moved closer to Ben—not out of fear, though she was terrified. She didn't want to lose him in the darkness. She was exhausted. If she lost him, she knew she would sit down. Sitting would be the same as signing her own death warrant.

As they plodded along, she admitted to herself she wasn't ready to die. Tears fell down her cheeks, and she wiped them away.

Ben's talk of miracles infuriated her.

How dare he?

She'd prayed for miracles when she was ten. All it had gotten her was orphaned. She would not call out for help again. God had abandoned her once. Why give him a second chance?

Erin's face swam into her mind, and she pushed it away. She should have called. She'd put it off the last few nights, knowing her sister would ask how her new romance was going. Looking at Ben's slumped shoulders, she regretted so many things—her bitter words not the least of them.

And what if God were to give her another chance?

She flung the thought away before it could fully form.

Foxhole faith. If there were a God, he should have let her die in the bottom of the ravine. She was no better than all the others—proclaiming no faith, then converting in her hour of need.

Except she didn't want to die. She wanted to live.

Ben stopped so suddenly she ran into the back of him.

"Something's wrong."

Dana's heart hammered so hard she could feel it in her throat.

"Stay here."

"No."

"Dana—"

"No. I'm going with you."

"I need to look—"

"I'm going with you."

All pretense of supervisor and employee was gone—had been for hours. She pulled her Glock out at the same moment he raised his rifle, although neither of them knew if it would fire straight.

They crept forward side-by-side, not even an inch separating them.

The trees thinned out. Ben pointed up, and Dana could see an entire canopy of stars for the first time in an hour. The walls of the ravine had spread out, not far, but enough for her to see they were entering some sort of clearing. Moving toward the edge of the woods, they saw what might have been a cave at one time.

In fact, they'd walked into a dead end. Built into the cave-like opening was a cabin, nearly identical to the one at Lake Abiquiu. She'd barely had time to process the thought when the sound of hoof beats reached them.

"He's coming," Ben said. "We need to get out of this clearing."

And then they ran to the cabin, because there was nowhere else to go.

Dana almost couldn't walk inside, she was shaking so badly.

Ben pushed her through the door, shut it silently, and moved to the window. "Dana, I need you to watch out this window while I check the room for explosives."

When she didn't move, he glanced back at her. "Dana?"

She didn't speak, couldn't have, but she did manage to walk to the window. She tried to raise her pistol, but her hand was shaking too badly.

"Here." He raised it for her, rested it against the frame of the glass. "You see anything, start shooting."

She swallowed and nodded once. Supporting the gun with her injured hand, she pulled the slide back with her right.

"Good girl."

She heard him moving around the room, shoving furniture aside, opening and closing the few cabinets in the kitchen. When he walked into the pantry, she cringed.

His boots rang against the floor as he walked back out into the single room, down toward the bathroom, and back into the main room again.

Finally, he squatted beside her at the window.

She glanced at him, then gazed back out into the darkness.

"There's no secret room, Dana. No sign of explosives. It looks like the other cabin, but it's not."

He put his hand over the top of the Glock, waited for her to ease her finger off the trigger. "Go and sit at the table. I've got this."

Seventy-five

I t was three in the morning when Drogan made contact. Ben knew because there was an old watch in one of the drawers. Surprised to find it ticking, he'd strapped it on.

Dana was still at the table, bottle of water in front of her. She hadn't spoken since he'd taken her position at the window. She hadn't moved in thirty minutes.

He heard the horse first, but couldn't see it.

Raising the Glock, he stepped away from the window. "Get down," he warned her.

Dana dropped to the floor like a stone falling to the bottom of a well.

A bottle hit the front porch. Ben ran outside, intending to knock it off before it exploded. That was when he saw the note wrapped around it.

Seventy-six

D ana stared at the bottle that Ben brought in. His gaze
never left her face as he tugged the note free,
smoothed it out, and set it on the table. The he switched on
the flashlight he'd found, though he cupped the light in his
hands. No use making them a easier target than they already
were.

Together, they looked down at the words.

The lettering was identical to the note they'd found in
the backpack four weeks ago. As if it would matter whether
there were fingerprints now, Drogan had again carefully cut
out letters from magazine pages to compose his message.
Which meant he had composed the message before he'd met
them in Elizabethtown. He'd carefully planned the entire
night.

It was easier for Dana to focus on those similarities
between the notes than it was to comprehend the words the
letters formed.

"Dana—" Ben put a hand on her shoulder, but she jerked away.

"Don't. Please don't say anything."

She stared down at the words, her death warrant. Essentially, she was reading her death warrant.

I'LL BE BACK FOR HER AT SUNRISE.

NO CONDITIONS. NO TERMS. NO WAY OUT.

She felt the blackness descend around her. Why did it have to end like this? And what could she have done differently?

Ben stood up, walked across the kitchen, and poured some of their water into a small pot. Turning on the stove, he set the pot on the front burner.

She watched him for a moment, then stared back down at the note.

He would kill her either way.

"I'm going with him," she said.

"No. You're not." Ben placed the med kit on the table between them.

"He'll either kill me in the morning, or kill us both in the morning." She couldn't look into his eyes, couldn't bear the depth of love she saw there. "Ben, do this for me. He'll let you through. I know he will."

When he didn't answer, she finally turned her eyes back to him.

"I'm not leaving, Dana. Nothing you can say will make me go. Do you understand?"

Slowly, she nodded.

"Now I need you to change my dressing."

It took her longer, working with only one hand. His wound was red and hot to her touch. As she removed the old bandage, it began to bleed again.

"I need to cut the shrapnel out."

"I'm afraid if you cut it deeply enough to remove the debris, I won't be able to use that arm at all when I need to. Clean it superficially, as best you can, then rewrap it."

His face lost all color when she applied the warm compress to the worst part of the wound. The muscle along the upper part of his arm had turned a dark purple, and the larger of the cuts began to ooze puss as well as blood as soon as she removed the compress.

They'd turned off the flashlight to save its batteries. She was working by the light of a single oil lamp they'd found on a shelf. When she'd suggested they should keep the room dark, he'd shrugged.

"He knows we're here. What difference does it make?"

She rewrapped the wound, and Ben pulled a fresh shirt out of his pack. It provided at least one more layer of protection.

Dana wondered if they'd live long enough to need it.

Then there was nothing to do but sit and face her regrets. Suddenly, she couldn't remember why it had been so imperative to move away from Erin. Had she really thought the ghosts of their past was stronger than the bond they shared?

And what of the man sitting across from her?

He'd stepped into her life, saved her more than once, offered her his love. She'd rejected him at every step.

Because she was his boss?

There had been a more burning reason, one that scraped at her soul. Watching him in the gas light, she wondered if she'd ever known anyone who possessed a more peaceful spirit.

Did she even believe they each had a spirit? And if she didn't, would she see her mother again? Would she see Erin?

She stood up and began pacing around the room and then worried Drogan would see her. She sat back down.

She'd never considered dying before thirty.

And she'd never expected to live to see thirty.

How was it she had come to set her standard in life so low?

Looking out at the darkness, she realized she wasn't surprised it had come to this. She'd been living without hope for a very long time.

Seventy-seven

B en didn't know what to say to Dana, so he prayed. He prayed for wisdom. He prayed for guidance. Mostly, he prayed for God to intercede.

He knew he couldn't beat Drogan alone.

Finally, he stood up and looked for oil to clean the rifle. No doubt he'd gotten dirt in the barrel when he'd clambered down the ravine after Dana. The fool thing might not work if he'd jammed debris in there.

He wasn't surprised to find a can of gun oil and some old rags under the kitchen sink.

Sitting back down across from Dana, he went to work disassembling and cleaning the rifle.

He didn't have a plan yet, but he knew what he wasn't going to do. He wasn't going to turn tail and run. He wasn't going to leave the woman he loved. And he wasn't going to allow Drogan to walk away, not if he could do anything about it.

So he cleaned the rifle, and he waited. The hands on the watch he'd borrowed read ten minutes until four.

He glanced occasionally at Dana, longed to pull her into his arms and tell her how much he cared for her.

Patience, he heard his granddad whisper.

Course Granddad hadn't known he'd be sitting in a madman's cabin with a deadline fast approaching.

God knew though.

Ben assembled the rifle, checked the sight, and tore it back down again.

God knew.

Seventy-eight

D ana glanced over at Ben, thought of Erin, and swallowed her pride.

Walking across the cabin floor, she squatted down in front of him. He was cleaning his rifle—again. The oil lamp threw plenty of shadows on the ceiling though it provided very little real light. She wondered how he could see well enough to work. But then she imagined he could probably clean the M24 in the dark. No doubt he had while he was in Iraq.

He set the cloth and rifle aside when she squatted in front of his chair. He didn't touch her. He hadn't touched her since she'd screamed at him earlier. She had herself to thank for the distance he kept.

She yearned for the feel of his hand in hers, the touch of his arm across her shoulder, even a casual brush of his fingers through her hair. But she didn't know how to ask for those comforts.

"What is it, Dana?"

She looked up into his face and swallowed. "Do you think he's waiting out there?"

"Yes, I do." Ben's eyes were calm. Had they ever been anything else?

Dana tensed, felt her head nod up and down, but something inside her cracked like a giant tree going down. Her mind flashed back on the old pine she'd run to so many years ago. Like every time before, she pushed the image away.

"So this was all a trap?"

Ben nodded, started to reach for her, then pushed his hands down to his side. "Yes, it was a trap. Don't be afraid, Dana."

"How can you say that?" It took every ounce of strength to force the words around the knot in her throat.

"Because we're going to make it through this."

She searched his face, saw he believed what he'd said, and stood. Moving to the other side of the small oak table, she sat in the chair. Ben once again picked up the rag and resumed cleaning the rifle.

"Do you have a plan?"

"I don't have a good one."

"Oh."

A whippoorwill's song echoed from the woods. Dana wondered how life could continue in all its normalcy when her life was in all likelihood about to end. And had she ever actually lived it?

"I've always been afraid," she said.

"Most people are."

"You're not."

Ben had been reaching for the bottle of oil. At her words, he stopped and stared at her. "Is that what you think?"

He snorted, poured a little oil on the rag, and continued cleaning the barrel of the rifle. The flicker of light from the lantern reflected off the gleam of the metal. "Every man and woman I've ever known is afraid at least some of the time, yours truly included."

"Of what?" Dana reached behind her for her hair and wound it nervously around and through her fingers.

Now Ben didn't meet her gaze, but focused more intently on the work he could do in complete darkness. "Missed chances. Maybe I could have said or done something differently when we were at Cimarron Canyon. I'm afraid of letting you down and of people dying because of my mistakes."

Dana looked across the tiny cabin and blinked away the tears that threatened to fall again. "But you're not afraid of dying."

"No." Ben sighed. Finally satisfied with the rifle, he set it gently aside. "I'm not afraid of dying."

Silence enveloped them, covered them like the corner they'd been backed into.

"Why?" Dana asked.

"Because He promised to be with us, Dana. My mother used to send me that verse from the Bible in every care package. God tells us, *Do not fear, for I am with you.* Every month I'd get the package. Every month the same verse. Finally, it sank in. And sometimes, yeah, I'd still be afraid. But I never really doubted whether He was with me. Even if I'd died over there, I know He would have been with me."

"I don't want to die tonight." Confessing the words split her heart wide open.

"This life isn't supposed to last forever. The next life is the one that lasts for eternity." He sounded older, wiser than he should have been for a man his age. When he looked up at her though, the old smile had returned. "Not that I'm hurrying it, mind you. I'd hoped to catch a few more fish, maybe settle down..."

He didn't finish the rest of the thought, didn't have to. They'd discussed it often enough.

"It might almost be worth dying if we could take Drogan out on the way with us, but to think he could get away. It's so unfair." Dana hugged her arms around herself, sat stiffly in the hard wooden chair. "I should have stayed with Erin. I want to see her again, Ben."

He lowered his head, and she thought he wouldn't answer her. When he did, his voice was gentler than she'd ever heard. He leaned across the table and looked straight into her eyes, all the way into her soul. "Then pray, Dana. Pray with all your heart."

"But it doesn't do any good when I pray." The tears fell like rain. She didn't even try to wipe at them. "I tried, remember? He doesn't hear me. You pray, Ben. I'll do whatever He wants. But your God doesn't hear me. You tell Him I need to see her again. Tell Him it isn't fair."

She was sobbing uncontrollably now. She didn't realize he'd stood and crossed the tiny space between them. Suddenly his arms were around her, and he had pulled her to her feet. He whispered into her ear, rocking her like a child.

"He does hear you, sweetheart. I promise you He does. I wouldn't lie to you. He wouldn't lie to you. And He promised to hear your prayers."

"But what about before?"

"What did you pray? Can you remember? Think back, sweetheart. I know you don't want to, but try to remember that night. When your mother died, what did you pray?"

She nuzzled into Ben's shirt and allowed her mind to remember, to go all the way back to the night she'd tried so hard to forget. "I woke up, and she was screaming. He was dru... dru... drinking."

She shuddered as her mind supplied the images she'd pushed away for eighteen years. "I grabbed Erin and her bear. We ran, ran from the house into the woods."

"And you prayed as you ran?"

She nodded against his chest, the night sounds around the cabin merging with the memories of that fateful night so long ago.

"What did you pray, Dana?"

"She was so heavy. I thought I'd drop her, and he'd catch us."

"But you didn't."

Dana shook her head, pulling in a deep, shaky breath. "No. We made it to the big pine tree. I set Erin down and turned to go back and help Mama. But he was there. He'd followed us."

"What happened then?"

Dana had no more tears, but the memories continued to play like a bad movie that wouldn't stop no matter how much she wanted it to. "He said I couldn't help her. Then he reached for us, but he fell and hit his head. When he didn't move, I picked up Erin and ran back to the house again."

"How did you manage to carry her back? You could hardly make it to the tree."

Dana looked up at him, pausing the replay of memories in her mind. "I don't know. That part is a blur. I remember picking her back up and running like the wind. I was terrified he would wake up and come after us, but he didn't. That's where the police found him later, still passed out cold."

Ben took her by the hand and led her back to the chair. "Sit down for a minute. I'll get you some water." Pulling the bottle from their pack, he uncapped it and handed it to her.

She took a small sip, then another.

"You think God helped me, don't you?"

"What do you think, sweetheart?"

"I don't know." She wiped at her face, pulled her hair back behind her shoulders. "I was so afraid for Erin. She was only three. I remember now. I kept praying I wouldn't drop her, and I didn't."

Ben smiled, but it was tinged with such sadness that Dana reached out and touched his face.

"Why did my mother have to die?"

"I don't know, Dana. There are evil people in this world. I'm sorry, so sorry, you experienced such violence as a child." Ben moved his chair in front of hers and sat down. Their knees touched. He pulled her hand into his lap. "I don't have all the answers. Only God does. I think though that as you were running away your mother's last prayers were for your safety and for Erin's safety."

Dana was silent for a moment, considering Ben's words. They were like a pearl found among a stack of family letters. "What makes you think she was praying for us?"

"Because of your name."

"I don't understand."

"I was telling my mother about you." Ben grinned rather sheepishly. "I didn't know how to tell you that I loved you, especially when you weren't speaking to me. So I told her about you. She told me your name, Dana, means bright gift of God. I think your mother was a believer, honey. I think with her last breath she was praying for you and Erin."

Seventy-nine

B en placed his rifle beside the cabin door. He checked the pockets of his Kevlar vest for extra ammo, though he knew it was there. He'd put it there five minutes before. He was stalling. The digital display on his watch read four-thirty.

He needed to go if he had any chance of being in position before the sky lightened.

Dana hadn't spoken in the last ten minutes. She sat there, staring into the night. The tears had dried on her cheeks where they'd fallen.

For a moment, he'd thought they might have broken through her fears. She had looked at him with such hope, but then she'd pulled her hand away and drawn into herself again. She'd been silent since then. He'd gone over his plan, as simple as it was. She had nodded and stared at him with eyes open wide, seeming to comprehend both the odds and that it was their one chance.

364

All he could do now was pray and use the skills God had given him to protect her.

He walked slowly across the room. His boots felt as if they'd been filled with lead. He stopped in front of her. She didn't even raise her eyes.

"Dana, I'm going now."

She continued staring into the darkness.

"Sweetheart, look at me." When she shook her head, he tugged her gently to her feet. "I want you to look at me."

He'd always been prepared for battle, had fought so many he had truly lost count. Looking into her tear-filled eyes nearly undid him, caused him to question walking out into the darkness.

Then he remembered what was lurking there. Knew in his heart Drogan would be coming for them, for her.

"I have to go, sweetheart. Do you know what you need to do?"

She nodded.

"I want to hear you say it."

When her gaze found his, he saw some of the old strength come back into them. "Leave the light on so he'll think we're both still here. Stay out of sight, in the corner. Keep the Glock close. You'll circle around and come up on him from behind."

"He'll attack just before the sun comes up. I'm sure of it. You won't have long to wait." Ben moved his hands to her face, longed to kiss her. "I wish I could stay with you."

She nodded, as if she understood.

He touched his forehead to hers, then pulled her into his arms. "I'll be right back," he whispered.

He didn't look back. If he had, he might not have found the strength to pick up the rifle and walk out the cabin door and into the night.

Eighty

As soon as the cabin door closed, Dana collapsed into the hard, wooden chair. The trembling started in her arm and spread through her entire body. Strangely, she didn't cry. Perhaps her tears were all spent.

She clasped her arms around her stomach and stared at the far wall of the cabin.

"This isn't fair," she whispered to herself. The words brought little comfort though, and the trembling didn't stop. She wondered if stress could bring on a seizure.

Maybe she should try walking around, but she couldn't find the strength to stand.

Memories of the photos in Drogan's first cabin came back to her in vivid color. Why her? Why had he fixated on her? Because she looked like Angela Dixon? It was not fair. Her whole life she had spent running, and she was suddenly, overwhelmingly tired.

"Then pray, sweetheart." Ben's voice came to her so softly, so gently, she turned to see if he had reentered the cabin.

Of course, he hadn't. She was still completely alone. What she saw instead must have been a result of the flickering light from the oil lamp, or so she told herself. Pushing herself up from the table, she walked across the room and stood in front of the crossbeams over the old, stone fireplace.

It looked as if it hadn't been used in years. The ashes from past fires were cold, sooty. Her eyes traveled up the bricks and mortar to where the beams met over the center of the wall.

They formed a perfect cross.

Surely, it was a coincidence of construction, but did she believe in coincidences?

She reached up with her hand and traced the place where the two beams came together.

They were actually no different from the other beams on the wall. They weren't raised or marked in anyway. But in the dim light, she could see the outline of the cross, as if it were carved there.

She walked around the room, thinking it would fade when viewed from a different angle. It never did.

"Pray, Dana." Ben's voice melted, became her mother's, and then another—one even stronger, more loving, more kind than she could have ever imagined.

"I don't know how," she whispered. And now the tears flowed freely. "I want to, Lord. But I don't know how. I loved her so much, and I should have stayed with her. I should have stayed."

She didn't realize the moment she dropped to her knees. She barely heard the words falling from her lips. "Help me, Lord. I can't do this alone anymore. Show me, and I will do it. Please just show me."

And then, she knew. There were no voices. The beams on the wall still looked like a cross, but they didn't glow with holy fire. And no angels sang that she could hear. But there was no doubt in Dana's heart, because she knew.

She didn't have to get through this night alone. And she hadn't survived that night so long ago alone either. God had been with her all along, just as he had been with Erin and with her mother. As the weight of guilt was lifted from her heart, she felt as though a stone the size of Gibraltar lifted from her back.

Wiping the tears from her cheeks, she rose to her feet, walked to the table, and placed her provisions in the remaining pack. Securing the Glock in her holster, she glanced one last time at the cross over the fireplace, then she stepped out into the predawn light.

Eighty-one

B en had taken up a position three hundred meters to the north side of the cabin. He was watching the clearing and front porch through his scope. Since the cabin was built into a hill facing east, Drogan had to attack from the north, east, or south. If he came from the north, Ben would hear him before he saw him. If he came from the east or the south, he'd see him before he entered the clearing. Such was the plan anyway.

The question was why. Why would he attack when he was outnumbered?

Because Ben and Dana were tired. Drogan had been hunting Dana for too long, and he knew that she was unnerved.

They were low on provisions. Drogan was planning to catch them at their weakest moment, which should be right now.

Right when Dana crept out the door.

Ben nearly fell out of the tree he'd positioned himself in. He'd specifically told her to stay inside, and he was confident she'd understood. So what was she doing?

Looking through his scope, he knew immediately something had happened. Though she still looked tired, Dana was moving with confidence. She had on her Kevlar vest and wore the pack of extra supplies. She also had the Glock gripped firmly in both hands.

Something had told her to move.

Ben scanned the clearing again and saw nothing. Dana crept to the east, toward the lightening sky and into the trees.

"Good girl," he whispered. By moving toward the glare of the sun, perhaps Drogan wouldn't see her. Or so Ben prayed.

He couldn't move now without risking his location, so he kept an eye on her position and continued to watch for Drogan. The situation might have changed, but their objective was the same. And with any luck, Drogan would think they were both still waiting inside the cabin.

Eighty-two

D ana didn't stop to question why she was moving steadily into the bright side of the woods. The confusion and doubt she'd lived with for the past eighteen years had been replaced by a deep calm.

She'd need to ask Ben about that as soon as they took care of Drogan. And they would take care of him.

She took up her position four feet within the canopy of the woods beneath a tall pine tree, but still within the glare of the sun. The irony wasn't lost on her as she leaned back against it and waited. Waiting wasn't something she had to do for long though. A twig snapped a hundred meters to her right. She turned her head without moving her body and found herself staring straight at Chance Drogan.

He was in a crouch, moving slowly toward the cabin. In his right hand was a detonator, and he smiled, actually smiled as he pushed the button.

The cabin exploded at the exact moment Dana raised her Glock. She never took her eyes off her target.

She did hesitate though. For one second she thought about taking the head shot. She wanted to. Instant death and the end to so much suffering—for him and for others.

Except that decision wasn't hers to make. She lowered her sight and aimed for the center of gravity as she'd been trained. He turned at the last second, and the bullet hit his left shoulder, propelling him backward.

She lowered her weapon as he fell. Walked to him and kicked the gun out of his reach.

Drogan's pale, blue eyes were open, staring up at her. Lying there on the ground, he looked exactly like what he was—a bitter, old man. He tried to speak, but no words came out. Dana kept her gun trained on him and waited for Ben.

Eighty-three

B en scrambled out of the tree as soon as pieces of the cabin stopped flying through the air. Gunshots had sounded from Dana's position. He skirted the clearing, ran toward her, and prayed he would get there in time.

He stopped a hundred meters off. Raising his rifle, he looked through the scope, prepared to take the shot if he could locate Drogan. All he saw though was Dana.

Dana alive.

Dana standing with her gun drawn, pointed toward the ground.

Dana looking saddened, but resolute.

He lowered his rifle and ran the rest of the distance.

As he entered the east woods, he called out to her. "Are you okay?"

"Yes, but he's not."

Ben placed the rifle on the ground next to Dana, then unzipped the pack, pulling out an emergency medical kit. "Just the single round?"

"Yes. His gun's over there." She nodded with her head in the direction the cabin had been. "I don't know if he had a backup weapon."

"I'm sure he does. Keep your weapon on him a little longer."

Ben snapped on a pair of surgical gloves from the med kit, then knelt beside Drogan and checked him for weapons. He discarded two pistols and a knife. Rolling the man over, he found another revolver in a paddle holster. The entire time, Drogan said nothing, though once he did glance from Dana to Ben, then stared up at the trees.

"Move his weapons and ours to the edge of the clearing. I'm going to need you to help me with his wound, and I don't want to worry about the firearms."

"What if—"

"He's lost too much blood, and there's two of us. Hurry."

While she did as he asked, he cut away Drogan's jacket and shirt.

"Why wasn't he wearing a vest?" Dana asked as she knelt beside him.

"I suppose he didn't expect to get shot."

Drogan's eyes locked with Ben's.

"Am I right, Chance? We weren't supposed to get close enough to deliver a shot. You kill from a distance, so you don't need a vest." Ben worked quickly, applying a field dressing to the wound.

Drogan didn't answer, but then Ben hadn't expected him to.

"The shot is a clean one. I saw an exit wound when I pulled his backup pistol."

Dana nodded and handed him more tape as he secured the dressing.

"We can't stay here."

"They'll see that explosion for miles. I expect someone will come to us. Hand me the morphine."

Drogan began to struggle as Dana reached for the syringe.

"What's wrong, Chance? You want to be awake for this part?" Ben sat back on his haunches and stared at the man he'd been chasing since he'd arrived in New Mexico. "Or were you actually thinking you could still get away?"

Drogan seemed about to speak, licked his lips, then tried again. All that came out was a croak.

"Give him some water, Dana."

Ben thought a change had come over her, but when she uncapped the water and held it to Drogan's lips, he was sure of it. There was sadness in her expression, as if she were looking at some broken thing she didn't know how to fix. But the anger and fear were gone.

Drogan drank two swallows, then pushed the water away with his right hand.

"Nam," he said. "Can't stand the stuff… ever since Nam."

Ben sat back, recapped the morphine, and placed it in the med kit. "All right. Have it your way."

Drogan stared at Dana as she placed the water back in their pack. Confusion clouded his eyes, turning them almost translucent.

"Angie?" he asked. "Angela?"

She turned and looked at him. "No, Mr. Drogan. I'm not Angela."

They stayed there, no one speaking, Drogan slipping into a light sleep. When the sound of an emergency chopper filled the air, Dana glanced at Ben.

"I'll stay," Ben hollered over the roar of its engine.

He watched her walk out into the sunlight. It was like watching a fawn take its first steps. She looked so strong to him and so beautiful. Something told him he was watching a new beginning.

Eighty-four

The second helicopter returned them to Elizabethtown where Ben's truck had been repaired. A paramedic cleaned Ben's wound and put a fresh bandage over it. They were offered a ride in an ambulance, but both chose to accept basic first aid with a promise to check in at the hospital as soon as they reached Taos. They spent the day helping the crew gather evidence, though proving Drogan's guilt wouldn't be a problem. Dana followed procedures though. They'd been drilled into her, and she wasn't one to question her training. By the end of the day, she was more than ready to accept a ride with Ben back to Taos.

As they drove toward town, Dana ran her hand across the leather seat. She wondered if it would be her last time to ride in Ben's truck. Something told her things would be changing between them. She didn't know if he would be leaving or she would be, or maybe they would both stay and things would be different.

She didn't dare hope he would confess his love again. A girl only received so many chances.

The peace she had found in the cabin hadn't left her though. Her faith was new, but it didn't wobble. God would show her the way.

"You're awfully quiet over there." Ben turned down the Clapton cassette and glanced her way.

"Am I?"

"Yes, you are. Not sleeping though. Normally, Clapton makes you sleep."

"Guess I'm not in a sleeping mood."

He seemed to consider her reply, then switched hands on the steering wheel, grimacing as he used the injured arm to drive. "You're different, Dana."

"I am?" She cornered herself between the leather seat and the door. That corner was starting to feel like home. She'd miss it. "How so?"

"Sassier, for one thing."

"I didn't think that was possible."

"See? Exactly what I mean." He ran his hand through the curls that had grown back at his neckline. "Something happened after I left the cabin this morning. I told you to stay put, but you didn't."

"True."

"So something did happen."

Dana smiled at him. He reminded her of a dog with a bone.

"Now there you go. Instead of arguing with me, like you normally would, you're just smiling like, like—"

"Like you're right?" she asked softly.

"Yeah."

"You are right." She ran her hand across the leather upholstery again. Tried to imagine what Ben's grandfather was like and how the Montana mountains looked when the sun rose over them. "I did do what you said, Ben."

"But—"

"You told me to pray, and I did. At first I thought I couldn't. Then…" She thought of the cross in the cabin that no longer existed. Decided to save that story for another time, if they ever had another time. "Well, I didn't really know how, but I just talked to God. Like you talk to me. And suddenly, I could remember my mama praying with me when I was a little girl, and it wasn't so hard. The scars I've tried to keep hidden, well, they just seemed to fade away."

She looked out at the mountains, turning a majestic purple in the setting sun. Then she looked back at Ben, and she waited.

"That's it?"

"What more do you need to hear, Marshall?"

It was his turn to be speechless, which she rather enjoyed. She let him flounder for a few minutes. Then she reached across the seat and covered his hand with hers.

"That isn't it, actually. I don't know how to explain what happened, and I don't want to minimize it by saying it wrong. There weren't any lights or angels or voices. Nothing like that. But it was as if this unbearable weight was lifted off my shoulders. Suddenly, I knew I was forgiven for whatever I'd done wrong eighteen years ago—"

"Dana, you didn't do anything wrong."

She cocked her head, considered his words, and shrugged. "Maybe you're right. I don't think it really matters now. What matters is the future."

Ben laced his fingers into hers.

Neither said anything for a few miles, and Dana went back to studying the landscape. Though it was harder to do so with Ben's thumb tracing a pattern on the back of her hand.

"Wow," he finally said.

She grinned at him. "I know. That's what I thought."

They passed a sign that read, SCENIC OVERLOOK AHEAD. Ben signaled and pulled off.

"Feel like sightseeing, Marshall?"

"Actually, I do." He parked the car in a space where they could watch the final moments of the sun setting over the mountains.

It reminded her of the night at Cimarron Canyon. Then the voice in her heart reminded her hope lay in the future, not the past.

She turned and looked at Ben, and when she did he pulled her into his arms.

"I thought you wanted to watch the sunset."

"I do," he said, brushing back her hair.

"It's that direction." She nodded toward the front of the truck.

"Uh-huh. I can see it in your eyes."

"What a beautiful thing to say, Ben."

"You could say something beautiful back." He kissed her gently on the lips, and she felt hope rise up in her heart like a nightingale in flight.

"What would you like me to say?"

"That you'll marry me."

"I will," she whispered, surprised to find she'd been hoping, even praying, that he would ask. She didn't know when she had begun to love Ben Marshall, but she was sure that what they shared was true enough and pure enough to last a lifetime.

They sat there in the truck, long after the sun had set and the moon had risen. They spoke of how the calm she felt was normal and how it wouldn't pass with the newness of her faith. They shared their dreams for a home and maybe, someday, children.

Mostly though, they looked out the window and watched the stars come out.

And they wished on them.

Both confident their biggest wish, their deepest heart's desires, had already been granted.

The End

Discussion Questions

1. Ben feels that God has directed him into the path of Dana Jacobs, but he doesn't know why. He does believe that "God will reveal His hand, but not until God is ready." What similar moments have you had in your life? Waiting is never easy. What did you do to deal with the time in between?

2. In Chapter 24, Ben and Dana go rock climbing—definitely an activity that requires trust between people. How does the image of Dana leaning back in the harness to descend the rock reflect our Christian faith? How is trust necessary in our relationship with God?

3. Ben describes St. Elmo's fire in Chapter 35. This is an actual natural phenomenon that has been observed from ships at sea during thunderstorms. It is a sign of electricity in the air and can interfere with compass readings. We sometimes experience a similar phenomena as Christians—a tenseness around us and things that can interfere with our spiritual compass. What can we do to weather such difficult times?

4. In Chapter 44, Dana discovers Drogan's fascination with her and she reacts by pushing Ben away. "She knew she'd unfairly lashed out at him, but she felt as if a bubble had descended around her. One which kept her from reaching out to him and kept him from being able to cross over to her." Sometimes when we're hurting we do push other people away. How can we cross that distance that we create?

5. In Chapter 46, Dana realizes she is "near a breaking point." We all have symptoms when the stress of life becomes too much. What does the Bible say about handing those worries over to God and how can we do so but still take practical steps to deal with current situations?

6. In Chapter 50 we finally learn more of Dana's history— the death of her mother and the conviction of her father. We learn why she feels totally alone and abandoned by God. What words of promise from the Bible assure us that we are never alone?

7. The scenes beginning in Chapter 70 are somewhat disturbing. Evil can be disturbing, and yet the Bible tells us repeatedly to NOT be afraid. Look up the phrase "Fear not" in a Bible concordance or via an internet search. Which verses speak to you the most?

8. Dana's conversion is simple—no angel's voices or blinding lights. Yet it profoundly changes her heart. What does the Bible say about our becoming a new creation?

Author's Note

This book is dedicated to my father's father—Benjamin Van Riper. He died before I was born, but I grew up listening to stories of his adventures both here at home and overseas. His life was the stuff of legends, and he inspired in me a sense of adventure that remains unquenched. I like to think that his life has colored my writing, and that I've been successful in sharing that sense of excitement.

I'd also like to thanks the folks who have helped this project see the light of day. My pre-readers—Britney Adams, Kristy Kreymer, and Dorsey Sparks. Kelly Irvin's input was appreciated. A special thanks to Barbara Scott for editing this project and to Ken Raney for the cover. Cait Peterson did the formatting, and her help was invaluable. As always, I appreciate my husband's abounding patience, and his willingness to throw together dinner, vacuum, and finish the laundry I barely manage to start.

I visited the Taos area 15 years ago, for my honeymoon. It was a magical place, and I tried to convey some of that here. I have never been an employee of Homeland Security, and although my research was thorough—I have taken creative license for the purpose of my story. Any errors are my own.

And finally … *always giving thanks to God the Father for everything, in the name of our Lord Jesus Christ* (Ephesians 5:20).

Blessings,
Vannetta

Also by Vannetta Chapman

Shisphewana Amish Mystery Series
Falling to Pieces (Book 1)
A Perfect Square (Book 2)
Material Witness (Book 3)

Amish Village Mystery Series
Murder Simply Brewed (Book 1)
Murder Tightly Knit (Book 2)

Pebble Creek Series
Home to Pebble Creek (free ebook short story)
A Promise for Miriam (Book 1)
A Home for Lydia (Book 2)
A Wedding for Julia (Book 3)
Christmas at Pebble Creek (free ebook short story)

Shorter Novels
A Simple Amish Christmas (Book 1)
The Christmas Quilt (Book 2)

Novellas
Where Healing Blooms, from the collection *An Amish Garden*
Unexpected Blessings, from the collection *An Amish Cradle*

Share Your Thoughts With the author: Your comments will be forwarded to the author when you send them to vannettachapman@gmail.com.

Submit your review of this book to:
vannettachapman@gmail.com
or via the connect/contact button on the author's website at:
www.VannettaChapman.com.

Sign up for the author's newsletter at
www.VannettaChapman.com.

Made in the USA
Middletown, DE
16 March 2017